THE BOOK OF SORREL

JJ MAKENZIE

Dedication

To Easton: you make my life more magical.

PROLOGUE

"PLEASE TELL ME ANOTHER STORY, Daddy," Sorrel entreated her father while snuggling closer to him on her canopy bed.

David looked over at the Minnie Mouse clock on his daughter's nightstand before he kissed her head, knowing exactly what she was doing. She loved nothing more than to prolong story time so she didn't have to go to sleep. "Little girls need their rest so they can grow tall and strong."

"I'm not little anymore—I'm five years old," she stated with authority.

David laughed deeply. "All right, my big girl." He could never tell her no. "I'll tell you one more story." He paused to think of which story he should tell her. One came to mind, but she was too young. Or was she? Sorrel was the most precocious child he had ever known. Perhaps she was ready. "Sorrel, my little love—"

"I told you, I'm not little, Daddy."

"You will always be my little love." He tickled her.

She squirmed and giggled. "Is Mommy your big love?"

He tapped her nose. "Mommy and you are the loves of my life."

"Will I have a love of my life too?" she asked so innocently.

As David had thought, she was older than her years gave her

1

credit for. "Yes, my sweet Sorrel, you will have a great love, but . . . ," he hesitated, "you must be patient and brave."

Sorrel puffed out her pink silk–covered chest. "I am brave. I jumped higher than anyone off the swings at the park today."

Silently he prayed that she remained courageous throughout her entire life. "You are a brave girl. And I want to tell you a story about a brave girl. A story you must always remember. This story is about a princess named Sorrel."

"Her name is just like mine," Sorrel squealed with delight. "I want to be a princess when I grow up."

He wrapped an arm around his daughter and squeezed. "You, my love, are meant to be a queen."

"Can I wear a crown?"

David laughed. "If you want to."

"I do." She settled against her father.

He held her close, wishing she would stay little and that he could always protect her. "While Princess Sorrel didn't wear a crown," he began, "she had beautiful chocolate-brown hair and eyes as blue as the ocean, just like you. She also had a special book."

"Like Mommy?"

"Yes, just like Mommy's book. This book was very special. Princess Sorrel had to do everything she could to keep the book safe. She could never show it to anyone except whomever the book told her to. And she had to obey the book. If the book told her to hide, she had to hide. When the book told her who to marry, that's who she had to marry."

"Why couldn't she pick her husband?" She sounded almost indignant.

David smoothed his tenacious five-year-old's brow. "Because, sweetheart . . . Sorrel was cursed."

"Did her wicked stepmother curse her, like in *Snow White*?" Sorrel asked.

He hesitated before whispering, "Her mother cursed her."

Sorrel looked up into her father's eyes, begging him to tell her it wasn't true. "Why would she do that? Mommies are supposed to love their children."

"Her mother loved her very much." He tenderly kissed her head. "She didn't want to curse her, but she had no choice."

Sorrel blinked several times, not understanding.

David thought for a moment about what to say. "Even though she had no choice, like with all curses, this curse could be broken."

"How?"

David's thoughtful brown eyes bore into his daughter's. "By obeying the book even if it scared her—and most importantly, by following her heart." He pointed to his daughter's heart. "Because she had the best heart, just like you."

Sorrel smiled. "Did she break the curse?"

David pressed his lips together. "She did her part. And . . . ," he swallowed hard, "you will too."

Sorrel's blue eyes swirled, understanding slowly dawning. "Am I cursed, Daddy?"

He pressed a lingering kiss to her forehead. He hated telling her, but knew the best way to keep her safe was to tell the truth. "Yes, my love. But never forget, you have the power to break this curse." He leaned back and held her beautiful face in his hands. "Promise me, Sorrel, promise me you'll always do what the book says. Promise me you'll break the curse."

With the resolve of a woman ten times her age, she placed her hands on top of her daddy's and firmly declared, "I will be brave. I promise."

ONE

"SORREL, SORREL, I HAVE THE best news," Annalise drawled while she practically dove over the counter to reach for me, pushing several other customers out of her way.

I caught her before she took a nosedive into my freshly-baked chocolate cupcakes with strawberry frosting just waiting to be put in the display case. "Whoa there. This must be some news." I struggled to right her and push her back over to the side where customers belonged. Though I considered Annalise more of a friend, really, those pesky health codes got in the way. You never knew when one of those sneaky inspectors would pop in, and heaven forbid I had anyone besides a paid employee back here. I mean, it wasn't like she was going to lick the cupcakes. Well, on second thought, maybe it was better if she stayed on the customer side.

Annalise exhaled loudly while smoothing out her *I Was Born to Love Luke Bryan* T-shirt. She was a huge fan of the country singer. She had proudly been to twenty-four of his concerts to date. When Annalise composed herself, she reached out a delicate hand riddled with faded bruises from IV lines. I held back my grimace. It wasn't the doctors' faults that what they

4

were taught in medical school was often barbaric and simply wrong—not everyone was lucky enough to be cursed like me.

Annalise took my latex-covered hand. "I'm in remission. They can't find any trace of the cancer in my colon. It's a miracle," she cried. "And for some reason, I feel like I need to thank you."

I cleared my throat and squeezed her hand. "I didn't do anything."

She smiled so big, her dimples sucked in half her face. "Well, maybe you didn't cure me, but ever since you gave me that energizing tea to drink every day, I've felt like a million bucks and some change. I can even eat without throwing it all back up."

"I'm so glad." I released her hand. "How about a cupcake, on the house, to celebrate?"

Her green eyes zeroed in on the chocolate-strawberry cupcakes on the rolling cart near me. "I've been dying," she giggled, "almost literally, to eat your goodies again."

I swallowed hard, thinking about when she'd told me about her diagnosis a few months ago. My mother taught me to be careful not to intervene in "mortals' lives." To never draw attention to myself. Yet my father taught me to follow my heart. I couldn't let Annalise die. And I was tired of living a life set by a bunch of rules that I wasn't even sure really existed. "How about I box up half a dozen for you to take home?"

"Ronnie would love that. I think if you'd agree to it, he'd leave me and marry you, just for your cupcakes alone."

I laughed off her silly insinuations while I prepared a box filled with an assortment of berry cupcakes that were popular in the spring and summer months. The strawberry, raspberry, and blackberry cupcakes, with swirls of varying shades of pink and purple frosting topped with real berries, looked so pretty in the box. I hated to cover them with the lid, though I had to say I loved my Love Bites logo. The *O* and the *B* were pink hearts, and next to the black letters they really stood out.

I handed Annalise the box. "Enjoy, and make sure you keep

drinking that tea. Let me know when you run out and I'll prepare another batch for you." Her body, though healed, would need the extra "nutrients" while it recovered from all the chemicals her well-intentioned doctors had fed her for weeks.

She eagerly took the box. "You're a doll. Thank you, darlin'. Thank you for everything."

While watching her walk out the door to the jangle of the bells, a sense of peace and purpose encompassed me. Maybe being cursed wasn't all that bad. I looked around the bakery at all the customers who filled the pink chairs and booths—I was obsessed with pink—and thought it wasn't a bad life. I made people happy.

Someone who could always make me happy popped in, carrying a ridiculous number of balloons, including a giant three and zero, telling everyone how old I was. She had the smirkiest of smirks on her gorgeous oval-shaped face. I was seriously jealous of her high cheekbones.

Josie began singing "Happy Birthday" in her sultry alto voice, which almost made me feel like I should be slowly removing my clothes. I'd always teased her that she'd missed her calling in life. Instead of a wedding singer, she should have been working in a strip club. She worked the song like she was Marilyn Monroe. It was fitting since she looked like her, too, with curly blonde hair, curves for days, and pouty red lips.

Several of my customers joined in, embarrassing me, which I was sure was Josie's plan. She knew I wasn't overly fond of my birthday, though she didn't know the half of why.

While the crowd serenaded me, I pretended to be overcome with joy, even putting my hands to my mouth, all while giving Josie an evil eye. She flashed me a mischievous smile as she finished singing, making sure to prolong the last "you."

While everyone clapped and shouted their birthday wishes, I took off my latex gloves, tossed them in the wastebasket, and asked Leann, one of my employees, to man the counter. I walked around the display case and met my best friend and occasional partner in crime. We did a lot of weddings together—I supplied the cake and she supplied the entertainment.

Josie met me and wrapped me in her arms, engulfing us both in a sea of Mylar and latex balloons, all in varying shades of pink and red. She knew me so well. Or at least she thought she did. If only I could tell her all my secrets. A cursed life was a lonely life, no matter how many friends you had.

"These balloons are giving my hair a bad case of static electricity," I half-heartedly complained.

"Well, you're welcome. Happy birthday."

"Thanks, Josie." I began to untangle myself from the ribbons and balloons. It was easier said than done. I felt like we were in a labyrinth. It didn't help when we started laughing so hard at the silliness of being trapped by balloons.

Once we had extricated ourselves, Josie placed the balloons on a nearby white hand-painted table. She immediately began to smooth out the flyaway hairs on my head. "How do you get your hair so shiny?"

"Um, it's a new shampoo. I'll make some for you, too, if you want."

Her brow quirked. "What else do you cook upstairs in your little 'lab'?"

It wasn't a lab; it was more like a test kitchen.

She held up her hand. "Please don't tell me if it's like meth or something. I don't want to have to testify against you."

I smacked her hand away. "I'm not cooking up illicit drugs."

She faux-wiped her brow. "Phew. Except, it kind of makes me hate you. I thought maybe you'd come up with some drug that prevented aging, and I was going to beg you for some." She patted my cheek. "How is it that the past few years I've known you, you haven't changed one bit? It's like you're eternally twenty-seven. And I'm over here using concealer like a weapon to fight the crow's feet that keep assaulting my eyes like some freaking ninja warrior."

I rubbed the back of my neck. She didn't know how close to

the truth she was. "You're gorgeous. Half the guys in here right now want to date you." That wasn't a lie. I think I owed at least a quarter of my business to her. Many a man came in asking if Josie would be dropping in that day. The answer was usually yes. To make ends meet between her wedding gigs, Josie delivered food for one of those food delivery apps. She even delivered for me. Sometimes people just needed a cupcake, or even an entire cake, fix. I could relate. Like, as in right now. I could use some sweet ecstasy.

Josie rolled her eyes. "I'm pretty sure all these guys come in here for you."

"I don't think so." I'd turned down every guy who had asked me out since I moved here. Not because I wanted to but because I had to break the curse, and never falling in love was the only way I knew how. Hence the name of my bakery, Love Bites. I thought the double meaning was clever, even if I was the only one who knew the snarky meaning behind it. Everyone else just thought it was a cute name for a bakery that sold wedding cakes.

"Oh really?" Josie sang. She turned my head toward the door, leaned in, and whispered, "See Mr. Tall, Brooding, and Handsome who just walked in here? He can't take his eyes off you."

I looked down at my pink, frilly apron, guessing that was why, except when I lifted my head, I was hit with the most enigmatic aqua eyes I'd ever seen. They drew me in like Scotty was beaming me up. I wouldn't have minded at all to be stuck on the starship *Enterprise* with the achingly beautiful, olive-skinned man, whose square face and strong jawline made me want to skim my finger across his freshly-shaved face and run my hand through his dark hair. His tailored black suit and slick haircut gave off the air of someone who wore an invisible barrier. It was both sexy and relatable.

The reasonable, curse-breaking side of me said to look away, though every other part of me begged to go to him. It was as if my feet, of their own accord, started walking his way. And partly it was Josie, who gave me a push. All I knew was that it wasn't me, because I was never this bold. His tractor-beam-eyes lured me over. Never once did those gorgeous things stray; it was as if he knew the power he held.

The stranger stood impossibly still at the door, waiting for me, even when other customers came in and out. In my head I kept saying *this feels weird*, but that didn't stop me from walking his way. I didn't even know what I was going to say. When I finally reached him, I took a moment to gaze at him. Up close he was even more attractive. An almost animalistic urge came over me to kiss him. It was like the depths of my soul called out that he would be the father of my children. That's when I came to my senses. I would never be allowed to choose who to love. And my kind only ever had one child—a daughter. A daughter that, I swore to myself, I would never pass this curse on to. I took a deep breath, trying to clear the daze I was in.

The man tilted his head and studied me. He probably thought I was a nutjob. He wouldn't be wrong after my bizarre behavior. Then he stepped closer. Some invisible thread between us wanted to stitch us together. Or so it seemed. Whatever it was, it made us both take a step back from each other.

"I'm so sorry," I blurted. "I thought you were someone I knew," I lied. "Excuse me." I turned to go back to Josie, who was fanning herself and grinning bigger than the time she'd run over her ex's foot on "accident."

"Are you Sorrel Black?" a seductive baritone voice asked.

I swallowed hard and turned back around. "I am. How can I help you?" *Please say it's to check if your breath is bad. I would do a thorough job. What? Why did I think that?*

"I'm here with the *Atlanta Daily Post*," he snarled.

Oh crap. I'd totally forgotten I was being interviewed by them today. But wait . . . "Where's Raine? She was supposed to do the interview." I'd made her wedding cake for her nuptials last month, and let's just say she was intrigued with my reputation for bringing out the truth in my couples during their wedding cake tasting appointment. I'd had more couples break up in here than all the seasons of *The Bachelor* and *The Bachelorette* combined. It was just an added service I provided, unbeknownst to my clients. I figured I was doing humankind a service and saving a lot of heartache. Just because I couldn't be happily married didn't mean I didn't want others to be. I felt it my duty to make sure each couple I provided a cake for was meant to be. Thankfully, Raine and her husband were a perfect match.

I was hesitant at first to do the interview because of the attention it would draw. However, word was already getting around about the fantastic breakups that had happened in my bakery. And oddly, it was as if I could hear my father telling me to do the interview when Raine had suggested it.

"Raine," the sexy stranger growled, "had to have an emergency appendectomy last night, so I was *forced* to take her place."

Forced? We would come back to that later. "Is she all right?"

"I'm told she'll live," he sounded put off by the thought.

Wow, this guy was a jerk. Totally hot, but nonetheless a jerk. "I didn't catch your name."

"Eric Knight."

"Okay, Eric, perhaps this interview should wait until Raine is recovered." That's what my mouth said, while my body was begging for him to stay. *We won't be seduced by a pretty package,* I sternly told myself. *We won't be seduced by any package.*

"I would agree, but like I said, I don't have a choice. So, let's get this over with, shall we? It won't take long. How interesting can a cake shop be?" His eyes darted all over my sweet little bright and airy place—designed to induce feelings of bliss. Maybe the special ingredients in the cupcakes helped. But no one would ever know.

I had to temper the ire building up inside of me, along with the stupid urge to kiss him. "That sounds like a challenge, Eric."

The corners of Eric's lips twitched up, involuntarily I would say, by how quickly he made himself scowl again. It was enough, though, to make him pause and assess me. Once his assessment was over, he folded his arms. "No one's been up to the task in years, but perhaps you'll surprise me."

"Well, Eric, get ready for the surprise of your life."

TWO

I HANDED MY APRON TO Josie. "Wish me luck."

Josie peeked over at the broody Eric Knight as he sat in the corner of my bakery, looking like he was waiting to interrogate me instead of interview me. He was tapping on his phone and then scribbling notes, frowning as he went. "Who is he?" Josie drooled.

"He's from the *Atlanta Daily Post*. Remember Raine Peters, the lifestyle reporter? She's the one who begged me to let her do a piece on the bakery after she came in for her wedding cake tasting."

"Oh yeah. She was marrying the professional hockey player."

"Yes. Well, apparently, she had an appendectomy last night, and they sent this guy over in her place."

"Lucky you." Josie wagged her brows.

"For some reason, I don't think so." There was something about him that was making me feel off-kilter. I'd stalled talking to him so I could grab a couple slices of my *special* cake. Eric seemed in need of an attitude adjustment, and I needed to compose myself.

Josie tilted her head. "Are you kidding me? You two looked to be having a moment there. I almost thought he might grab you and lay a big one on you." Her southern roots came out.

Though her drawl wasn't as prominent as most people's in Riverhaven—Tennessee's best-kept secret—due to the fact that her daddy was a Yankee and she was raised up north.

I didn't mention that I had thought I was going to kiss him too. I'd never felt an urge so deep. Thankfully, I'd stopped myself. That would have been quite the beginning for an article about the bakery . . . *The owner is crazy and has no inhibitions.* That would be great for business.

"I think he would rather eat me for lunch than kiss me," I whispered.

"Ooh. That sounds like fun."

I playfully smacked her. "Get your mind out of the gutter." I bit my lip and stared at the attractive man who was furiously jotting down notes on a pad of paper. "Can you hang around for a bit?"

Josie placed a hand on my shoulder. "Everything okay?"

"Yeah, you know, just in need of some moral support." Like the kind that would keep me from accosting the stranger. When I'd said I thought he was someone I knew, that wasn't a 100 percent lie. I did feel like I knew him, though I couldn't place him.

"Does a moral supporter get free cake and lemonade?"

"Doesn't she always?" I grinned.

Josie tapped her full lips. "Why yes, she does. Now go and do me proud." She nudged me with her hip.

I shuffled over to the counter. Mateo, one of my pastry chefs, happened to emerge from the kitchen. I say *happened to,* but he'd probably heard Josie, and we all knew he had a thing for her. I think Josie liked the Latin lover too. Mateo knew how beautiful he was, and he made sure to tell everyone his name meant *gift of God.* He translated that into him being God's gift to women. Don't get me wrong, he *was* handsome, with his flawless bronzed skin and athletic build. Too bad for him that Josie liked to be the only godlike one in a relationship. That didn't stop them from relentlessly flirting, though.

"Hey, Mateo, will you please plate two slices of the French yogurt–and–blackberry cake I made this morning?"

"Sure thing, boss. Then can I take ten?" His dark-brown eyes drifted toward Josie sitting at the table with all the balloons, applying some of the lemon pressed lip gloss I'd made especially for her. Thanks to me, she would never get a cold sore again.

"If you must," I teased.

He hopped to it and dashed through the swinging wooden doors that led to the kitchen. He was back in no time with two slices of cake, garnished with mint leaves, on my signature pink plates.

"Thank you. And please behave. I don't want Josie filing any sexual harassment claims against me."

He slapped a hand on his chest, offended. "Me? She's the one always coming on to me. But I like it." He flashed me an impish grin before zooming toward my best friend. Those two just needed to make out already and get it over with.

I watched Josie pretend to be uninterested in Mateo before I took a deep breath and walked toward Mr. I-Look-Disgruntled. I set the plates on the table. "I thought you might like a sample of what we offer here."

Eric sneered at the slices of cake like they had killed one of his loved ones. "I don't do refined sugar."

"Well, I guess it's a good thing, I don't either." I took my seat across from him. "Everything we make here is completely organic and unprocessed. I make a chocolate frosting that's so good, you would never know it's made with avocados and no sugar." Though I did use raw sugar and other natural sweeteners in some of my cakes and frostings. What mortals failed to recognize was how their bodies were designed to tell them exactly what they needed and when they needed it. Instead, most of the time, they tried to fill it with whatever was convenient, usually processed food. Or worse, denied themselves, sometimes out of shame. If only they realized that if they ate intuitively, they would naturally be satisfied. They would even find their bodies

14

needed some good old-fashioned dessert from time to time, and that was okay.

Eric looked unimpressed by my claim. So much so that he pushed the scrumptious cake topped with the prettiest blackberries to the side, picked up his fancy wooden pen, and tapped it against his pad of paper filled with notes. When I looked too closely at what he'd been writing, he covered it up with his hand.

I sighed audibly. He really needed to eat the dang cake. It would make him happy, or maybe in his case just less surly. If only I'd used more gotu kola in my blend this morning when making the cake. Although, too much wasn't a good thing for most people. Once I'd accidentally doubled my own special blend and I had a bunch of customers behaving like laughing hyenas. It had made everything funny to them, including people sneezing.

"So, you bake cakes," he started off.

"What an insightful question. Did they teach you that in Journalism 101?" I teased.

His ears reddened, but his eyes said I amused him. He shifted in his seat. "Did you always know you wanted to own a bakery? Is that better for you?"

"I suppose it will do." I found flirting with him came too easily. "The answer is no."

"Then what made you open this place?"

I looked around my beloved bakery at all the happy people chatting and smiling. "It just felt right, like I was meant to?"

"Meant to?" He said it like it was a foreign notion.

"Yes. Haven't you ever known deep inside that you were supposed to do something?"

He paused for a moment. His eyes drifted down. "Some of us aren't that lucky."

The tone of his voice made me want to reach out to him. I almost did. What was wrong with me? "That's too bad. How did you know you wanted to be a lifestyle reporter?" I found myself wanting to get to know him.

"I'm an investigative journalist," he scoffed, offended.

I laughed at how seriously he'd said that. "An investigative journalist? Are you here to take down my bakery? See if I'm cooking the books or illegally filtering money into campaign funds through bake sales?" I joked.

The corners of his mouth twitched. If only he would really smile, it would improve his mood. Though maybe it was a good thing he didn't; I bet he was dashingly handsome when he smiled, if he ever did. I had a feeling he forced himself not to.

"Like I said before, I'm here on behalf of Raine."

"Couldn't they have at least sent the sports guy? Or what about the woman who writes the advice column?"

His hands clenched. "Believe me, I'm not happy about this arrangement either. Can we just get on with it?"

"Maybe you should have some cake first." I pushed a plate toward him.

"No thank you." He flipped through some pages on his notepad. "County records say you opened this bakery three years ago. Is that correct?"

He'd seriously looked that up. Is that what he had been over here doing while I was getting the cake? "That's correct."

"What did you do before then?"

I tucked some hair behind my ear. "Traveled."

His eyes narrowed. "This is your first business?"

I nodded.

"Where did you go to school? I don't see any of your credentials on your website."

I clasped my hands together and laid them in my lap. "I didn't. My mother taught me almost everything I know."

"She must be some teacher."

"She *was*."

"Was?"

"She died five years ago," I stuttered.

He cocked his head like he could hear the lie in my voice.

I felt my face flush. Why was this guy throwing me off my game? Normally I could tell that lie with ease.

He made a note without offering any condolences like most people would. Instead, he got right back to business. "Not only does your website lack credentials, but there are no photos of you. In fact, I don't see you on social media at all. And why did you stipulate that we couldn't take your photo for this piece?"

"I'm camera shy," I lied again.

He perused me, taking his time. "I have a hard time believing that."

I leaned forward. "Why is that?"

His eyes penetrated my own, making my heart pound as if I'd run a marathon. "You're beautiful," he whispered.

Oh. I wanted him to whisper more words. I wanted him, which was ridiculous.

He shook his head as if he were trying to shake me out of his thoughts, the way I should have been trying to cast him out of my own.

"What's your annual revenue?"

"Is that really important for this story?"

"As a journalist, I cover all angles."

"I can see that." Though I couldn't understand why. "Are you sure you don't want some cake?"

"Positive," he growled. "Annual revenue?" He wasn't letting that go.

"I don't know," I stammered. "My accountant keeps track of that."

His brow quirked. "You don't care about your bottom line?"

The answer was no, but I only shrugged.

He jotted down another note. "I see you purchased this place for $1.2 million. Does that sound right?"

I cleared my throat. "I don't like discussing money. I was told this was going to be a feel-good piece." I avoided answering his question, again.

It was clear from his smirk and the "aha" look in his eye that he knew he'd rattled me and was quite delighted about it. "Hmm. I guess that depends on what your definition of *feel-good* is," he quipped before getting back to interrogating me. "I don't see any loans or liens on the property. I can't believe a place like this is not only flush after three years, but has no business loans to date."

"You got me, I'm a loan shark on the side," I teased, hoping he would see how ridiculous his line of questioning was.

No such luck. He lifted his pad of paper and made some more notes.

"Hey, I'm not really a loan shark. I'll sue you for libel if you put that in there."

He shrugged it off like he'd been threatened with that before. "Let's say you're not into anything illegal—how does someone as young as you front an endeavor like this?"

"First of all, I'm not fronting anything. I own and run my own business. Secondly, I'm thirty, probably around the same age as you. Which makes me wonder what happened to make you so cynical. Maybe you need some more sugar in your diet." I gave him the snidest pressed-lip smile.

He sat up straight as a pin. "I'm doing my job, Ms. Black. And you're awfully defensive."

Defensive? Of course I was being defensive—he intimated I was into something illegal. "Well, Mr. Knight, if being a jerk is part of your job description, you deserve a raise." I pointed at his stupid pad of paper. "You can quote me on that." I scooted my chair back and stood. "I think this interview is over."

"No problem." He glared. "I have other ways of getting the information I need."

My jaw dropped. What kind of information did he need? I made wedding cakes for goodness' sake. "You have *fun* with that. Except, I wonder if you know what that word means. Maybe you can do some research on that."

"Oh, I'll be doing research." He held up his fancy phone that looked more like a tablet.

I gripped the back of my chair, white knuckling it while wearing the face of someone calm, cool, and collected—not cursed. "I don't know what you think you'll find except what an idiot you are for investigating a woman who bakes wedding cakes, but go ahead," I dared him, all while hoping he wouldn't call my bluff. As careful as my family had been to keep our secrets, I would be naive to think it was foolproof, especially in this digital age. It was getting harder and harder to hide our youth and longevity. Hence why I tried to keep myself off social media. Josie hated that I would never let her post selfies of us. I always used the excuse that I thought social media was what was wrong with society and didn't want any part of it. Why hadn't I said that a minute ago to the egotistical man sitting across from me? Still, with all that said, this bakery was purchased on the up and up, and I wasn't lying about my age. At least not yet.

Eric stood ever so slowly, pressed his strong hands on the small table between us, and leaned forward, just inches from my face. As much as I loathed him, the strange urge from before to kiss him welled up inside of me, even more intensely this time. So much so, I gripped the chair until it hurt, forcing myself not to lean forward. It didn't lessen the magnetic pull and vibrations that bounced between us. In his shocked eyes I could see he felt it, too, yet he didn't move away. Instead, he inched forward with steel determination etched on his refined features.

"One thing I'm not, and that's an idiot," he punctuated each word, slowly and deeply. It was mesmerizing. As was his minty breath that drifted between us, acting like one of my elixirs, soothing me into a place I didn't want to be. Except every part of me wanted to erase any distance between us. What was wrong with me?

No! I had to scream in my head. Coming to my senses, I stood tall and put some distance between us. "That's debatable," I zinged back.

"I'm up to debating you anytime, Ms. Black. I have a feeling we'll be seeing each other again very soon."

"Don't count on it."

"I think you'll find it's you who has miscalculated." He flashed me a cocky grin before he gathered his phone and notes.

I stood stunned for a moment, not knowing what to say. I was right about his smile—it was dashingly handsome, and I hated myself for being drawn to him. More than that, I was stunned because honestly, I never miscalculated. I always innately knew what to do. It's why I'd agreed to do the interview. It felt right. I didn't see him coming. At all. Why was that?

"Don't let the door hit you on the way out," I said, which was—let's admit—a lame comeback, but it was all I had in me. "And by the way, I'll be filing a complaint with the paper and canceling my online subscription."

He chuckled so deep and rich I felt it in my chest. "You do that. See you later."

"Ugh." I so badly wanted to chuck the cake at his head. Instead, I turned to find everyone in the bakery silently staring at me with wide eyes, wondering what that was all about. I wondered the same thing. Perhaps, though, I should have been a little more discreet. I hated that I had let him get to me. I was normally even-keeled.

Josie was to me in seconds. "Are you all right?"

The answer was no. No, I wasn't.

THREE

ERIC

ERIC WALKED OUT INTO THE bright sunshine and threw his shades on, pleased that yet again he'd found another juicy story where others would never think to look. Maybe being forced to take this assignment wasn't going to be the joke he thought it would be. Though he still resented being told what to do. He'd been working on an important piece about illegal sweatshops in downtown Atlanta. Hopefully he would be able to get back to that soon. *After all, it shouldn't take long to shake down the gorgeous Sorrel Black,* he thought.

An image of her filled all his senses. She was more than beautiful. Something about her, he had to admit, threw him off. He was usually a pro at getting people to talk. He normally pressed until he got the answers he wanted, yet he'd kept imagining taking the raven-haired beauty in his arms and getting lost in her deep-blue eyes. He'd imagined some other things, too, that would have gotten him in trouble with the paper for crossing professional lines. He kept trying to shake those very unprofessional images, but she'd gotten under his skin in a way no woman had in a long time, maybe ever.

He had a feeling he wasn't the only man to find himself

overcome by her. He'd noticed the longing looks of the other men in the bakery. For some unknown reason, he seethed about it on the inside. This primitive, territorial desire had almost overtaken him in there. Why he'd felt this need to have her and protect her, he had no idea. But he'd fought it off. Besides, he had a feeling Sorrel Black didn't need anyone's protection, and he had given up on women a long time ago.

Those thoughts propelled him to the next phase of his plan—get to know everything he could about Sorrel Black. Who knew? Maybe this piece would catapult him to the next level. Maybe he would finally get some national recognition. Perhaps that was why he was forced to take the assignment. Unfortunately, the powers that be would control the piece's fate. But he would do everything he could to make sure his article got the glory it deserved. Because the instincts that made him so perfect for this job were telling him that Sorrel Black had a secret worth uncovering.

Eric walked down the gray cobbled streets in search of a place to eat a late lunch and hopefully interview some of the locals about Sorrel. Riverhaven was reminiscent of his younger days in Prague, he thought. He found himself almost getting sentimental as he walked past the tightly-knit brick buildings that housed everything from frozen yogurt shops to clothing boutiques. His days in Europe were some of the best and worst of his life. He had seen things—and knew things—he wouldn't wish on anyone. Things he didn't wish to be part of. He supposed they had made him cynical, like Sorrel had accused him of being. He'd been accused of worse, so he let it slide off his back. Almost. He didn't like that Sorrel thought poorly of him, though he knew she had every right to. It wasn't going to stop him from getting his story.

Eric decided to eat at the Riverview restaurant, not far from Love Bites. He would give Sorrel this: it was a clever name for her bakery. The Riverview restaurant boasted a healthy fare, which was hard to find in the south. Most places in these parts—

even in Atlanta where he lived, two hours away—fried everything. Portions were insane, too. Another reason to miss Europe.

The hostess seated him outside, as he'd requested, at a table on the terrace that overlooked the river. Eric wasn't looking forward to the sweltering summer days that would be upon them soon. He wanted to take advantage of the mild May weather while he could. And it wasn't often he got to eat in such a picturesque place. He usually ate at his desk or in his car, depending on his assignment. *The lone wolf,* they called him at the office.

While he waited for his food, he observed the kayakers and several people taking a stroll across the stone bridge— reminiscent of Europe with its medieval flare—that spanned the lazy river. Riverhaven was just the kind of town to hide in, he thought. So quaint that no one would suspect a criminal lurking among them. Not to say Sorrel was a criminal, though he wasn't ruling it out as a possibility. Which was why when his attractive server, who had flirted with him when she'd taken his order, returned with his quinoa Caesar salad, he used it to his advantage.

"Carly, is it?" he purred her name. "Do you have a minute to chat?"

She bit her lip and looked around at the mostly-empty tables on the terrace. It was well after the lunch rush and before the dinner crowd arrived. "Well, okay." She took the seat across from him, flapping her fake eyelashes so much it was going to give him a case of vertigo. Even so, he would endure the eager younger woman if it got him closer to his end goal.

He leaned in a bit. "How long have you lived here?"

"Gosh, my whole life," she drawled.

"How long have you worked here?"

"Since high school. My momma owns this place."

This was good news, Eric thought. "So, you know most people around here?"

"Yep." She smiled. "At least all the locals. We get a lot of tourists in here. Are you visiting or moving here?" Her tone begged for him to say he was going to increase their population and not only by one.

Eric leaned back and gave her a dazzling smile. "I might be around for a while."

Her bright violet eyes lit up.

"Can you recommend a good bakery?" He tried to keep it subtle. "I have a sweet tooth." He didn't lie. He was just good at controlling his cravings—all of them.

She clapped her hands together. "Oh my goodness, yes! Love Bites is the best place ever. When you eat there, I swear it's like you leave feeling healthier, even though you're eating cupcakes. And don't even get me going on Sorrel, the owner. She's the nicest person I've ever met."

"Did you say Sorrel?" an older woman seated at the next table over asked.

Eric gave this new player in his game his attention. That was enough for the white-haired woman to turn her chair toward them. "She is the sweetest thing." She spoke with her hands, waving them all over the place. "I came down with a case of that terrible crud that was going around here a few months ago." She turned to Carly. "Do you remember that? I thought I was going to cough up a lung. They almost had to put me on oxygen."

Carly nodded gravely. "So many people were sick."

The older woman slapped a hand across her large bosom. "That dear Sorrel brought me, and at least a dozen people I know, homemade soup, the likes of which I've never tasted. My golly was it amazing. She even spoon-fed me. How precious is that?"

Carly reached out to the woman and patted her hand. "That is the sweetest thing I've ever heard, but it doesn't surprise me. That Sorrel is something special."

"Amen. After that soup, I felt like a real person again. Not sure what was in it, but it cured me, I'll tell you that." The older woman swatted her knee.

Eric held up his hand. "Excuse me, did you say her soup cured you?"

"Well, yes, darlin'. A little TLC and food are good for the soul."

"So, it wasn't really the soup?" Eric confirmed.

The woman waved her hand in front of him. "You're missing the point."

"Which is?" Eric asked.

She leaned in conspiratorially. "There's something about Sorrel."

"Yes, ma'am, you're right. You just have to try Love Bites and meet Sorrel," Carly gushed.

"Sorrel! Sorrel!" another woman joined in who happened to be walking by. "Oh. My. Gosh. I. Love. Her. She saved me from marrying that two-timing louse Hunter Dupree last year. I'll be forever grateful to her."

Eric's brow quirked. "How did she manage that?" He tried to sound like somebody more interested in gossip rather than a calculating bastard, which he knew he was.

Sorrel's newest fan pulled up a chair right next to him. She gave him an appraising look before holding out her manicured hand. "I'm Sadie, by the way," she said seductively.

Perfect. He had another admirer. He gave her hand a quick shake. He didn't have time for female distractions. But he knew he had to play nice to get the information he needed. Though he had been hoping for more incriminating evidence, not a damn pep rally for the beautiful creature he couldn't stop imagining holding in his arms. *Focus.* "Nice to meet you, Sadie. Tell me your story."

She sat up straight, showing off her posture, which in turn gave a better view of every curve she owned. No doubt she was looking for someone to replace the ex-fiancé. "Last year," she began, "that pig Hunter and I went into Love Bites for our cake tasting, and after we tried the chocolate raspberry truffle cake—"

"Ooh, that's one of my faves," Carly interrupted.

All the women nodded in agreement.

Could Sorrel walk on water too? Eric wondered.

"Anyway," Sadie continued, "Sorrel took both our hands, and as calm as an ocean breeze she said, 'I think, Sadie, there's something that Hunter needs to tell you.' I thought for sure it was going to be that the idiot had wrecked another truck or some nonsense. However, after he spluttered for a few minutes, he confessed to sleeping with Bethany Jenkins not once, but pretty much the entire time we were engaged." She slammed her fist on the table. "I can't believe I was going to marry that fool. My daddy said he was a loser."

Eric tilted his head. "So, there were rumors about him going around?"

"Oh no," Sadie swore, "for as stupid as Hunter was, he was good at hiding his indiscretion."

"Then how did Sorrel know?"

All the women looked at each other, debating with their eyes if they should say what was obviously on the tips of their tongues.

"Ladies," Eric coaxed.

The older woman leaned in and whispered, "Well, some people around these parts say it's witchcraft, but the good Lord knows she's too sweet for that to be true."

"Witchcraft?" Eric chuckled. These small-town people were something else, always wanting to blame everything on the devil instead of people's human nature. He was quite confident whatever Sorrel was into was more illegal than evil. He knew evil, and she wasn't it.

FOUR

SORREL. MY MOTHER'S PIERCING VOICE could wake the dead, or in my case, dead asleep.

I shot straight up on my couch where I had fallen asleep, clutching the wretched silent book, wishing it would, for once, speak to me. Help me know what to do about that reporter, Eric Knight.

Sorrel, can you hear me?

I closed my eyes and focused on the sound of her voice, wishing so much we could speak in person and not only in our minds. As far as the world knew, Elizabeth Black had died in a tragic scuba diving accident in Palau, Micronesia, five years ago. Her body was never recovered. I didn't even know where she lived now or what new name she'd assumed, all for my protection. Yet, I didn't feel protected. I felt cursed, living a life where I never aged past twenty-five, which made it impossible for my mother and me to stay together. It was getting harder and harder for people to buy that we were mother and daughter, no matter how many gray streaks my mother put in her hair or the horrid makeup she applied each day to age herself.

We had stayed together as long as the book directed. Long enough for her to pass the book on to me on my twenty-fifth birthday. The day appointed by this curse that each new descendant, all female in my family tree's straight line, inherited the book our magic was tied to. It had been the day I was supposed to find out which mortal I would be forced to marry. It was the day the book stopped working.

I rubbed my tired eyes. *I can hear you.*

Happy birthday, my love.

I picked up my phone to check the time. It was just before midnight. It made me wonder if my mother was close by in the same time zone as me. Or did she just instinctively know I was alone, and it was a good time to contact me, as she didn't know where I lived either. I hated not being able to share everything about my life with her. She didn't even know I owned a bakery. She felt the less info we shared, the safer we would be.

Thank you. I leaned my head back on the couch, exhausted.

You're worried. I can feel it. Did the book finally say something to you? So much hope and trepidation filled her voice. She hated that she'd passed down this curse to me, yet she feared what the book's silence meant for me—and her.

The book is ever silent. I ran my hand across its ancient cover that had been woven together with the brightest, greenest leaves I'd ever seen. I'm not sure what species the leaves were, but they were indestructible, as far as I knew. Inside the book, the pages were made of a substance like white animal skin, and every word was written in gold. There were pages and pages of instruction on things like how to prepare elixirs to cure everything from acne to the flu, even serious diseases. The last page, though, had been added later, but how long ago, no one exactly knew. Family legend stated it was when the curse began. It was when the messages began to appear, directing the life of the keeper of the book. The only messages the page contained now were ones to my mother from years ago, including the directive to marry my father.

Maybe you're right, Sorrel; maybe the curse will end with you.

Dad always said I would be the one to break it.

Mom sighed. *Your father was a mortal who told you fairy tales because he desperately wanted to give you hope.*

Why do you speak of him like that? You loved him and he loved you.

Did he, or was it the curse I thrust on him and you? Guilt riddled her words.

I knew Mom worried Dad had loved her only because the curse made him, but I didn't believe that. I saw the way my parents used to look at each other when they didn't know I was watching. And even though I was only nine when my father unexpectedly died of a heart attack, I knew love existed between them. It was the kind of love I wanted. The kind my father promised me I would have. Though maybe my mother was right. Dad only told me the stories about Princess Sorrel, who I realized as I got older was really me, to help me deal with the curse in the only way he knew how to at the time.

He loved you. I pleaded with her to believe me. For my own well-being, I had to believe that was true.

Perhaps, she conceded.

Mom, do you think the curse is already broken? I mean, the book has quit sending messages, and it's not like we were ever hunted down by the Selene family. For years I'd been warned about the importance of keeping the book safe. The legend was that many years ago, in a land and time unknown, there had lived three families, all part of the Praeditus, or the Endowed. The Aelius family, the Tellus family, and the Selene family. Each family was blessed with powers and given a book.

The Aelius family received its powers from the sun. My family, the Tellus family, was given its powers from the earth. It allowed us to use the things from the planet to heal and help by pushing our energy into herbs and plants of all kinds. The Selene family was blessed by the moon. Though the families' gifts came from different sources, they all worked in harmony just as the sun, earth, and moon do. As time went on, the Aelius family believed our families' gifts should help all mankind, not just our kind. Then the Aelius queen fell in love with a mortal. Against the wishes of the other two families, she married the mortal and had children with him. The Tellus and Selene families feared this would expose them all and that mortals would exploit them. So they banded together to destroy the entire Aelius family.

As the last remaining member of her family, the Aelius queen sought her revenge by cursing the other two families, using the powers of the books. Since her line wasn't allowed to continue, she would make sure the other two lines suffered the same fate. The Tellus family was limited to one daughter for each generation, and for the Selene family, one son. In sweet revenge, each cursed son or daughter would be forced to marry a mortal. It was a double-edged sword. Not only did marrying a mortal mean they would be diluting their powers with each generation, but it also shortened their lifespans. No longer would they live for over a thousand years like their ancestors before them. As an added cruelty, it meant never knowing if the mortal they were bound to truly loved them, or vice versa, because the power of the curse brought them together. Regardless, each cursed child was forced to watch their mortal companion age and die while they stayed young for years and years.

The last part of the curse was that the remaining two lines would be sworn enemies from that time forward. Legend held that each ruling family from the Tellus and Selene sects went into hiding with the family books, while the remaining members hunted each other into oblivion. According to the legend, there was one way to break the curse. If either the Selene or Tellus family found the book of their enemy, they could destroy it, killing the remaining members of that line. For the curse dictated that, in the end, only one family would remain.

For all I knew, it was mostly all a fairy tale, reinvented as it was passed down from generation to generation. My mother couldn't even tell me what powers the other lines supposedly possessed, other than that the Aelius family had something to do with light and life and the Selene family, darkness and death.

It's dangerous to think the curse has been broken, Sorrel.

Why? We wouldn't know how to destroy the other family's

book even if we did find it. Not like we had ever tried. I had no desire to.

Perhaps it's like the binding ceremony: it only appears in the book once you've met the mortal you're meant to marry.

You mean forced?

Yes, she let out a heavy breath.

My snow-white cat, Tara, jumped on my lap, pushing the book out of the way. She was an attention whore. I stroked her soft fur until she purred. *Mom, even if I did find the other book, I could never destroy it. How could I kill anyone?*

This is why I insist we stay apart. To lessen suspicion about who we really are. We don't know the heart of the other family. What if they are willing to kill you . . . and me?

Why did she have to put it like that? *How could I live with myself? Dad said I was meant to heal, not hurt.*

And so you have, I'm sure to your detriment.

I curled up and held Tara close. *There's a man investigating me, a reporter,* I admitted.

My mother went silent, but I felt the anger and worry inside of her. *I told you to be careful.*

I have been. I only help people when I feel like I'm supposed to. Which was pretty much all the time, but I hid that thought from her.

You and your feelings, Sorrel. They're going to get you into trouble. It sounds like they already may have.

Dad told me to follow my heart. It's all I have to go on.

What about reason? You're recklessly putting yourself in danger.

From a family we don't even know exists? Or from the mortals you're so prejudiced toward?

I'm not prejudiced, she fumed. *There are stories in our family of how cruelly mortals have used us—the mortals we've been forced to marry and those who've been suspicious of us. And if it weren't for a mortal, our family would have never been cursed.*

31

Was it the mortal's fault or the pride of our family? I retorted.

She remained silent.

I'm sorry, Mom. I don't like to argue with you.

You're a special woman. Your father was not wrong there. You have his heart, for which I'm thankful. But what of this reporter?

I thought about Eric Knight. So many conflicting emotions surrounded him.

You're attracted to him. I can feel it. It's strong, Mom interrupted my thoughts. *It feels like when I met your father.*

I bolted up, jostling Tara. *Really?*

Yes. You feel as if you can't help the attraction.

That's exactly how I feel, except I can't stand him. He's awful.

Mom laughed. *You sound like you're having a hard time convincing yourself of that. Are you sure the book hasn't spoken to you?*

Positive. I mean, you don't think he's the one, do you?

Mom thought for a minute. *There's a way you could find out if the curse is broken.*

How?

Sleep with him, of course.

Mom! I could kill him if I did. The curse made sure we never strayed outside of who it picked as our mate. If anyone of my kind had sex with someone besides the person we were bound to, that man died. My mother once told me a story about my great-great-great-grandmother who had fallen in love outside of the curse. She gave in to her desire and consummated the unsanctioned relationship. The next day the man was run over and killed by a stagecoach. There were also stories of men being driven mad after sleeping with my ancestors, to the point of killing themselves when the curse made them realize they could never be with the woman they loved—or rather, were consumed with.

Sounds like a win-win situation to me, Mom deadpanned.

I can't believe you think I should risk a man's life. Besides, I want to share that experience with someone I love. But, I sighed, *I don't believe that will ever happen. The curse will die with me.*

I fear you may be right, she cried. *I'm sorry I cursed you.*

I'm not, I half-lied to make her feel better. *I've helped a lot of people.*

You are too good, daughter.

I don't know about that.

Promise me you will be careful with this man; your emotions run strong for him.

I'll try.

If you don't want to sleep with him, you could always seduce him and convince him to forget about you, she suggested. *We have our ways. I believe on page ten there's a great little elixir that will do the trick.*

Good night, Mom.

She laughed before I felt her go silent and leave my thoughts.

I scratched Tara's ears in the semidarkness while flipping the book open, which had fallen off to the side when Tara had jumped on my lap. I turned it to page ten, curious about which elixir my mother was referring to. I hadn't memorized them all yet, like she had. The words for the elixir appeared in English, a part of the book's magic. The language changed depending on who the rightful heir was. Or so I was told. Honestly, I didn't know what to believe anymore. All I knew was I wouldn't be using the elixir meant to induce arousal.

If ever a man fell in love with me, I wanted it to be of his own accord. And for some unfathomable reason I couldn't explain, I wanted it to be Eric.

FIVE

"ARE YOU HAVING FUN?" I slid into the chair across from Eric. The rumor swirling around Riverhaven was that he'd been interviewing anyone and everyone who would talk to him the last few days. Now he had the audacity to show his pretty face in my bakery. Which wasn't all bad. While I resented him, I was still drawn to him. So much so, I had to keep my hands clasped together on my lap for fear of accosting him. The last few nights I'd been dreaming about him. Like very real, steamy dreams. Dream Eric was an amazing kisser and spoke beautiful words. "What I wouldn't give to know every part of you," he'd whispered in my ear last night while his fingers skimmed over my flesh. Though his touch was light, I could feel it deep within. Almost as if he were the only person meant to touch me. You know, while I was unconscious. That didn't sound right, or legal.

Eric stared at my lips, amusement dancing in his eyes like he knew what I was thinking. Or perhaps was himself wishing what I wished. That my dreams would come true. He laid his pen down on his notepad with a smirk so conceited it warranted being smacked off. "Didn't you accuse me of not being able to have fun, Ms. Black?"

It was back to reality. Back to *mostly* despising him. "I suppose I did. So, what brings you here today, then?"

34

He leaned in, a rich, spicy scent rolling off of him. I recognized the intoxicating artemisia in his cologne. It was better known as wormwood. I had used it to help those suffering from malaria when I visited India during my travels. The way he smelled and the way he looked at me made my hands itch to come out and touch his stubbled cheeks like I had in my dreams. But I had to remind myself that this man was not the man *of* my dreams, just the man *in* my dreams.

"I thought perhaps it would be *fun* to see you again."

His seductive tones sent a shiver down my spine. "Is that so?" I stuttered.

"Yes, as much as I've enjoyed interviewing your sycophants all week, I wanted to get up close and personal with my subject."

I had to press my lips together before I said, "I would like that too. Very much." Thankfully, my head reminded me what a jerk he was. "Sycophants?"

"Flatterers and fawners," he cockily clarified.

"I know what the word means. I may not have taken Journalism 101 like you, but I'm not uneducated." My education might not have come in the halls of higher learning, or in any school for that matter, yet I was well-learned. My classroom was the world, and at my mother's and father's feet.

His eyes dropped. "I didn't mean to offend you."

I tilted my head. "Are you sure? What do you call interviewing all my *friends* and *acquaintances*?"

He picked up his pen and tapped it on the pad of paper. "I call it a challenge. I've never met someone as admired and loved as you."

"You sound disappointed."

"I'm skeptical. You know what they say: 'If it sounds too good to be true, it usually is.'"

I shrugged. "Maybe you're right. But . . ." I leaned in and spoke softly. "What if what you see before you *is* who I am? A woman who sells tea and cake."

He thought for a moment, his eyes searching my own. "You

don't know how much I wish that were true. But I don't live in fairy tales."

"You think I'm make-believe?"

"Well, according to your fans, you cure diseases, make Christmas wishes come true, and leap tall buildings in a single bound."

"You forgot X-ray vision and super speed," I teased him.

He chuckled, and I remembered the way he laughed in my dreams. It was melodic and heartfelt, not sarcastic like now. "Please accept my apologies for underestimating you."

I pushed my chair back and stood. "You shouldn't under-estimate me."

He looked up at me with narrowed eyes. "I don't."

"Good. Now that we've cleared that up, what can I bring you? These tables are for paying customers only."

He gave me a half smile. "Touché, Ms. Black."

"Please call me Sorrel." That's what he'd called me in my dreams.

"Sorrel," he crooned.

Oh, was that sexy. I grabbed onto the chair.

His grin said he knew it affected me. "I'll take some tea."

"What kind?" I breathed out, trying to compose myself and wondering why I felt so overcome by him.

"You choose." He had no idea the power he'd just given me.

My father's words rang in my head that those who were given great power must use great restraint. I had never used my gifts as a weapon. I was to heal, not hurt. And as much as I wanted to make him forget about this ridiculous story he was writing, I wouldn't do it by supernatural means. However, I might give him a little something to make him happier, but that was only because I was a good person.

"I'll be right back." I turned to leave.

"I look forward to it."

I stopped midturn. "For a second there, you fooled me. You almost sounded sincere."

"Believe me, there is hardly a thing I look forward to more than your return."

There was dream Eric in the flesh. My mouth dropped open, only to make a squeaking sound. I pointed to the counter. "I'm going to go now," I eeked out, hardly able to speak.

Josie was waiting for me near the end of the display case. I had texted her when Eric walked in about thirty minutes before, telling her I needed reinforcements. She was shaking her head at me. "Hey there." She clapped loudly in my face, bringing me back to my senses. "What was all that about? Looks like you were on a date. Did you forget that he's enemy number one?"

"I know, I know," I whispered, mad at myself.

"He's trying to seduce you." Josie glared at the man who was now fixedly staring at his phone while simultaneously writing notes at a furious pace. What had he found? Surely it couldn't be about me. Honestly, besides having weird abilities, I had a boring history; you know, other than traveling the world in search of exotic plants and curing people.

"What reason would he have to seduce me?" I kept my voice low in the hope that none of my other customers heard what we were talking about. The town was already abuzz about the reporter. Some people had purposefully sought him out, offended on my behalf. I'd heard sweet Fran, who was a regular customer of mine, had even set her German shepherd on him, though apparently Eric was some kind of dog whisperer and it all came to nothing except him being licked half to death. I was almost jealous of the dog.

"Oh, I don't know. Maybe because you're hot and he wants to sleep with you," Josie responded too loudly.

I elbowed her.

She lowered her voice. "He's probably waiting to offer you a deal. Sex in exchange for him keeping his mouth shut."

That would be a fatal error on his part. And it made me sick to think that was his plan. My insides squirmed imagining he was that kind of man. Sure, he was a jerk, but sexual coercion was inexcusable. "There's nothing for him to keep his mouth shut about."

Josie patted my arm. "I know. Seriously, you're so vanilla."

"Thanks for that."

She laughed. "You know it's true. You don't even date."

I stared at Eric, thinking about the dates we had shared in my dreams. Last night it was a picnic at Emerald Falls, above the town. It started out cute and innocent, and then we ended up in the water, and let's just say it became a hot spring. Apparently, I had a better imagination than I ever knew. So much so, I couldn't wait to go to bed tonight. I shook myself out of those thoughts. "I need to get to work," I commented.

"All right. I'll keep an eye on the reporter. Do you want me to seduce him? I'm not above some bribery." She wagged her brows.

"No," I said way too fast.

She flashed me a crooked grin. "You like him."

"Of course, I don't." I blushed. "I gotta go." In haste I headed back behind the counter to make Eric's tea.

Josie giggled before sauntering Eric's way and taking a seat at his table. She said nothing, just folded her arms and gave him the look. The look only a southern woman could give. It had been known to put the fear of God in many a child, and man, I was told. However, Eric hardly paid her any attention. Whatever game he was playing, he was good at it. But he had no idea who he was up against. Josie stretched out her legs and propped her feet up on the table. Normally, I wouldn't have wanted her to do that, for sanitary reasons, but I let it slide. Seeing the shock in Eric's eyes was worth it. His shock, though, was soon replaced with determination. He went right back to work as if she weren't there.

All my employees and customers were glued to the cat and mouse game going on in the corner. If anything, I think Eric's presence would be good for business, at least in the short term. What if he did find something to raise suspicions that I wasn't normal? Would people start to believe it was witchcraft, as a few people already suspected? Would I get figuratively burned at the stake? Maybe I would be forced to leave and take on a new identity before I was ready. I'd hoped to stay in Riverhaven until I was thirty-five. It was the first place that had felt like home in a long time. The first time I'd had a best friend other than my mother. Mom had always cautioned against forming attachments to mortals, yet all I'd found myself wanting to do was get close to people.

I had Leann drop off Eric's tea at his table. I chose a rose damiana tea that would not only help him relax but maybe soften his heart a bit. I could never be sure. I had a feeling he was a tough cookie to crack. Maybe he hadn't gotten enough love as a child. Something told me he hid who he really was behind his beautiful, hard exterior. I could tell that he carefully watched his emotions. Even when he'd told me he couldn't wait for me to return, I could see how it agitated him that he'd expressed how he truly felt. I wasn't the only one with secrets to keep. Or maybe it was just the nature of his job.

While Eric and Josie proceeded with their battle of wills, I got ready for my next wedding cake tasting appointment. During each appointment I offered a variety of flavors, everything from carrot cake to fresh strawberries-and-cream cake. But there was always one special cake. Today it was the lemon-berry cake. I'd added an elixir infused with enhanced valerian and blackthorn to it. No one would be able to the detect the extra ingredients, but once digested, it would encourage the partaker to be honest with themselves and hopefully their partner. Sometimes they needed a little coaxing on my part. I could tell if one or both partners needed to share something. It was all in the tint of their skin. The redder the tint, the bigger the indiscretion. However, while the elixir had the power to bring out the lies in people, the opposite was true as well. If the couple were truly in love, with no secrets between them, the elixir would have them professing their heartfelt feelings for their intended. I loved when that happened. And I hoped for Gabrielle and Richie's sake that today only feelings of love would exist.

What I hadn't accounted for was Eric staying for the show. Apparently, he'd run into Gabrielle yesterday while he was interviewing people. She'd blabbed about their appointment, and he wanted a front-row seat. That was disappointing. I'd thought he'd come to see me. I really needed to stop thinking like that. I was going to have to make myself an elixir for clarity and sanity soon if I couldn't get control over my thoughts.

I tried not to let his presence throw me off my game when the happy couple arrived. They really were cute. High school and college sweethearts. They'd both barely graduated from the University of Tennessee. Neither of them stood taller than five feet, five inches, even with their cowboy boots on. While they waited for me to bring out the samples of cake, they gazed into each other's eyes. They were off to a good start. I hoped it stayed that way. No telling what Eric would write if he saw an epic breakup in here. It made me almost reconsider adding the "special" cake to the tray, but it wasn't fair to Gabrielle and Richie not to.

When I arrived with the samples, Eric had pulled his table over to be near them and was "interviewing" them. "Why did you pick Love Bites to make your wedding cake?" Apparently, my tea hadn't worked the way I'd hoped. I would have to up the dosage for him next time.

"Because Sorrel's the best." Richie pecked Gabrielle on the lips. "And my girl deserves the best."

"Aren't you worried about this bakery's reputation?" Eric said in front of me with no qualms at all.

Gabrielle nuzzled her nose against Richie's. "Not at all. We know we'll never break up."

I pushed Eric out of the way and set the pink platter full of neatly arranged samples in front of the lovely couple. "Are you ready to begin?"

The eager pair nodded.

"Why don't we start with the lemon berry?" The properties within the elixir needed time to work.

"Ooh, I love lemon berry." Gabrielle picked up the small fork and took a rather large bite. While she chewed, she groaned in pleasure.

Richie also took a decent-sized bite. "It's good," he said with a full mouth, "but it's kind of girly. I'm more of a chocolate guy."

"We can have more than one flavor, silly." She wiped some frosting off his lip with her thumb.

Eric looked like he wanted to vomit at the cuteness.

Josie, who had come over with Eric, was rolling her eyes. She wasn't into mushy stuff either.

It didn't bother me. In fact, I was quite jealous, knowing I would never have this moment. Even if the book ever did tell me who to marry, there would be no ceremony or reception. No announcements or fanfare. I would speak the words of the binding ceremony, and that man would be forever lost to his own family as if he had never existed. His life from then on would be ruled by the curse and the power of the book. It almost felt like slavery. My dad had never complained, but he'd been an orphan.

"Try the chocolate ganache cake next," I suggested.

"Now we're talking." Richie dug in. He closed his eyes and savored the decadent flavor. "This is heaven right here." He pointed at the cake with his fork.

Gabrielle gave him a big smooch. "I'm so glad you like it."

"I love you, pookie bear." He tapped her nose.

"I love you too," Gabrielle cooed.

"Nothing is keeping us apart," Richie declared.

"You're so right, baby . . . except . . ." Gabrielle pressed her lips together hard, but her neck started to splotch pink as if she were embarrassed. "Except for . . . ," she fought the words coming out of her mouth. "Except for I hate your momma," she blurted, before her hands flew to her mouth.

Richie dropped his fork. His cheeks flushed. "Well, I hate it when you treat me like a child!"

The startled couple stared at each other, not sure what to make of each other's revelations.

Josie grabbed a cupcake and watched like she lived for these moments.

With wide eyes, Eric looked between me, the couple, and the cake, all very suspiciously.

When it began to settle in that maybe all wasn't as rosy as it seemed for the nauseatingly cute couple, the fireworks began.

"How can you hate my momma?" Richie seethed. "She's been nothing but nice to you."

"Nice?" Gabrielle mirthfully laughed. "She cuts me down behind your back all the time. And I wouldn't have to treat you like a child if that woman had ever taught you how to fend for yourself. Dirty underwear goes in the freaking hamper, and for the love of God, would it be so hard to put the toilet seat down, or clean it for that matter?"

"Okay, okay." I reached out and took a hand from each of them. "These are very good things to know about each other. The important thing now is that you remember why you fell in love and work through your issues *together*." While they obviously had some problems, I didn't think it warranted them breaking up.

They both ripped their hands away from me, folded their arms, and pouted like children.

Eric gave me a look like, *What are you going to do now?*

Oh, I had my ways. "Gabrielle, do you remember when you came in to set up this appointment and you told me you knew Richie was the one when you had a period mishap in tenth grade and he came to the rescue, telling you it was a natural part of life and you shouldn't be embarrassed? Didn't he give you his jacket to tie around your waist before walking you home?"

The corners of her mouth twitched. "Yes," she whispered.

"And, Richie, I think I recall hearing that Gabrielle helped you get through school, even learning all she could about dyslexia because you struggled with that."

Richie looked adoringly at his bride-to-be. "Yeah, she did." He placed a hand on her cheek, and she leaned into it.

"I think I'll give you two a moment alone." I gave Eric and Josie a pointed look and nodded toward the counter, hoping they would follow.

Eric immediately followed me, but Josie stayed put, grabbed another cupcake, and indulged.

Once we were out of earshot of the couple, Eric seemed at a loss for words. He opened his mouth several times to speak, only to end up spluttering. Finally, he said, "I want a sample of your cakes to have them analyzed. You must be drugging them."

I laughed. "I'm pretty sure that's illegal. But go ahead. I'll give you a slice of everything I sell. You won't find anything unusual." That was true. My gifts only unlocked the true potential of the ingredients I used. "I think it's more of a placebo effect. You know how these rumors start and people just buy into it?"

He shook his head like he wasn't buying the lie I was trying to sell. "What's your secret, then? Extortion?"

"Nah, too time consuming." I laughed. "Besides, why would I extort people to break up? That would be bad for a wedding cake business."

"It's great publicity." He snapped his fingers. "Maybe that's it—this is all just a publicity stunt."

"Why didn't I think of that?"

"You're mocking me."

"You're making it easy."

He stepped closer to me. The closeness didn't go unnoticed by me or the burgeoning butterflies in my stomach that were multiplying rapidly. He leaned in as if he were going to kiss me, but then at the last second, he veered to the side of my face, toward my ear. "I don't like to be mocked," he whispered, and his breathy words spread a trail of heat from my ear, down my neck, to the tips of my toes.

My hand, I swear, took his without my consent. Surprisingly, when we touched it was as familiar as my father's hand had been to me, yet different. Eric's touch filled me with this indescribable hope for the future. And when his fingers intertwined with mine, I felt a connection like no other, like coming home. It was even stronger than in my dreams.

Eric pulled back slightly and looked down at our hands, as if he couldn't believe we were touching, but he didn't pull away. No, he held on tighter, though his eyes said he couldn't explain why.

For a small moment, no one else existed but him and me.

"Eric," I whispered, as if we were an intimate couple, "please believe me," I pleaded. Something inside of me told me that he would protect me. "I'm just a cake maker."

He pulled me closer and raised his other hand as if he wanted to stroke my cheek. But we were interrupted by Josie shoving some papers in my face.

"Snap out of it, Sorrel. This guy is playing you," Josie snarled.

I let go of Eric's hand, though no part of me wanted to. That was, until my eyes were able to focus on what was on the papers. It was a copy of my father's coroner's report. Eric had scribbled on the top, *Both her mother's and father's deaths are suspicious. Is Sorrel somehow involved?*

I lost the ability to breathe. How dare he? I glared at Eric. How could I have ever thought he would protect me? I didn't even know him. What had happened to my instincts? "How could you?" I was hurt in a way I had never felt before. In a way I didn't understand. "Get out of here." I shoved the papers against his chest. "I don't care what you put in your stupid article, but I never want to see you again." I shook, on the verge of tears.

Eric trapped the papers and my hand, holding them firmly against his chest. "I have to cover every angle," he defended himself. "It's not personal," he begged me to believe him.

I ripped my hand away from his, making the papers fall to

the floor. "That's where you're wrong. The deaths of my parents were very personal to me. And when did baking cakes and helping people become a story worthy of digging into my past?"

He had to think for a moment. "I don't know . . . but I know there's a story here. There are a lot of questions and holes in your past. A lot of things no one can explain about you."

There were a lot of things I couldn't explain, either, but . . . "Sometimes, there's beauty in not knowing how or why good things happen. But people like you will never understand that, because you live off bringing others down. So, go ahead, Mr. Knight, keep digging. Maybe eventually you'll find the truth— that you're just a jerk."

SIX

ERIC

ERIC REPEATEDLY PUNCHED HIS PILLOW, unable to sleep. All he could see every time he closed his eyes was the scathing way Sorrel had looked at him after seeing those damn papers. He had gotten careless, leaving them out for her annoying friend to find. But when Sorrel had beckoned for him to follow her, it's all he wanted to do. He had a feeling he would have followed her off a cliff if she'd asked. It's why the moisture he'd seen in her eyes plagued him. A woman's tears had never affected him before, but the way she bravely held them in stung him in a way he'd never known. In a way he couldn't explain.

All of this had nothing on her touch. When she'd taken his hand, it had surprised him at first. But that had quickly been replaced with a feeling of never wanting to let her go. He could still feel her slender fingers interlocking with his, as if that was what they were made to do. What a crazy thought. He sat up and flipped on his bedside lamp, running his fingers through his hair. This woman had overtaken his every thought. This need to protect her swelled within him. But the only person he needed to protect her from was himself. She'd accused him of being a jerk. She had no idea he was that and more.

He picked up his watch to look at the time—one a.m. Apparently sleep would elude him again.

Little did Sorrel know that she had been keeping him up the last several nights. He wasn't complaining. He'd enjoyed their time spent together in her dreams. He glanced over at the ever-empty side of his bed. What he wouldn't give to have her there, asleep on his bare chest like she had been last night in her peaceful slumber. He almost hated himself for delving into her dreams. He knew what a violation it was, but he had to know her. To find out if she was truly as good as everyone said she was, as good as he had seen with his own eyes.

He thought about how she treated everyone who came into her bakery like they were family. How her smile lit up a room and how her touch made others happy—even himself, though he'd done a poor job of showing it. He'd forgotten what it felt like to feel that way. It almost frightened him, as he knew it could never last.

He scrubbed a hand over his face. There were too many questions surrounding her. Or were there, really? Was he making something out of nothing because all he had been taught his entire life was to be suspicious of everyone around him? His blood boiled thinking about how much he resented his upbringing, yet he fell right in line with it. Even the career he was forced into required an unhealthy dose of suspicion. It was why, when he was ordered to take this assignment, he had assumed there was a scandal involved.

However, even in her dreams she was the same woman she portrayed in life—sweet and astonishingly innocent. He was taken aback by how shy she was. Like she had never felt a man's touch. She'd been hesitant to touch him, but once she had, she'd giggled. It was a beautiful sound. Not once in her dreams had she given him any reason to doubt her. He'd tried to use his powers of persuasion on her, to no avail. Either she was telling the truth, or she was the best liar he'd ever met. He'd gotten even the cleverest of men and women to talk before. But with Sorrel, he found himself wanting only to listen to her ramble on about her travels around the world. She saw good in everyone and everything, even him. She said she could tell, deep within him, that he wanted to do the right thing. He wasn't even sure what that was anymore.

Damn it, this woman, he thought while sinking back into his pillow. Why had she possessed him? He wanted to go to her now and apologize. He wanted to take her in his arms, in the flesh, and hold her close, if only to listen to the sound of her heart. However, he knew how dangerous that could be. And he would at least protect her physically from himself. But he could have her in her dreams, if she would allow him to. She'd been cautious, not letting it go too far.

He wrestled with himself over whether or not to invade her dreams. He knew it wasn't right, yet, she called to him. He wasn't hurting her, he rationalized. Or was he? The devastating pain in her eyes flashed in his mind. He knew she felt the inexplicable connection between them too. It made him want to go to her even more. One more time, he lied to himself.

Eric closed his eyes and focused on her. The way her raven hair bounced as she walked and the way her eyes penetrated his own. The feel of her hand. For him, finding her dreams was like walking down a hall with many doors, feeling his way toward the one that would lead to Sorrel. Of course, hers was pink. She seemed obsessed with the color. But somehow it suited her. He ran a hand down her door, telling himself one more time that he shouldn't. But before he knew it, he was opening it. At first, just a crack.

There she was, in a vineyard again, wearing a white cotton dress that showed off every curve she was graced with. The way the sun shone upon her made her look more angelic than usual. An insatiable desire filled him. But before his appetites overtook him, he wondered why she was always dreaming about the vineyard. Every night he'd found her there, walking with a man she never let him see. A man he was jealous as hell of. He wanted to be the one holding her hand and sharing confidences with her. But his secrets would frighten her. He was sure if she knew who he really was, and what he was capable of, she would change her tune about the good she saw in him, even if it was only in her dreams.

Once Eric stepped closer and shut the door, Sorrel detected his presence almost instantly. As soon as she did, she was no longer in the vineyard. They were now standing on the stone bridge that spanned the river near her bakery. The man whom she obviously cared for was gone too. It was probably a good thing; Eric wanted to beat him to a pulp.

At first Sorrel smiled at him, her eyes alight, but that quickly turned into a scowl. She turned from him and walked in the opposite direction. He immediately chased after her. "Sorrel, wait."

"Leave me alone," she begged.

He couldn't, wouldn't. He easily caught up to her and gently took her hand. He could tell she was fighting within herself about whether she should pull away.

"Please, don't go," he pleaded.

"Why do I keep dreaming about you?" She desperately wanted to know.

He pulled her closer. "Because you want to." That was true. His ability was totally dependent on the willingness of the participant, for lack of a better word.

"No, I don't." She was trying to convince herself.

"Sorrel." He brushed her hair back. "I'm sorry for hurting you."

"You're just saying that because this is a dream. I should wake up."

"Don't." He panicked. "Not yet." He craved all the time with her he could get, even if it wasn't real. But compared to his real life, he would take this imitation any day of the week. "I truly am sorry." For the first time in a long time, he meant it.

"Then you won't write your story?"

"I have to write the story," he sighed. His editor was expecting something big. Unfortunately, that was his own doing. He'd used his powers to persuade him to let him have this assignment, but only because he had to. Now his boss thought it was all his idea and was patting his own back for how brilliant it was that Eric had dug up some possible dirt.

Sorrel yanked her hand away from him. "How could you even think that I had anything to do with the deaths of my parents? I was a child when my father died," she cried. "And you have no idea how much I miss my mother."

He gathered her in his arms and let her sob into his bare chest. At first she resisted, but soon she melted into him. Her tiny frame shook against him. He'd never felt more worthless in his life, and that was saying something. He hated that he was the reason for her anguish. Every part of him wanted to make it better. But how? He'd started this damn ball that had taken on a life of its own. Stopping it would mean possibly losing his job and his editor thrusting another ruthless bastard on her. More and more he was hating the damn book that ruled his life.

After her sobs became tiny shudders, she leaned away from him. "Why are you always shirtless in my dreams?"

He laughed and ran a finger down her cheek. "I thought you liked it."

She bit her lip and blushed. It was adorable. "I do," she quietly admitted. "But I shouldn't."

"Why?"

"Because I can't have you."

He tilted his head. "Why not?"

"I need to go," she rushed to say.

He held on to her. "Is it another man?" He sounded like a pathetic teenager begging his crush to not give up on him.

"No." She gave him a sad smile before standing on her tiptoes and barely brushing his lips. "Goodbye."

He reached for her, wanting more than a casual peck on the lips. He wanted to taste her and caress every part of her. But she was gone, and he was left alone in his bed. He pounded a fist against his mattress. He'd been hoping for more of a romantic interlude. He could only blame himself, though, after she'd seen the coroner's report he'd requested. She had every right to hate him, even though the report was inconclusive. The coroner had listed the cause of death as a heart attack, but that was because he hadn't had any other choice.

The retired coroner from Tulare, California, was easily persuaded to talk, and David Black's death still baffled him. He had said he'd never seen a healthier person and couldn't find one shred of evidence as to why the thirty-two-year-old had passed away so suddenly. There were no signs of foul play, but there weren't any natural causes to be found either. He'd also found it odd how his widow and little girl had left town immediately after having David's body cremated. He spoke, though, of how enchanted he had been with little Sorrel. Apparently, she'd always had an effect on people. Eric could hear the smile in the coroner's voice when he spoke of how lovely Sorrel had been. How she'd tried to comfort her mother.

Eric could easily picture her trying to help her mother. Who had comforted her, he wondered? He wished it could have been him. Oddly, he'd lived not far from her at the time, in Fresno. Except, it would have been in bad taste for a twenty-year-old stranger to comfort a young girl. And he'd gone by a different name back then. The book that ruled his life had mandated it. Cursed him to live a solitary life.

He rubbed his chest. He found himself aching to be with Sorrel. To have enchanting daughters with her who would look exactly like the beauty who had come to haunt his every thought. But he knew if the book ever told him who to marry, he would have a son, only one. And he hated to think of bringing Sorrel into his sordid affairs. She would only end up despising him, like his mother despised his father. Perhaps this abhorrent curse would drive even the lovely Sorrel insane, like it had his mother. Not that his father, grandfather, and great-grandfather were any better. They were consumed with hunting down some ancient enemy who probably never even existed, in search of another book that had never been seen. They were in Paraguay now on some wild goose chase. Some rumor about a woman living to be 110 without aging and only eating raw plants her entire life.

He was glad to be done with the lot of them. Once the book had become his, sixteen years ago, it instructed him to move away from his reprehensible family. But it had failed to mention the one thing it was supposed to tell him. He reached under his bed and pulled out the blasted book, hidden in the shadows where only he could find it. Unfortunately, he couldn't deny the book's power. He'd tried to disobey its wishes, to the detriment of not only himself but also the only other woman he'd ever cared for. He would never forgive himself for Karina's death. He would never let Sorrel become a victim of his recklessness.

Eric set the heavy book in his lap. For as beautiful as the moonstone-covered book was, with its pearly sheen that glowed under the lamp's light, it held the power to make nightmares come true. Within the book were instructions on the art of persuasion and how to enter a person's dreams, induce sleep, and move among the shadows. He even had the power to control water and steal life. Each gift could be used for good or evil. His family had mostly used them for the latter. In his own way, he had too. His abilities made him good at his job. He'd rationalized it was for the greater good. That he was taking down people who needed to be brought to justice. But what about Sorrel? Was she deserving of his wrath? Something inside him told him no.

Then why had the book sent him to her?

He flipped to the last page. On the onyx pages, written in silver, were the instructions he'd been given for the last sixteen years, each one time-stamped like a journal entry. For once he wished it would tell him something he truly wanted, like, *Bind yourself to Sorrel,* no matter how guilty he would feel about punishing her with this godforsaken life he'd been forced to lead. He'd feel even worse for whisking her away from a life she clearly loved, but she would be his. Deep down he had this inexplicable feeling they could make each other happy. That was, after he ruined her life by writing an exposé on her.

Eric brushed his hands across the words that had ruled his life. The first message he'd ever received was, *Your path has yet to unfold. You must prove yourself worthy of the destiny meant to be yours.* It was as frustratingly cryptic as the most recent one. *Take Raine Peters's assignment. The story to be told has been in the making for many years. But how it ends will be up to you.*

He knew exactly how he wanted it to end, but like he'd told Sorrel, he didn't believe in fairy tales. He wasn't meant for a happy ending.

SEVEN

I TOOK MY HEELS OFF and slung them over my shoulder before I walked up the steps to my apartment above the bakery, happy to have another successful wedding in the books. The cool feel of the metal steps soothed my tired feet. The breeze off the river made it all the more pleasant. I was looking forward to slipping into the tub and drinking some strawberry wine. As happy as the wedding had made me, I was still reeling from Eric's betrayal, which was ridiculous. I barely knew the man. Yet, I felt scorned and found myself wanting to drown my sorrows in a lavender-infused bath.

For the first time in my life, I had an inkling of how it felt to be mortal. I'd watched hundreds of rom-coms over the years and had wished for butterflies in my stomach and cheesy love songs to play on repeat in my head. I'd longed for the anticipation of seeing the object of my desire. I'd experienced all those things with Eric, but it wasn't real. So why did it feel like it was? Why did my heart hurt for a man who didn't exist? The Eric in my dreams was a figment of my imagination. Except when I'd touched him yesterday, he'd felt more real to me than anything.

This is insane, I berated myself. I should probably be thinking about an exit strategy, not what I would do with Eric in my dreams tonight if my brain should make him appear. Kudos to my brain for making that happen every night. Despite my fantasy life, I worried how deep the reporter would dig. More than that, I was furious he thought my father's death was suspicious. He died of a heart attack, plain and simple. Not to say Eric wasn't right about my mother's death. Even the authorities questioned it, but they never recovered her body, and since I didn't benefit financially from her death, I was never a suspect.

My father had been left a fortune by his parents, who had died when he was very young. Most of that fortune was carefully hidden in banks all over the world. My mother had access to her own wealth, curated over time by our family. Living for as long as we did had given us an advantage when it came to accumulating wealth. And there were plenty of countries around the world who were more than happy to overlook the oddities of our lineage as long as we both mutually benefited. I might have to take advantage of that soon, depending on what Eric wrote up about me.

The thought of leaving Riverhaven killed me. Half the town was ready to boycott the newspaper on my behalf and call for Eric's head on a platter if his article disparaged me in any way. I was afraid that would be a losing battle. I'd called the editor and complained, only to be belittled. He said he had implicit confidence in Eric, and if Eric thought there was a story worth telling, he would bet his last dollar that he was right on the money. There was a story to tell, but not the one Eric was looking for. The real story was one that would probably turn the good people of Riverhaven against me. My abilities weren't natural, and the only way to explain them would be to attribute them to something unholy. Not even I could explain where they came from. I knew my family legends weren't going to fly. Not even I believed them. It didn't matter how beautiful my gifts were. Or how I wished I could share them with the world, to heal every sick person I came across. If my secret got out, I would be ostracized, or worse—exploited by governments and corporations.

Maybe I should have listened to my mother and secured a

"safe house" nearby, just in case. We'd always had one wherever we went, no matter if it was Tahiti or New Zealand. I always thought it was overkill because the Selene family had never once appeared. But my mother feared mortals more than anyone. Perhaps she wasn't wrong. But for now, my heart was telling me to stay. I would say it had never steered me wrong before, but it had told me to do that interview with Raine. Why had I felt so strongly that I should? A better question was why I felt so strongly for the man who could ruin it all for me.

When I reached the top of the steps I stopped, suddenly feeling like I wasn't alone. My shoes fell from my hand, and I swallowed hard. I stared at my door but didn't see anyone, yet I couldn't shake the feeling that I was being watched from the shadow of darkness that shrouded the corner where I had placed a large potted plant. Maybe I should have gone through the bakery and used the indoor entrance.

I grabbed my cell phone, ready to dial 911. "Is anyone there?" I timidly called out, feeling silly for talking to myself. Riverhaven was a safe place, and aside from its one nonmortal resident, completely boring, just the way I liked it. "Okay," I said to myself as I approached my door, still not seeing a single soul. "I'm going to open my door now, and I know like ten different kinds of martial arts, but I'd rather not kick your butt because I don't want to get any blood on my pink blouse. You've been warned." I swore I heard a snigger, which had me opening my door at lightning speed and rushing in to close it just as fast. I immediately flipped on the lights, locked the dead bolt, and leaned against the door, my heart about ready to beat out of my chest. I melted into the floor, my head falling onto my knees. I stayed that way for a couple of minutes, trying to calm down by convincing myself I was hearing and seeing things. It didn't help when someone loudly knocked on my door. I jumped and a decent scream escaped me.

"Are you all right in there?" A distinctive masculine voice— one that had filled my dreams—came through loud and clear.

"What are you doing here?" I asked through labored breathing and massive heart palpitations. "And how do you know where I live?"

He paused for an uncomfortable moment, making me feel as if I had almost imagined his voice, just like I had imagined someone lurking in the shadows. Maybe I really was going crazy. First, I was falling for the dream version of my enemy. Second, I wasn't totally repulsed by said enemy; in fact, I was kind of excited he was on the other side of my door. Third, that was utterly insane, but it was like I had no control over myself.

Finally, he cleared his throat, which made me feel better, or at least that I wasn't crazy for imagining his voice.

"Everyone in this town knows where you live, and I came to apologize."

I grabbed my stomach as more butterflies erupted. He'd apologized last night in my dreams, and I'd woken up wishing he would in real life. Wishing so many things I shouldn't, because we could never be together. I could never be with anyone. Yet all I'd wanted to do since I met him was be with him.

"Well, thanks, I guess," I eeked out, hopefully loud enough for him to hear. It was taking all I had in me not to open the door.

"Sorrel."

The way he said my name made goose bumps appear all over my body.

"Will you please open the door? I'd like to give you a proper apology. And I believe I have your shoes."

I smiled at how absurd I'd been, dropping my shoes because I was afraid of a shadow. "You can leave them at the door."

"Or I could hold them for ransom until you let me apologize."

I really did love those Italian leather pumps, but were they worth the angst Eric stirred in me?

"Sorrel, I don't blame you for not wanting to see me, but . . . I . . . I had to see you," he admitted.

I stood, turned around, and leaned my forehead against the door. Did he feel the pull too? "Are you still going to write your article?"

"I have no choice," he sighed.

"Then we have nothing left to say."

"I don't believe that's true. Neither do you."

I unlocked the door and whipped it open to glare at the beyond-handsome man who was in tight jeans and, unfortunately, not shirtless, though his snug tee did him justice. "You listen here, you don't speak for me. You don't even know me."

He held out my heels like a peace offering. "I thought maybe it would be a good idea if I changed that, considering I'm writing a piece about you."

I snatched my shoes. "Maybe you should have thought about that before you started accusing me of murdering my parents."

"Now you're exaggerating." He smirked.

"Maybe I am." I gave him a small smile. "But you have to admit, you've taken this too far."

"Prove me wrong," he dared me.

I tilted my head and studied him. "And when I do, what happens then?"

"I'll think of something."

"Why should I believe you?"

He stepped closer, waves of magnetic heat rolling off him. My body craved giving in to the attraction. He reached up as if he wanted to rest his hand on my cheek; instead, he balled his fist and let it drop to his side. "You shouldn't believe me."

"That's comforting."

"Don't get comfortable around me, Sorrel."

My brain knew that was good advice, but my heart didn't want to heed his warning. There was an undeniable comfort in his touch, even in his presence. I really was going crazy. "I won't," I lied.

"Hmm." He pressed his lips together. I don't think he

believed me. "Why did you scream when I knocked?" he changed the subject.

"Um . . ." I blushed. "It's silly. I thought I saw something in the shadows and heard someone laugh."

His eyes danced with amusement.

"Did you see anyone?" I had to ask, even though I knew it made me sound all the crazier.

"Just myself." He smiled. Like a genuine smile. It was breathtaking.

It was official. I was certifiable. "Okay. Um . . . good night." I had no idea what else to say. It was either that or, *Take off your shirt, please.*

He leaned against the doorframe, in no hurry to leave. "You didn't let me apologize."

I bit my lip. "I suppose I didn't. You may proceed."

His sexy smile appeared again. "It could take a while."

I held my stomach. All sorts of butterflies were taking flight. "Like long enough that you might want to sit down for it?"

He took a step, crossing the threshold. "Would you mind if I stayed for a while?"

I shook my head no because I'd lost the ability to speak and I couldn't think of anything in that moment that I wanted more.

EIGHT

I STOOD IN MY KITCHEN, staring at Eric, perplexed by not only his unexpected appearance but also by my cat who, until this very moment, had liked no one but me. She sat on his lap as if she were claiming him as her own. I couldn't blame Tara; if anything, I was jealous of her.

Eric sat on my couch lazily stroking Tara while looking around my apartment as if trying to take it all in. "Nice place," he commented. "I'm surprised it's not decorated in pink."

I grabbed a bottle of strawberry wine and two glasses and headed his way. It was hardly a walk. The kitchen and living area flowed together. "I thought for resale value, I should keep it neutral." My entire apartment was decorated in shades of cream and gray and accented by several plants, making it look like a mini jungle.

"Smart thinking."

"You don't like pink?"

"Not until very recently." He grinned.

My cheeks flushed while I nodded toward my sliding glass door. "Would you like to sit out on the terrace? It's a beautiful night."

He stared down at Tara, who was purring louder than I'd ever heard her. "I'd love to, but I'm trapped."

"Tara loves the terrace. I grow catnip."

"You drug your cat, too." He chuckled.

I narrowed my eyes at him.

He threw his hands out. "I'm teasing."

"Uh-huh." I headed for the door.

Eric, with Tara in tow, quickly met me there and slid the door open for me. We were immediately hit with a cool breeze that carried with it the smell of jasmine and magnolia with a hint of mint. Tara nuzzled Eric with her head one more time before jumping out of his arms and heading straight for the planter box full of catnip.

"Thank you." I walked out into my own personal oasis.

"Wow." Eric looked around in amazement. "I've never seen a balcony botanical garden. Did you grow all this?"

"I did." I loved this space, which was lit up by bistro lights strung overhead. It was bright and colorful. I'd planted every flower imaginable from marigolds to hibiscus. I had lemon trees and planters bursting with strawberries. And trellises crawling with an assortment of berries. Not to mention medicinal herbs of every kind.

Eric stared between me and his surroundings, stunned. "I don't think I've ever met anyone quite like you."

I shrugged. "I'm just a girl who loves flowers and pink everything."

His aqua eyes captivated my own. "You're so much more than that."

My heart erratically skipped several beats. "I bake and decorate cakes too," I squeaked out.

"I think I remember something about that," he teased.

I held up the bottle of wine. "Do you want a glass? I promise I didn't drug it," I smirked.

"But I suppose you made it yourself."

"That I did."

"What other talents do you have?"

I stepped closer to him, only the bottle of wine and glasses separating us. "I guess you'll have to do some more research to find out." I shouldn't flirt with him, but it came so naturally.

He leaned in, his warm breath cascading down my neck. "Don't tempt me, Sorrel," he whispered.

It took me a second to catch my breath. "Do I tempt you?"

"I think you know the answer to that." He stood upright and took the bottle of wine from me—bringing me back to my senses. "Let's have a drink, shall we? I believe I still owe you an apology."

We both took a seat at the small table near the ledge. It provided a spectacular view of the river, which was illuminated by moonbeams. Lovers walked along the shoreline while others stopped to dip their toes in the water. Such a happy scene.

"You smile so easily, Sorrel." Eric poured each of us a glass.

"I like seeing other people happy."

"Like I said, I've never known anyone like you before." He downed a rather large gulp of wine.

"It bothers you. I bother you."

He studied me for a moment. "You intrigue me. I want you to prove me wrong. Make me believe that you have nothing to hide. You're pricking my conscience."

"You have one?" I giggled.

He held up his glass as if to toast me. "Believe me, I'm as surprised as you."

"I'm not that surprised." I took a sip of my wine, berating myself for spouting such nonsense. It was nonsense I believed, but I had no idea why.

He cocked his head. "You're naive."

"Perhaps, but I know people. And something tells me that deep down you're more than a brooding, egotistical, selfish reporter."

"So, this is what you really think of me?" His pearly whites glistened in the mood lighting.

I had some other thoughts, but I kept them to myself.

"I am sorry, Sorrel. I'm only doing what I've been told to do."

"Yeah, your boss," I snarled, "he's a real charmer."

THE BOOK OF SORREL

Eric barked out a laugh. "I heard you called him. You're not the first."

"A lot of good it did me." I gripped the table. "I just don't understand why. Why me? I'm not hurting anyone or doing anything illegal. This was supposed to be a fun piece."

He skimmed the rim of his glass with his finger. "How do you get people to confess their deepest secrets?" His tones bordered on persuasive and seductive.

I thought for a moment about what to say. "Honestly, I don't know." That was true. I had no idea where these powers came from. I mean, how could the earth gift a book to someone? But I knew something flowed through me. I'd felt it my entire life. It had only gotten stronger after I turned twenty-five and the book became mine. Though it never spoke to me, I could feel something different coursing through me. Like I was tied to something I couldn't put my finger on. I supposed it was the book. Actually, it felt like the pull I felt toward Eric. Odd.

"You don't know?" Eric was obviously skeptical.

"Haven't you ever met someone who you just wanted to tell everything to, no matter the consequences?"

Eric cleared his throat. "Yes," he reluctantly admitted. "She's sitting in front of me."

"Maybe you can answer your own question, then. Why do want to tell me your secrets? And I know you have some, because I've found that those who make it their business to find out the secrets of others have the biggest ones to keep."

His jaw dropped, but he quickly recovered. "You're right, I shouldn't underestimate you."

I flashed him a disarming smile. "I'm harmless."

"That's where you're wrong."

I bit my lip. "Is that a compliment?"

"Yes," he said in a soft, low voice.

I tucked some hair behind my ear. "So, what else can I say to prove you wrong?"

He tapped his fingers against the table. "Tell me about your father."

I had to hold my anger back. He had no right delving into my past like that. He had no idea how many times I'd played that event over and over in my head—my dad stumbling through our back door, holding his chest and reaching out for me. He kept saying, "I'm so sorry. Please forgive me." Only my father would apologize for having a heart attack. But I reminded myself this was my opportunity to make Eric see how ridiculous this all was, so I held back my diatribe. "My dad was a wonderful man. He loved the outdoors and making wine. We owned a vineyard when I was younger."

"A vineyard?" That piqued Eric's interest.

"In California, in a small town called Tulare. No one's ever heard of it."

"I have," he said casually. "I lived in Fresno."

"Really? When?"

"A long time ago." Something in his tone said he didn't care for the place.

"My father used to take me to the underground gardens there. Did you ever visit them?"

"No. My family wasn't into any sort of culture."

"That's too bad. My father could tell you stories for days about the man who built the gardens. He was from Sicily, I believe."

"You remember that?"

"I remember all the stories my father told me. He made most of them up. Fairy tales about a Princess Sorrel."

That elicited a smile from Eric. "It has a ring to it. Tell me about her."

I looked up at the stars and thought back to my days of walking in the vineyard with my father, hand in hand. "Princess Sorrel was strong and beautiful, of course, because all princesses are. And she went on adventures. She did her best to always help people, even if she was scared or it put her in danger." I didn't mention the crazy book she possessed that ruled her life.

"Did this princess have a prince?"

"Yes." I smiled. "He was handsome and brave. He did all he could to protect Sorrel, and she him." I gazed out over the water. If only that part of my father's stories would come true.

Eric's fingertips grazed my own. "Are you okay?"

Even the slightest touch from him sent sparks through me. "Yes. I just miss my father. He was the best man I've ever known. His death was a tragic shock." I made sure to hit that point home.

Eric placed his hand on top of mine. "Sorrel, I spoke to the coroner in Tulare."

I yanked my hand away, but he was too quick and captured it in his own. "Why would you do that?"

"Please hear me out. The coroner was baffled by your father's death. Can you think of any reason why that would be?"

"Of course. My father was a young, healthy man."

"It was more than that. He couldn't find any conclusive evidence as to why he passed away so suddenly."

"Maybe because the coroner was a bumbling idiot. I remember meeting him, and he seemed incompetent. Did you check his background?"

Eric tugged on the collar of his tee. "No. But you were a child—how would you know if he was incompetent?"

"My mother thought he was an idiot. And I would have to agree."

Eric released my hand. "Your father was an elusive man."

"What is that supposed to mean?"

"I mean the only records I can find about him are his passport and a death certificate."

"So? What more do you need?" More like, why did he need them at all?

"Where did he go to school? Where did he work?"

"His family moved to France when he was young, but when he met my mother, they moved back to the States. And I told you we owned a vineyard."

"Hmm."

I could see him making mental notes. "Any other questions?" I asked, annoyed.

"What about your mother's death? Very suspicious as well."

I rubbed my face in my hands. "I'm sorry my parents didn't die in a more palatable manner for you."

"Sorrel," he spoked in hushed tones, "I don't mean to upset you. Your life is shrouded in mystery. You obviously have wealth, yet there's no paper trail. And until the last few years, there's no record of you anywhere other than your birth certificate and a driver's license. In this day and age, that's quite the feat."

"What's so wrong with wanting to live a life unfettered by the demands of 'normal' society? My parents gave me a beautiful upbringing. I was able to travel the world and study cultures by experiencing them. I was able to learn from the brightest minds through reading books. I know I didn't have the usual child-hood, but that doesn't make it wrong. In fact, most people would say it was a gift." Or in my case, a curse. I folded my arms in a huff.

A stupid grin washed over Eric's face.

"Why are you smiling like that?"

"You're fiery. I didn't expect that."

"You seem to bring out the worst in me." It was true. I was never like this. I barely ever raised my voice unless it was to tell Josie to quit stealing the cupcakes. Even then, it was more in jest.

He finished off his glass of wine. "I seem to have a knack for bringing out the worst in people."

"Perhaps if you didn't interrogate them or bring up their most painful memories, that wouldn't happen."

"Sometimes, I don't have a choice," he sighed.

"What about now? Have I changed your mind?"

The corners of his mouth twitched in a wicked manner. "I think we're going to have to spend some more time together for me to be sure."

It suddenly felt like noon on a summer afternoon rather than a cool late-spring night. "My head is telling me to say no and that I should loathe you, but . . . I don't. Why is that?" I found myself being more honest with him than I intended.

"I don't know, but I'm glad for it."

"Eric." I leaned toward him.

He did the same, bringing us within inches of each other.

I stared at his lips, aching to touch them with my own. The pull toward him deepened with every breath I took. "Do you feel the strange attraction between us?"

He nodded.

"What should we do about it?" My vote was that we should kiss on it, but I wasn't well-versed in these kinds of situations.

He sat back in his chair. "We must be careful."

My cheeks burned with embarrassment. "Right." Except that felt wrong.

NINE

ERIC

ON SUNDAY MORNING ERIC FOUND himself once again in Riverhaven, walking over the stone bridge that would lead him straight to Sorrel. His pace was light and quick. He blamed it on his assignment, but he knew that wasn't the real reason. He craved any time he could get with the beauty who was making him doubt his skills as an investigative reporter. She about had him convinced there wasn't a story to tell, other than how maddeningly attractive and good she was. He wanted to kick himself for not checking the coroner's credentials first. When he had, late last night, he'd found a few blemishes on the doctor's record. Enough to make Eric question the validity of David Black's autopsy report. And he believed Sorrel when she said she didn't know why people told her their secrets, though he knew exactly why. It was her smile and the way her eyes penetrated his that invited him to speak. And her touch could soothe even the toughest soul—his soul.

Not to say he didn't still have questions; the book always had a reason for what it did. And he knew it didn't send him to Sorrel to give him a treat. Though he wouldn't mind tasting her. No, the book was an evil bastard that loved to taunt him, to remind him he was never worthy enough for the miserable destiny it was planning for him. But one thing it wasn't, and that was a liar. The book said there was a story to be told. He still didn't know what the book meant when it said the ending would be up to him. If it were up to him, he would have taken Sorrel in his arms last night when she'd leaned in, begging him to kiss her. He wanted to do that and more. He hated that he had to rebuff her. The embarrassment was apparent in her cheeks. But for her own protection, he had to. Sorrel had no idea how alluring her innocence was. And he feared the strong attraction between the two of them would lead to a beautiful but deadly encounter if he wasn't careful. The thought of Sorrel's blood on his hands made him shiver in the warm sunlight.

If only she would let him have her in her dreams, but there she had been coy. Was it because of the man she always walked with in the vineyard? Last night when she had said they'd owned a vineyard when she was a little girl, it had given him hope that the man was her father; however, he couldn't be sure. There had to be a reason she never let him see who she was with. He was determined to discover why she thought they couldn't be together in her dreams.

Eric paused when he reached the other side of the river. He looked out over the gently flowing water. It was the first time in a long time he'd appreciated the beauty of water instead of the need to control it. Normally his fingers would be itching to, at the very least, direct its current. But this morning he'd let the peaceful flow settle his soul, as if that was what his power over water was meant to give him all along. Or maybe the peace had more to do with the woman who was headed in his direction. Sorrel and her friend Josie were running along the river's path. The sun graced Sorrel's lithe body, dressed only in running shorts and a sports bra. Her sweat-beaded, creamy skin shone, making him want to bask in the glory of her.

When Sorrel saw him, she stopped in her tracks, taking deep breaths in and out. Her friend questioned why she'd stopped, until she followed the direction of Sorrel's gaze. Josie gave Eric a sneer that would have frightened most men. But Eric wasn't just any man, and he only had eyes for the gorgeous creature who was having a hard time keeping her smile to herself.

Josie jabbed Sorrel with her elbow. "Stop acting like you like him."

Sorrel pressed her lips together and looked down at her running shoes, doing her best to act unaffected. But Eric knew better, because he was just as affected by her. Even more so this morning with the little clothing she wore to cover up her lean, toned body that had curves in all the right places. She was a vision. It was all he could do not to run to her, pull her sweaty body up against his, and undo her messy bun. How his fingers longed to run through her hair. His mouth ached to taste the salt on her lips from the perspiration dripping off her.

"You have a lot of nerve showing up here, buddy." Josie interrupted Eric's salacious thoughts as he sauntered toward them. When he reached the beautiful pair, she poked his chest. "We protect our own here in Riverhaven. So why don't you go crawl back to whatever . . ." She trailed off, now fascinated with his chest. She kept poking it, but in different spots. "Dang. You're rock solid. Like, wow," her voice became breathy. She went from poking him to practically massaging his chest with her curiously strong hand.

Eric's brow quirked. "Excuse me."

Sorrel grabbed Josie's hand. "Sorry, she's still learning to keep her hands to herself."

Eric wished Sorrel would take some lessons from her uninhibited friend and use them in her dreams.

Josie unabashedly stepped away from him. "Just because you're freakishly hot, doesn't mean you're welcome here."

"I think we should let Sorrel be the judge of that." He gave Sorrel his best smoldering smile.

Sorrel looked between her friend and Eric, rubbing her

neck. "Well, I mean, maybe we should find out why he's here," Sorrel squeaked.

Josie rolled her eyes. "You're hopeless. I'm going to finish my run." She pointed her finger at Eric. "I will hurt you if you mess with her."

Eric shoved his hands into the pockets of his jeans. "I was just hoping to finish our interview while I take her to brunch."

A wide smile lit up Sorrel's face before her hand flew up and covered her mouth. Eric was both amused and frustrated by how conflicted she behaved. She was the same way in her dreams. He knew she had every right to be. In fact, she should run the other way from him. He was confused as to why she hadn't yet. As conceited as it sounded, Eric knew how good looking he was. He didn't think, though, that Sorrel was someone who valued looks over substance. No, from all his interactions with her, he could tell she was someone who esteemed a person's heart.

Honestly, he was beginning to wonder if the book wasn't playing some part in their unnatural attraction. Not to say he doubted why he was bewitched by her. One only had to look at her and talk to her for five minutes to know why. But he questioned why she was just as drawn to him. Which made him more suspicious that the book was playing a role, as his heart was undeserving of her. What nefarious purpose did the book have? Maybe he should turn around and leave. He almost did, but then Sorrel owned her smile and said, "I'd like that, but I need to shower first."

Eric's first thought was to ask her if she wanted company, but he knew that wouldn't go over well with Sorrel or Josie. And he had to protect her from himself. It was going to be easier said than done. "I'll wait." Eric was happy to oblige.

Josie whispered something in Sorrel's ear before turning to scowl at him. "I won't be far," she warned as she jogged off.

"I get the feeling she doesn't like me," Eric joked.

"I don't know. By the way she was petting you, I think you

could easily change her mind." Sorrel drank deeply from her pink water bottle.

"Do you run often?" Eric asked, fighting the urge to make the water in her bottle cascade down her chest. He remembered how beautiful she'd looked the night he'd coaxed her into the water during one of her dreams. The way her T-shirt had clung to her, showing off her figure. The way her dark hair was made darker by the water and how it contrasted so beautifully with her creamy, smooth complexion.

"A few times a week," she answered. "Do you want to wait in my apartment while I get ready?" She bit her lip as if she were afraid it was too bold to ask a man up to her place. Surely this woman had a thousand suitors knocking down her door.

"If you're comfortable with that."

She nodded, though her cheeks turned crimson. "Tara will be happy. Once she came off her catnip high, she kept looking for you after you left last night."

Eric stepped closer. "Will it make you happy, Sorrel?" He wasn't sure why he asked her that, but all he wanted to do was make her happy, even though he knew it was impossible.

She rubbed her red, blotched chest. "I think so."

He tilted his head. "You don't know?"

"I don't know anything about you," she whispered, "other than I want to know everything about you. But that makes me sound crazy."

"Then we're both crazy."

"Are you using me?" Her voice pleaded with him to tell her no.

"Is that what Josie whispered?"

"She's worried you're trying to seduce me and will hold the article over my head if I don't give in to you. She thinks I'm naive."

"I would agree with her on that account, although I like that about you. But the answer is no, I'm not trying to seduce you."

At least not in the flesh, he thought. "I need to finish my research and turn in something to my editor by the end of the week."

"Yeah, of course," she sounded disappointed. She marched toward her apartment. "You know I could sue you for libel?"

He followed her, chuckling. "You haven't even read the article yet."

She stopped and looked him squarely in the eyes. "Will I want to?"

A thousand thoughts crossed his mind. Everything from how she'd made him question his judgment to the little voice in his head that told him there was a story to tell. Yet none of that mattered, because when he peered into her soulful eyes that begged him to do right by her, this overwhelming desire to protect her consumed him. "Yes," he found himself promising her, before he could stop himself. And suddenly, the consequences didn't matter, only the grateful smile she flashed him before she threw her arms around him.

"Thank you." She squeezed him tight.

Without hesitation, he wrapped his arms around her, pressing her sweaty body to his. The touch of her bare skin beneath his hands was more pleasurable than it had been in her dreams. He deeply breathed in the scent of almond and honey from her damp hair. It was more intoxicating than vodka. When she buried her head in his chest, he almost lost all reason. He was seconds away from sweeping her up into his arms and capturing her lips. Beckoning her into the water, where they could live out not only her dream but his greatest desire.

Thankfully Sorrel pulled away from him, though with regret in her eyes. "I'm sorry. You told me not to get comfortable with you. It was wrong of me to touch you like that."

He could hear the internal debate in her voice. The argument raged inside of him, too. Still, he knew she'd done the right thing, no matter how much he wanted to disagree with her and pull her back into his arms.

She took another step away from him. "I hope you'll forgive me."

He clasped his hands behind his back to stop himself from doing something reckless and reaching for her. "There's no need to apologize."

Relief washed over her beautiful face. "In that case, would you mind if I made you brunch? I'm particular about what I eat."

His mouth said, "That would be great." But his mind yelled, *What in the hell have you done?* Not only was he going to have to write some feel-good piece, which meant entangling himself further with the adorable creature in front of him, but his boss was going to have his head. He was going to have to think of something to appease him. And what about the book? What would it do?

TEN

I SMOOTHED OUT MY BLOUSE and took at least twenty deep breaths—in and out—feeling like a naughty schoolgirl who had sneaked a boy up to my room, terrified of getting caught by my mother. I could hear her now. She would say I was inviting trouble, going against the rules set by a book that no longer spoke. But I couldn't stop thinking about being in Eric's strong arms and hearing the way his heart thudded against his taut chest. It was like listening to the beat of my favorite song. A song I'd never heard before, yet I recognized its rich melody. I wanted to run out of my bedroom, throw myself in his arms again, and play it on repeat.

Unfortunately, he was a temptation I knew I could never give in to. "Rules are meant to keep you safe," I could hear my mother say. Even my father had begged me to always follow the rules of the book. However, he had encouraged me to listen to my heart too.

I stared at my nightstand with the hidden drawer that kept my secret. A salvia plant sat on top of it that my mother had given me as an added precaution. Infused with our energy, the plant would make anyone who tried to steal the book fall into a state of deep hallucination, thus forgetting why they were there. I almost laughed at how silly it seemed. However, I wondered how my father would feel if I told him my heart wanted Eric. I pictured Dad taking my face in his hands and saying, "Sorrel, you must break this curse." I closed my eyes and sighed. He was right. And I knew what that meant—I would die alone. Besides, Eric obviously wasn't looking for a relationship with me. He kept warning me to keep my distance. But, like an idiot who had no control over herself, I kept throwing myself at him.

These were helpful thoughts, no matter how embarrassing they were. He was here to finish interviewing me. He would write his article, and we would probably never see each other again. The thought physically pricked my heart. I rubbed my chest, begging myself to get ahold of these unrealistic desires. I knew what my destiny was, and I wouldn't endanger anyone's life with a careless act. But would making out with Eric once be so bad? *Knock it off, Sorrel.*

I opened my bedroom door and was hit by a sweet scene. Tara was cuddled up against Eric's chest, purring at a ridiculous decibel level. I would purr for him like that, too. *Really, Sorrel, stop it.* "Thanks for waiting," I said, before I stopped myself from pushing my cat out of his arms and cleaning him with my tongue.

Eric perused me, taking in my white shorts and paisley peasant blouse before flashing me a smile. "No problem. Your cat kept me company."

"I see that." I eyed his black tee. "I have a lint roller if you're interested." Tara looked up at me as if she were offended that I'd even hinted that she shed.

Eric placated her by petting her head ever so gently. His actions didn't fit the brooding tough-guy persona he gave off, but honestly, I wasn't surprised. Something deep within me knew he wasn't the man he sold to the world. It made me wonder why he felt the need to hide who he really was.

Eric stood, making sure not to jostle Tara. "Are you sure I can't take you out to eat? I don't want to trouble you."

"It's no trouble at all. I love to cook. Besides, I can make a Greek asparagus omelet that will make you want to sing."

He chuckled. "I have no doubt."

"Do you want to help?" I bit my lip.

He tilted his head. "No one's ever asked for my help in the kitchen before."

"Really? Not even your mom or dad?" *A girlfriend or wife?* I wanted to add.

He stiffened at the mention of them. "Never."

"That's a shame."

"They were never out to win parent of the year." The pain in his tone was apparent.

Maybe this was why he came off as an unfeeling jerk at times. He really hadn't gotten enough love as a child. "I'm sorry."

"You need to quit apologizing to me." He set down a disgruntled Tara, who refused to leave him. She weaved in and out around his feet. Eric was entertained by my lovesick cat. "I'd love to help you."

That made me smile more than it should have. "Follow me." I flicked my head toward the kitchen.

Eric and Tara both followed.

I went straight to my fridge and pulled out most of the ingredients we would need.

Eric looked around my small but functional kitchen with high-end appliances. "Have you always lived here by yourself?" he casually asked.

"Yes."

"No roommates . . . live-in boyfriends?"

"No. I'm afraid I snore too loudly," I teased. It made me sound more normal.

His eyes narrowed. "Why don't I believe that?"

I shrugged.

"What motivated you to move to Riverhaven, then?"

I opened a cupboard to retrieve my cutting board. "Is this all for the article, or do you personally want to know?"

"Both," he easily admitted.

I berated myself for the little thrill that gave me. *You're going to die alone*, I reminded myself before setting the cutting board down. "Grab the chef's knife there." I pointed at my cutlery set. "We can chop vegetables and talk at the same time."

"Good thinking. I'm starving." Eric slid the knife out of the wooden block.

I handed him the asparagus. "Would you mind cutting these spears into two-inch pieces?"

He held the asparagus between us like it was some sort of romantic offering. "Not at all," he said so dang sexily I stopped breathing. This was what came from never having a real romantic relationship. You get turned on by asparagus.

"Um . . . thanks," I eeked out before turning from him to catch my breath. I seriously needed help.

"You didn't answer my question."

I grabbed a glass bowl to crack the eggs into. "Oh. Well, it sounds weird, but a few years ago while I was in Phuket eating lunch at a local restaurant, I overheard a husband and wife talking about selling their café here. I was intrigued." And something told me to eavesdrop on them.

"Why were you in Thailand?"

"Because the beaches in Phuket are stunning." Also, because they grow the best turmeric. It was perfect for relieving swelling. I'd even used it to treat headaches. But Eric didn't need to know that.

"You like the beach."

"Love it." I cracked an egg with one hand.

Eric was meticulously cutting the asparagus into even pieces. "Why didn't you move to a coastal area, then?"

"It's beautiful here, too, and the Jensens, the couple who owned this place before me, made me a deal I couldn't refuse." More like they desperately needed the money and I knew I should help them. They'd been in Thailand meeting with a supposed investor in a last-ditch attempt to save themselves from financially drowning. They'd maxed out a credit card to make the trip. Then the investor ended up being a conman. Poor Mrs. Jensen was so distraught that day.

He stopped chopping and gave me a pointed look. "And where did you get the money?"

"You're not going to let that drop, are you?"

He shook his head.

"If you must know, I'm a trust fund baby." It sounded so pretentious, but it was true. "My father came from a wealthy family. Unfortunately, they died when he was young, and he was left the sole heir."

"How did they die?"

"Are you going to pull their coroner's reports too?" I cracked another egg into the bowl without looking. My eyes stayed fixed on Eric's.

Eric leaned in. "Perhaps," he said. But the way his eyes lit up said he was teasing me.

I rolled my eyes and finished the task at hand. "Honestly, I don't know a lot about my grandparents. My dad didn't like to talk about them. I got the feeling they weren't the best people." Which was sad, because my dad was perfect in every way.

"I can relate," Eric admitted quietly.

Before I could stop myself, there I was touching him again. My hand landed on his defined arm. The smooth feel of his olive skin made my body sing like Aretha Franklin doing her rendition of "(You Make Me Feel Like) A Natural Woman." My mom used to listen to that song all the time when I was younger. I remembered the coy smile she would give my dad every time she turned it on. Now I knew why, and it kind of grossed me out. I wondered, though, if my mom had ever wanted to shout out to my dad, "You make me feel so alive!" Because that's exactly what I felt like doing in that moment. Instead, I said something just as dumb. "Do you want to talk about it?" Of course he didn't. He just said he could relate to my father's feelings about not wanting to talk about his parents. But when I touched him, I got the feeling he wanted to tell me something.

Eric's gaze fell on my hand, then smacked me square in the face. "Yes." He blinked several times. "I mean, no."

I dropped my hand, severing our weird connection. Mad at myself for not being able to keep my hands off him. Maybe Josie wasn't the only person with a problem. Did they have self-help groups for that?

Eric turned from me and started chopping the asparagus again, this time with a vengeance. "It was your mother who taught you how to bake, right?" he asked, flustered.

"Wait." I needed a second to compose myself and think. "I don't want you to mention my money in your article. I don't want my friends to see me any differently."

"Fine," he hastily agreed.

"I've upset you."

He laid the knife down and pressed his palms against the granite, closing his eyes. "You vex me."

"That's a strong word." I tried to keep the hurt out of my voice but failed.

He opened his eyes and turned toward me. "That wasn't meant as a slight. It's just ever since I've met you, I want to . . ."

"You want to what?"

He let out a heavy breath. "Never mind. Who taught you how to bake?"

"Like I told you before, my mother. And a phenomenal pastry chef by the name of Gaston Ansel, from New York City." I shouldn't leave Gaston out. I still used many of his decorating tips.

"I thought you said you didn't go to culinary school?"

"I didn't. I met him when my mother and I stayed in New York the summer I turned seventeen. My mom loved the art museums there. She made me write a research paper each week about every artist from Manet to Picasso. As a reward for a job well done, we took private lessons from Gaston. The man made a chocolate framboisier cake that could make a grown man cry."

Eric chuckled. "You've lived quite the life, Sorrel."

For being so cursed, I knew how lucky I'd been. "I suppose I have."

"Riverhaven must seem tame to you."

"Not at all. Just the other day, Clive Jones brought his prized pig into the bakery for a birthday cupcake." I giggled thinking about the pig with a big red bow on her head.

Eric joined in and laughed deeply. "I'm sorry I missed that."

"It could have really added something to your story."

Eric's laughter ceased. "You're all this story needs," he said under his breath.

"I'm interested to read what you write about me. To see how you see me."

Eric set the knife down and hesitantly tucked some tendrils of my hair behind my ear. "If only you could know how I see you."

Aretha Franklin was going off in my head again. "Then what?" I whispered.

"Then there would be a much different ending to this story."

I had a feeling that was a story I would want to read.

ELEVEN

ERIC

THE LAST THING ERIC WANTED to be was holed up in his car in front of the Gold Phone Booth—one of Atlanta's most exclusive nightclubs—waiting for Ivy Davies to arrive. She was the executive vice president for the upscale Palmer department stores that dotted the south. She was also rumored to be the mistress of Clayton Palmer, the owner and CEO. Eric's skin crawled just thinking about the man. Clayton Palmer painted himself as a family man and upstanding citizen. He was one of the most admired and respected businessmen in the city. In reality, he was the scum of the earth. And Eric's ticket to protecting Sorrel. After Eric got the scoop on the illegal sweatshops being run by Clayton Palmer, his editor would forget Sorrel had ever been on their radar.

If only Eric could forget about Sorrel. Not that he wanted to, but it would make his life a whole hell of a lot easier. For one, he wouldn't be sitting there pining for someone he could never have, playing over and over in his mind their time spent together yesterday. He couldn't help but smile, thinking about how she'd not only made him brunch but a birthday cake, too, when he mentioned he'd never had one. Why celebrate your birthdays when you live for as long and as miserably as his kind did? At least that was how his mother and father looked at it. Sorrel thought it was a crime and remedied the situation, even though his birthday wasn't until September. She'd found it "cute" that he was only twenty-eight and younger than her. Though she did say he acted much older. She was nothing, if not observant. What would she think if she knew he was really forty-one? That he would never age and would live for at least another hundred and fifty years? As much as he wanted the beauty, he would never wish her a life of watching herself age while her husband remained youthful. It had driven his mother to the point of madness.

Eric closed his eyes and thought of much more pleasant thoughts. A vision of Sorrel eating some of the strawberries she was using to make his cake filled him with unspeakable pleasure. The way her luscious, begging-to-be-kissed lips covered the bursting ripe berries had him needing to take a cold shower. It had almost thrown him over the edge when she held one up for him to taste. She had no idea how sexy she was, which only made her more desirable.

Not only had the woman baked him a cake and sung to him, but she'd dragged him all over town delivering her homemade stinging nettle-and-peppermint tea to half the residents of Riverhaven, who were suffering from seasonal allergies. She was a damn saint and beloved by everyone. Eric was sure the town would eventually canonize her, or at the very least rename Riverhaven in her honor. She'd even gotten most of the residents to forgive him for his indiscretion of ever doubting her. She'd blamed it on a lapse in judgment and not eating enough cake.

Eric leaned his head on the steering wheel. He knew very well it wasn't a complete lapse in judgment, but none of that mattered. All that mattered was that Sorrel was happy. Maybe she was right—there was something beautiful in not knowing why good things happen. And Sorrel was good. He felt her light shining into his dark soul.

He sat up and sighed. His dark powers would come out tonight. The ones he tried to keep in check. The ones he hated because he'd seen his father use them all too often. He'd been trying to take down Clayton Palmer in a more civilized manner, but that was before the book had interfered and sent him careening into Sorrel's life. His looming deadline for Sorrel's story meant there was no time left. Clayton's mistress and his repugnant associates were going to talk, all on the record. They weren't going to do it willingly, though they would never realize it after Eric was done with them. Eric appeased his guilt by reminding himself that Clayton Palmer was the vilest of humans. The man was getting rich off exploiting the weak. He used immigrants—many who didn't speak English and none who had any working knowledge of the legal system—to work in deplorable conditions sewing clothes for his department stores. Many of the workers were underaged and trafficked. All were too afraid to go to the authorities for fear of being deported, or worse.

Eric saw a flash of headlights and was alerted to Ivy arriving in her Mercedes, which probably cost more than double his annual salary. The middle-aged woman. who had more plastic in her than a Tupperware store, stepped out of her vehicle in a silver sheen dress and tossed her keys to the valet before slinking into the club. That meant it was showtime for Eric. He straightened his black silk tie and did one more check in his rearview mirror. He tried smoothing the cowlick on the crown of his dark hair that never wanted to behave. How he wished he was getting ready to meet Sorrel for a date instead of seducing Ivy Davies. But he needed names, and she was the first key to unlocking the downfall of Clayton Palmer.

Eric exited his vehicle and slid into his black suit coat. The club had a strict dress code. He looked across the street at the understated brick building with a gold telephone booth outside of it. It looked like nothing special on the outside, but he knew inside it was a rich person's paradise. Well, for some rich people.

He could never imagine Sorrel here. The quirky heiress obviously wanted to remain anonymous in her do-gooder ways. He almost wondered if she or her late father were Robin Hoods, robbing the rich to give to the poor. If she was, he didn't want to know. For once in his life, he just wanted someone to be who they professed to be.

Eric strutted across the street in the humid night air, acting as if he belonged at such a ritzy joint. The book had always chosen careers for him that, despite his two rounds of college, kept him from being wealthy. He was hoping in his next go round of life, the book would be kinder, but he knew that bastard had it out for him. It most likely took pleasure in keeping him in the lower middle class, just like it probably took pleasure in giving him a taste of the most incredible woman he'd ever met, only to keep her from him.

He walked in through the golden phone booth entrance and was greeted by a tall, cool brunette dressed in a body-hugging burgundy dress. She had a tablet in hand, ready to check the guest list. The list Eric wasn't on.

"Hello," Eric purred. He caught the name on her name tag. "Shaylee, is it?"

Shaylee flashed him a brilliant smile. "Name."

Eric ran a finger down her silky bare arm, though it gave him no pleasure; in fact, it made him feel ill in a way he'd never experienced. Almost as if his body were telling him his touch was meant for someone else. He knew who he wanted that someone to be. However, he had no choice but to touch the hostess if he wanted access to the club. Eric caught the gaze of the pretty brunette, which was exactly what he needed. He held her eyes with his own while focusing intently on what he needed her to see. Energy built up inside of him—energy that contained the picture she needed to see and the words she needed to speak. Once it was fully formed, he pushed the energy into her.

Shaylee blinked and twitched as if she'd been hit with static electricity, but she did exactly what Eric had silently instructed her to do. She looked at her tablet and scrolled down her list. "I see you here, Mr. Knight." She gave him a toothy smile. "Enjoy your evening."

"Thank you." Eric moved past her, half-hating himself for manipulating the woman, yet knowing tonight it would be the most harmless thing he would do. He flexed his hand as if it would remove the sensation of Shaylee's skin from his fingers. It was odd—he'd never had that reaction before. Normally the feel of a pretty woman's skin would give him some pleasure, but everything seemed to be different, ever since the book had pushed him headlong into Sorrel's world.

The club had a masculine bent to it, with several leather couches grouped in different seating arrangements throughout the place. The smell of cigars and brandy lingered in the air. Eric weaved his way through the crowd toward the bar when he spotted Ivy Davies sitting in a private corner near one of the hearths, deep in conversation with a portly, bald man wearing an Armani suit. Eric stopped and ordered a dry martini from the bar—Ivy's favorite drink, according to one of his informants—before making his way over to the pair.

With drink in hand, Eric sauntered over to Ivy, who looked bored talking to the gentleman who only had eyes for her. He probably didn't know she was sleeping with her boss. At least Eric could put the poor man out of his misery.

"Ivy," Eric interrupted. "It's been a while since we've seen each other."

The pair looked up at Eric from their seats on the leather couch. The portly man sized him up, and defeat flashed across his face, evidence that he knew it was best to retreat. He graciously stood and said his goodnights. Ivy, on the other hand, tried to place Eric, but it was obvious from the confusion in her eyes that she couldn't. That didn't stop her from inviting him to join her. Eric was, after all, irresistible—unless your name was Sorrel, though even she had her moments.

Eric cozied up to the woman who had slits for eyes, like the venomous snake she was.

Ivy pressed her hand against the couch and leaned in. "For the life of me, I don't remember your name."

Eric smiled, not at her but at her gray roots. Someone had missed a hair appointment. "Eric. We met last year at the Mayor's Gala. I'm with the *Daily Post.*"

"Oh, yes," she lied.

Eric swirled the martini before taking a sip and then offering it to her. "If I remember correctly, dry martinis are your favorite."

A look of unadulterated pleasure washed over her face. "Mmm. I think I'm remembering you now." She took the glass from him and sipped from it.

Eric hated to, but he rested his hand on her knee. "I was hoping you would."

Ivy downed the rest of the drink before placing the glass on the table in front of them.

"Would you like another?" Eric offered.

"Maybe later." She grabbed his tie and pulled him closer. "I was thinking maybe we should get reacquainted."

"I'd like that very much." Eric caressed her knee while his stomach roiled. He needed to act quickly before he vomited. He conjured up the energy inside of him—filling it with the story and script she should follow. He was thrown off for a second when the vixen started nibbling on his ear. His first instinct was to swear and push her away, but then he remembered who he was doing this for and soldiered on. He focused back on the energy within him and leaned away, capturing Ivy's eyes. While she stared longingly into his, he let go of the energy within him, transferring it to her like a tidal wave crashing against the shoreline. She shook like a thrill had gone through her. It emboldened her to kiss him before his silent instructions worked their magic.

When her collagen-filled lips hit his, it was as if she remembered something and thankfully disengaged. Eric wanted to wipe his mouth off and gargle with bleach. It wasn't only that he was repulsed by the woman—his body wanted to expunge every touch that wasn't Sorrel's. However, time was of the essence, so despite Eric's aversion, he leaned in close and whispered in her ear, "I'm going to record you, and you will verbally give me permission to. Then you're going to tell me how your boss is luring people to work in his sweatshops and how he's getting away with it."

Fear filled Ivy's eyes. She shook her head. "I can't."

Eric squeezed her knee, his fingers pressing deeply into her skin. His fingertips could feel the rush of blood. Blood that was mostly made of water. His powers began to seize control of the life force that flowed through her. The water within her cells began to swell—he could feel it, and so could she. She placed a hand on her forehead. The headache always came first; next she would feel nauseated, and then she would have difficulty breathing. He was slowly poisoning her with water. If he let it go on too long, it would send her into cerebral edema and eventually she would die. It would be so easy. He'd seen his father take more than one life. But Eric swore that would never be him. He hated himself for even going as far as he had. So much so, he backed off a little.

Ivy reached for him. "What are you doing to me?"

"Nothing, darling," he whispered. "You want to tell me about Clayton, don't you? Clear your conscience," his tones were seductive.

She nodded, unsure.

"This is all your idea." He pushed the thought into her mind. "You asked to meet me here."

"I'm so glad you came," she said, zombie-like.

Eric knew he had control of her now. With his free hand he got his phone out and pushed *Record.* "You are aware I'm recording this conversation and you agree to it?"

"Yes," she stated.

"Tell me where the workers in the factory come from," Eric asked.

Ivy had the audacity to smirk. "From all over the world, even first world countries. Young girls are so naive. Most of them are runaways and stupid enough to believe anything."

It was all Eric could do not to burst every vessel in her body.

"Who hires these girls?"

"We have special contractors."

"You mean traffickers?" Eric didn't mince words.

That wiped the smirk off her face. "Yes." She hung her head.

"Where do I find them?" Eric seethed, debating with himself whether the traffickers would live when he got his hands on them.

Ivy prattled off several names and even addresses. He was disgusted by how involved she seemed to be. She went into detail about how they got these girls into the country and the lies they sold them about making a better life for them here in America, only to pay them a few dollars an hour. She then explained the dummy corporations and "subcontractors" they claimed to use to cover it all up. With every detail, Eric had to fight himself to not just finish her off; he even fleetingly considered the sickening thought of sleeping with her. That way he wouldn't be the one to kill her—the curse would. *No. No.* He wasn't that person.

Flashes of Karina flooded his mind. Her bloodied and mangled body after a *freak* factory accident where she worked in Prague haunted him. It had happened the day after they'd made love for the first and only time. He'd convinced himself the curse must have been broken or perhaps wasn't real, as the book hadn't told him who he should bind himself to on his twenty-fifth birthday. And Karina had been tempting him for months. Teasing him about being a virgin. He would never forgive himself for giving in to her. Just as he would never forgive himself if he killed the snake in front of him. He would let her slither away, at least from him. She wasn't going to be so lucky with the authorities.

"Is there anything else you would like to say?" Eric growled.

"You'll protect my name, right?"

Eric let out a mirthful laugh, giving her all the answer she needed. There was only one woman he would be protecting tonight.

TWELVE

I FELT ERIC BEFORE I saw him. I squeezed my father's calloused hand. "I want you to meet Eric."

Dad smiled at me. "Not yet."

I sighed, disappointed. "I don't understand why you don't want to meet him. I think you would like him."

Dad placed a warm hand on my cheek. "I know I will. But you're not ready for it, and neither is he. Don't let him in the vineyard yet." And with that, Dad and the vineyard vanished. Before I could think about what Dad had said, my new favorite voice beckoned me.

"Sorrel," Eric called.

I turned and was suddenly out of the hot sun. Eric was in my living room, sitting on my couch, dressed to the nines. He took my breath away. "What are you doing here?"

"I needed to see you." He sounded distressed.

It was then I noticed he was shaking. I rushed to his side and took his hand. As each finger interlocked, my heart knit together with his, piece by piece. "What's wrong?" I could feel him tremble.

He turned toward me, and with his free hand he brushed his thumb across my cheek. "You're so beautiful."

"Thank you." I blushed. "You're beautiful too." I especially liked him in his black suit. It offset his clear aqua eyes.

"I'm not beautiful. I've done ugly things, Sorrel. Things I'm not proud of."

I should have been concerned, yet more than anything I felt a need to comfort him. "It can't be that bad. I'm sure whatever it is, it's a misunderstanding."

He closed his eyes and shuddered. "No, Sorrel. I'm not who you think I am."

"Who are you?"

He pulled away from me, leaned forward, and rested his arms on his knees. His face fell into his hands. "You can never know."

I rubbed his back, able to feel every muscle through his suit coat. "I know who you are. I can feel it."

He turned and met my gaze. "You're too trusting."

"That may be, but I can feel your heart. And it's good." *It belongs to me,* I wanted to say. I felt that with all that I am.

"How can you feel my heart?"

I shrugged. "I don't know, but you should believe me," I implored.

Eric leaned his forehead against mine. "If only I could. But I did terrible things tonight."

"What things?" I whispered, unsettled.

"Whatever was necessary to protect you."

"Protect me from what?"

"Me."

"I don't want to be protected from you." He needed protection from me.

"Sorrel," he spoke my name with such tenderness. "We can't see each other anymore."

"Why?" I cried, even though my head said that was for the best. I had to break the curse. But my heart was telling me something entirely different.

"It's not safe. I don't want to hurt you."

I placed my hands on his stubbled cheeks. "You won't." Deep down I knew that was true. How, I didn't know.

He didn't disagree with me. Instead, his lips teased my own. His minty breath invited me to draw closer to him.

"If only I could have you. I would do my best to make you happy." He barely brushed my lips before capturing them, crushing them against his own. In his hunger he pulled me onto his lap and gathered me in his arms, making sure there wasn't any space between us. I wrapped my arms around his neck and begged him with a sweep of my tongue to deepen the kiss. He obliged and tasted me deeply, making me gasp. He groaned against my lips before releasing them.

Eric ran his strong hand through my hair. "What I wouldn't give for this to be real."

"This is real."

He chuckled. "I'm glad you think so."

"It's not?" I was so confused.

"No. It's not. And I have to go. I won't come to see you anymore," he said, determined, yet sorrow wove through his words.

I grabbed the lapels of his jacket. "Please stay." Now I was sounding like a desperate schoolgirl, but I didn't care. We belonged together. In my soul, I knew it.

He took my hands and kissed them. "I can't. But don't worry, you're safe now."

"I'm braver than you think." My voice pleaded for him to stay.

"I believe you." He brushed my lips one more time. "If my life were my own, and given the chance, I think I would find myself very much in love with you. Goodbye, Sorrel."

"Wait. You can't say something like that and leave." But leave, he did. He vanished into thin air. A pain so deep filled me that I cried out, waking myself up. I sat up straight in bed, rubbing my chest and breathing hard, feeling like a piece of my soul had just torn. It was only a dream, I told myself over and over again. The most realistic dream I had ever had. I touched my lips. I swear they felt swollen from Eric's kiss.

Feeling unsettled, I flipped on my bedside lamp. Tara curled up against me. "I think I'm going crazy," I said to her. She nudged me, letting me know she expected to be adored. I absent-mindedly stroked her head while snuggling back under the covers. I felt like a child who was afraid after a nightmare, though it wasn't exactly a bad dream. He did say he could love me. But it wasn't him. It was a figment of my imagination brought on by loneliness and an intense desire for the sexy reporter.

I closed my eyes, needing my mother. I wondered if she was awake. *Mom,* I called out. No response. Perhaps she was sleeping. Maybe that meant she was in a nearby time zone. *Mom,* I tried to reach her one more time.

I still can't get a moment alone in the bathroom.

I laughed at her. *I'm sorry. Does this mean it's daytime where you're at?*

Sorrel, don't ask me questions like that.

So, you're having nighttime incontinence problems?

I'm still your mother, young lady.

Okay, fine. You know, bladder control problems are nothing to be ashamed of, I teased her, knowing full well her body was functioning properly. The curse wanted to make sure we lived as long as we could under its control. Or at least it used to. I had no idea anymore.

Tell me what's wrong, Sorrel.

How do you know something is wrong?

Because I know my daughter. Is it the reporter?

I could hear the fear in her voice. *Yes, but he's no longer investigating me.* I tried to put her mind at ease.

You have feelings for him.

No. I mean, yes. I know it's wrong.

It's not wrong, my love. It's dangerous.

I snuggled Tara. *I know. But he's different.*

Different how?

I could hear the skepticism in her voice. *I don't know how to explain it. I feel different around him. Protected.*

Do you feel like you need to be protected? She was in a panic.

Of course I do. I'm cursed.

Mom sighed. *Sorrel, I am sorry for that, but no mortal is going to protect you from your destiny.*

Right. My destiny. To be alone.

I'm afraid so.

Tears pricked my eyes. *Maybe when I'm ready to move on from Riv—*

Don't speak of where you live, she begged.

Please, Mom. I want you to know where I am and what I'm doing. I think you would be proud of me. I want to see you again.

She paused before she spoke. *Sweet daughter, I am proud of you. More than you know. But my highest priority has always been your safety, and it will continue to be. Even if that means never seeing you again. There's less chance of us drawing attention to ourselves if we're apart. Have you checked the book again?*

No, I said, frustrated and hurt. *And I haven't gotten that tingling feeling you described when the book has spoken.*

Maybe it's different for you. You should check the book.

Why? So I can be reminded that I'm meant to be alone?

Mom let out a heavy breath. *I know what that's like too. I feel your and your father's absence every day of my life. But I stay away because a tiny shred of hope lives in me that maybe you can break the curse and live. You don't know how much I wish for you to live the life you deserve. How much your father wished for it. And as long as that hope resides in me, I will sacrifice my happiness so that you may have a chance at your own.*

Tears streamed down my face. Not only because of my mother's love but because I knew, in the end, neither of us would get our wish. There was no reason to hope. *I love you, Mom.*

I love you, more than you will ever know—until you have a child of your own. Her voice was filled with pain.

We both knew I would never have the pleasure. *I would name her Lizzy after you,* I cried.

Heaven help us if we ever have another Elizabeth in the family.

I knew heaven wouldn't help us. I wasn't sure I believed in a heaven when I felt like I was doomed to hell on earth. *Good night, or good day, Mom. I'm sorry I interrupted you in the bathroom again.*

You can interrupt me anytime. Don't get too caught up in the reporter. He won't be the last man you have feelings for. It's normal, and mostly hormones talking. Make yourself the elixir on page twenty-nine. You'll be over him in no time.

I didn't disagree with her, but I knew she was wrong. No elixir was going to make me get over Eric. I didn't want to.

Thirteen

Eric

ERIC TOOK A BREAK FROM typing and stretched his back in his tiny cubicle. His eyes drifted toward the date on his laptop. It had been three weeks and four days since he'd seen Sorrel. That was how he was counting the days now. He'd done the right thing, he had to remind himself. She was safer and probably happier this way. He couldn't think about the tears in her dreams or how easily she had let him pull her close and kiss her. However, he'd meant what he said. If his life was his own, he could easily see himself in love with her. Hell, he was already halfway there. The restraint he'd had to exercise not to visit her in her dreams, or in person, was nothing short of miraculous. She silently beckoned him, day and night.

"There's the man of the hour." Devon, his boss, or Devon the Douche as most of his coworkers called him behind his back, patted him on the shoulders.

Eric swiveled around in his chair to face the overly sun-tanned man who was obsessed with teeth whitener. "Devon, to what do I owe the pleasure?" Eric knew how to play the game.

Devon handed him today's paper. "I thought you would appreciate this."

Eric took the paper, and on the front page was a picture of Clayton Palmer and Ivy Davies leaving the courthouse with their hands covering their faces. He hoped they would get what they deserved. A lifetime behind bars or, better yet, working in the same hellhole they had subjected hundreds of women and girls to.

"Palmer department store stock has plummeted, thanks to you," Devon gloated. "I still don't know how you got Palmer's hired goons to talk, but I don't care. We're making national news, and online subscriptions are way up."

Eric didn't want to think about how he'd gotten them to talk. He'd come close to killing them after they'd confessed to doing more than just delivering the girls. Murderous thoughts still raged within him. He hoped the victims would get the help they needed now that the factory had been raided and shut down. He was afraid they would become nameless faces in the system that had already failed them once.

"Glad to hear it. I guess that means I'll be getting my raise this year?"

Devon chuckled. "I'll see what I can do. For now, I have to prep for my CNN interview. You don't mind that I'm doing it, right? I figured you wouldn't want the spotlight."

And this is how he'd earned his nickname.

"It's all yours," Eric growled.

"I might need some notes from you. I don't want to make us look bad." He ran a hand over his slicked-back hair.

"Whatever you need." Eric went to turn back around, done with the conversation and his egomaniacal boss.

"You should check out page forty-three. Your little article about the bakery came out today. Who would have thought you had a soft side? That Sorrel Black must be smokin' hot. Did you get more than some cake out of the deal? You know what? It's better I don't know. After all, I'm all by the book."

Eric clenched his fists, ready to throw a punch. "Don't ever speak her name again."

Devon smirked. "That answers my question. Don't make me have to write you up. I'd hate to lose my star reporter." He walked off, whistling like the weasel he was.

Eric contemplated showing up in Devon's dreams tonight and scaring the hell out of him. Unfortunately, he feared he was becoming more and more like his father—using his ungodly powers for his own will and pleasure. Yet, none of this had given him any pleasure. Except for his time with Sorrel. Even that was now torturing him. The book had had its fun at Eric's expense, as usual. But at least she was safe.

Eric turned around and flipped through the paper. It wasn't like he hadn't memorized every word he'd written about Love Bites and its beautiful owner, but there was something satisfying about seeing his work in black and white. He hoped Sorrel would read it and take it for what it was—a love letter and his final goodbye.

SORREL

I knew I was being ridiculous, and I'd promised Josie I would fangirl over her next set at the Hannover's wedding, but I was itching to read Eric's article for the hundredth time since it had come out a couple of days ago. I kept a firm grip on my phone, telling myself to just enjoy the wedding that I'd made the most beautiful naked wedding cake for, decorated with my favorite— pink roses. My thumb kept brushing over the screen, ready to click my email app, while thoughts of Eric swirled in my brain. I hadn't seen him in weeks, not since I'd made him a birthday cake and we'd laughed and talked all night. I'd thought he would have at least called. So, he didn't have my number, but he knew where I worked, and he had the bakery's number.

Maybe it was because of the big story he'd written that exposed a huge illegal sweatshop ring in Atlanta. One of my customers, Sadie, had mentioned it to me, and I had been obsessively following it ever since. I was proud of Eric, as odd as that sounded. And I was glad to know he could use his cutthroat ways to take down real criminals, not cake makers with weird lineage. But I got the feeling it wasn't his big story that was keeping him away.

I couldn't stop thinking of the dream I'd had about him. It was weird how it had come true, at least the part where he said he was never going to see me again. It was an unfortunate coincidence, I kept telling myself. Except I hadn't dreamed about him again either. No matter how hard I'd tried, Eric never appeared. It was like he had vanished, just like in my dream.

I knew it was all for the best. Or at least I tried to make myself believe that. I was failing miserably. Honestly, it hurt that he hadn't contacted me. I thought we had a connection. Apparently, it was one-sided since he didn't even tell me that the article he wrote had been published. Raine Peters, the lifestyle reporter who was supposed to have written the article, had emailed me with a link.

Dear Sorrel,

Eric asked me to make sure you got a copy of this. He was certain you had canceled your subscription. He mentioned something about you two getting off on the wrong foot. I'm not surprised. He's a bit of a heavy-hitter around here and keeps to himself. I'm still not sure how and why he got assigned to cover this story in my absence. But I have to admit, he did a better job than I would have. In fact, I'm kind of jealous of his prose. You must have really impressed him. Which isn't surprising. I tell everyone I know they should make the drive from Atlanta to Riverhaven just for your cupcakes and the chance to talk to you.

I hope this article brings you tons of business. You're a real gem.

Toodles,

Raine

Her note was sweet, and I was glad she was feeling better

after her appendectomy. She had been in the hospital longer than she'd expected. If only I could have sneaked in and given her some of my special vegetable juice with fenugreek and almond oil, she would have healed in a jiffy. Better yet, if I'd known earlier, I could have given her some and she'd still have her appendix. I knew I couldn't save the world, but I wished I could. It would help me to feel better about my lonely existence.

I gave a big thumbs-up to Josie, who was on stage singing her heart out for the newly married couple and half the state of Tennessee. She was belting out a fabulous rendition of "Signed, Sealed, Delivered I'm Yours." Not to mention she was totally rocking it in her tight coral dress. I wasn't sure she saw me among the large crowd of inebriated wedding goers, but I pretended she had and scooted off to an empty table near the cake display, where only crumbs of my masterpiece remained.

In the glow of the lantern centerpiece, I clicked on the link to Eric's article. Butterflies erupted in my stomach just knowing I was going to read his beautiful words. Words that, on one hand, led me to believe he liked me as much as I liked him but, on the other hand, confused me. Why couldn't he have at least sent the article to me? It was as if he was purposely avoiding me. Like my dream was real. Which was insane, right? My dad used to tell me that dreams were important and I should pay attention to them. Now, as an adult, I assumed he meant that in a metaphorical way—because when I was a little girl, I used to dream all the time that I lived in a castle made of mostly windows and that my pink teddy bears were real and could talk to me. Dad used to laugh when I told him that. He would say, "Your world will be as magical as you want to make it." Eric was pretty magical. At least in my dreams. No. Not just there. His article made my heart sing.

When I walked into Love Bites, I expected I would be writing an uninspired story about another wedding cake baker whose highest aspirations were to be discovered by a televised baking competition where they manufactured drama and chose the winner before the contest even started. But this hardened reporter was pleasantly surprised by the owner, Sorrel Black. From the first moment I met her, I knew this wouldn't be a run-of-the-mill, feel-good story. Because there is nothing run-of-the-mill about Sorrel.

To start with, her bakery looks like a dollhouse decorated in every imaginable shade of pink. It invokes feelings of hope and happiness—two words I would use to describe the owner herself. Even her customers seem to feed off the energy of the place, and her. You will hardly find a face there without a smile. That is, unless you happen to be daring enough to book a wedding cake tasting appointment with her. Then you should be prepared to have your deep-seated secrets come to the surface. Sorrel has an uncanny way of bringing out the truth in future brides and grooms. Some say it's the cake. I would say it's the way Sorrel can look into your soul and make you wish you were a better person—the person she can see deep inside of you. She will have you longing to do anything to become that person, even if it means facing the truths that scare you the most and announcing them to the world. But don't worry, all is not lost, she has a gift for healing rifts, too. Just a touch of her hand calms the most agitated hearts.

To top that off, her cake, though deliciously sinful, will make you feel so good you won't think twice about treating yourself to the extra calories. Her customers swear on their Bibles that it's the best health food since God created kale. It's no surprise, as Sorrel has traveled the world looking for the best ingredients and has studied with one of New York's finest pastry chefs. I would say the protégée has become the master.

However, all of this isn't what truly makes Sorrel special. What makes her unique is her ability to treat every customer like they're her best friend, and her community like they're her family. I was privileged to join her one sunny afternoon while she delivered her specially-made tea, that helps with seasonal allergies, to half the residents of the sleepy town of Riverhaven.

You would have thought that the Queen of England herself was visiting the lucky recipients of Sorrel's kindness, by the way they revered her. I heard story after story of how Sorrel had helped them in their time of need, whether it was her cure-all soup or just a hand to hold after losing a loved one. Though she wouldn't like the praise or recognition, she deserves every bit of it. I, for one, will always count myself a lucky man for being able to meet her. And though my time with her was brief, I'll never forget it. But don't take my word for it. Visit Love Bites yourself and see if Sorrel doesn't have you believing in magic.

I wiped my eyes and set my phone down. To see myself through his eyes made me want him all the more. Yet, it made me wonder what I had done to cause him to fall off the face of the earth. As odd as it sounded, I felt as if a piece of me were missing with him gone. That was more than odd. It made me sound downright certifiable, but it was true. Ever since he'd walked into my life, something inside of me had changed. I couldn't put it into words, but I certainly felt it.

Josie interrupted my pity party. I was a terrible friend. I hadn't even noticed that she'd quit singing. She pulled up a chair next to me and rolled her eyes at my phone. "Why don't you just contact him?"

I clicked out of my app. "I thought you didn't like him."

She crossed her long, lean, mostly bare legs. "I don't, but I get the appeal. Heck, if you didn't like him, I would totally have a one-night stand with him." She wagged her brows.

"You're so romantic," I teased.

"Romance is so overrated." She stared at the newlyweds groping each other near the buffet table while people congratulated them. "No matter how good the relationship is in the beginning, eventually you wake up one morning and have to stop yourself from smothering him with your pillow. And that's only because you don't want to share a shower with a dozen women in prison."

"All relationships can't be like that." I played with some of the heart-shaped confetti scattered around the table.

She shrugged. "It's all I've ever known. Though I might not be the best example. I did, after all, marry a man who was required to wear a hot dog costume to work and greet every customer by saying, 'We have the best wieners in town.' To make it worse, he thought he was talking about himself."

I laughed. "You could always date Mateo."

"And have a normal relationship? I'm not sure what I'd do." She tilted her head. "Why haven't you ever dated anyone? And don't try to sell me that malarkey that it's because you're saving yourself for Mr. Right. There's no such thing."

"What if there is?"

She patted my hand in that *Oh, you poor naive girl* way. "Honey, there are billions of men in this world. Odds are that more than one of them can make you happy."

"What if I want more than someone who can make me happy? Happiness is fleeting."

"What more do you want?"

I wasn't sure I could put it into words. And honestly, I basically had zero experience, unless you counted my very brief—all of four hours—relationship with a handsome Swiss man on the train from Zurich to Saint Moritz. And when I say *relationship*, I mean we'd made out for two of those four hours, and I never saw him again. "I just want to feel connected. Like I'm his person and he's mine."

She puckered her lips and narrowed her eyes. "And you think Eric Knight is that person?"

Yes. "No." I waved off her ridiculous, spot-on insinuation.

"Good. Though I have to give him props for how beautifully he captured you in his article. If someone wrote about me like that, I would probably marry him . . . and then divorce him after a few months." She giggled. "But you deserve someone as good as you." She pointed near the open bar. "Speaking of which, the best man has been eyeing you all night. I hear he's a doctor from Nashville."

I took a peek, and sure enough, the handsome man with

tousled blond hair was looking my way. Sadly, it was hard to take him seriously since he was wearing a camouflage tuxedo, like all the men in the wedding party. "He's cute," I commented.

"Cute? Um, he's freaking gorgeous."

"Why don't you go ask him out?"

Her eyes lit up like an evil genius. "Do you mind?"

"Why would I?"

She popped up and patted the bun on top of my head. "Someday you're going to meet your person. I just hope I'm around to see it."

What if I had already met him?

FOURTEEN

ERIC

ERIC SET HIS LAPTOP ON his coffee table, so tired the words on the
screen had begun to blur. Devon already had him on a new
assignment investigating a local hospital's misuse of government
funds, allowing himself to take all the glory for the Clayton
Palmer scandal. The guy really was a douche. If Eric could quit,
he would. Unfortunately, the book had always directed his
career path, even if it didn't always make sense. When he had
lived in Prague, he'd been forced to finish his political science
degree, which had been useless to him. He'd ended up working
an IT job until the book told him to come back to America and
pursue a career in journalism. At least this job was more
satisfying. Anything was better than answering phones all day,
trying to explain to people how to fix their internet connections.

He leaned his head against the back of his cracked, faux-
leather couch and rubbed his eyes before closing them. Visions
of Sorrel filled his mind, so much so he almost gave in and went
to her in her dreams. He was sure she would be walking in the
vineyard, but he could convince her they should be on the beach
and she should wear a bikini. Pleasure like no other overcame
him as he thought of them together on the warm sand with

hardly a thing between them. After resisting the call to go to her, he drifted off to sleep. If only he could dream of her on demand. Unfortunately, he found himself in his old childhood room, frightened.

He was a child, covering his head with his ratty old blanket while he cowered on the stained mattress lying on the floor. He could hear his parents screaming. His mother, Portia, was accusing his father, Vincent, of cheating on her again, thereby killing the woman who lived below them. His father readily admitted to sleeping with the woman, then blamed it on Portia for growing fat and ugly. Vincent swore he would have killed Portia by now except the curse prevented him from doing so. Eric held in his sobs. If his father heard him crying, he would punish him for being weak. Selene men were supposed to be strong and emotionless. Bastards. They were supposed to fight for what was rightfully theirs and never stop until they broke the curse and killed off every living member of the traitorous Tellus family. It didn't matter what they had to do, even if they had to give their lives—they would see the Tellus family die.

But Eric didn't want to be like that. His breathing became more labored before he remembered he wasn't a little boy anymore and this was a dream. He needed to wake up. He came out from under the blanket, trying to come to his senses. He almost had, until someone pounded on the dilapidated door with peeling gray paint.

"Open up the damn door," his father shouted. This was no dream.

"No," Eric whispered. He pushed himself back into the corner, as far away as he could get from the man who he'd always promised himself he would never become. He covered his head with his hands, worried that was exactly who he had become. He had used his dark powers to extract information and inflict pain. He had almost killed two men. Did it matter if his intentions were good? That he had done it to protect the purest thing he had ever known?

The pounding became louder. "Don't make me kick down this door," Vincent shouted.

Eric slowly stood and smiled, remembering something. "You can't. This is my dream. And I'm not a child." He would no longer be a willing victim.

Vincent barked out an evil laugh. "Finally learning some control, son? It's about time."

"I'm waking up now," Eric informed him.

"That's too bad. I suppose I'll have to make a personal visit. It's been so long since we've seen each other. When I get there, you can introduce me to Sorrel Black. She sounds like someone I should meet."

Eric faltered; his blood ran cold. How did he know about Sorrel? A better question was, why was he interested in her? Though he loathed to, he walked toward the door, in the name of protecting Sorrel. He grabbed the handle and cursed under his breath before opening it. There stood his father. It was as if he were staring into a mirror. Except for their clothing—his father always wore all black, no matter the season—they were almost identical. But Eric liked to think his eyes weren't as dark and cold as his father's.

"Father." Eric tried to control the rise of bile in his throat.

Without an invitation, Vincent strutted through the door.

The dingy room now held a small wooden table with two slatted chairs. Each man took a seat and faced each other, sizing up their opponent.

Tired of the staring contest, Eric started off with, "Why the hell are you here, and what is Sorrel to you?"

Vincent slapped his hand against his chest, the place where his heart should have been, but Eric had never seen any evidence that he had one. "I'm hurt, son. I came here to tell you how proud I am of you."

"That's a first," Eric scoffed.

"Well, you've finally done something befitting of our family," Vincent replied, unabashedly. "I've been following your work at the paper. You stole power from the unworthy—those who would gain it on the backs of others. People just like the Aelius family," he spewed.

Eric clenched his fists, hating himself and the book. He'd thought he'd protected Sorrel by writing the article about Clayton Palmer. Instead, it looked like he'd thrown her in the path of someone much more dangerous than his boss. What depraved game was the book playing with him, and, it would seem, with Sorrel?

His father began to ramble about the Aelius family. "Those mortal-loving children of the sun ruined our lives. And those cowards, the Tellus family . . . if only they'd done their job and assassinated the Aelius queen before she sacrificed herself to curse us all, we would be living like royalty now, the way we were meant to."

Eric mostly tuned him out; he was well aware of all the tales passed down from generation to generation, meant to breed hatred for a people he had never met and wasn't really sure existed. He despised hearing about his own bloodthirsty relatives who were willing to step in and kill the Aelius queen, though they were too late. Eric only cared to hear one thing from his father tonight. "What is your concern with Sorrel?"

A wicked grin filled his father's face. "Like I said, I've been following your work. I find it entertaining that my son can take down large corporations yet still write sappy drivel. Albeit interesting drivel."

Eric tilted his head. "Interesting how?"

Vincent leaned forward, his clasped hands resting on the table. "Tell me about Sorrel."

That was the last thing Eric wanted to do. "You obviously read the article. There's nothing else to know."

"Except, you have feelings for her. I read between the lines, and I hear it in your voice and see it in your eyes." Vincent drummed his fingers against the table. "What is the book saying nowadays?"

109

"Nothing of consequence." Eric tried to keep a straight face and a steady voice. His father was a human lie detector. A man who lived his life in the dark and shadows, a liar himself.

Vincent narrowed his eyes. "Is it still speaking in riddles?"

Eric shrugged. Riddles were one way to put it. It was odd that the book was so elusive with him at times, yet had always been so direct with the previous heirs.

"Why did you write the article about the bakery?" Vincent wasn't going to let it go.

"I was assigned to," Eric responded dryly.

Vincent leaned back with a knowing smile. "There's more to the story. Tell your father," he demanded.

Eric's pulse raced. His father was a master at instilling fear in people, at pushing just the right button to make them panic. Sorrel was his button, and Eric feared for her. "There's nothing to tell."

Vincent folded his arms. "I see . . . obviously I still need to teach you a lesson. There are no coincidences in the life of a Selene."

Eric swallowed hard, thinking about how the book had sent him to Sorrel.

"Are you not at all suspicious about the cake lady?"

Eric had his suspicions, but nothing that would be of interest to his father. "Why would I be?"

Vincent shook his head in disgust. "I've raised a fool. Did my training over the years teach you nothing?"

"Other than to be a sadistic bastard? No."

His father laughed maniacally. "You flatter me." He paused. His laughter ceased, and his eyes bored into Eric's. "Let me give you another lesson. The cake lady might be who we've been looking for all these years."

It was Eric's turn to laugh. "You think she's part of the Tellus family? You've gone crazy, old man."

"Have I? You yourself described her as magical."

"It was a metaphor." Though Eric agreed, every part of her was magical.

"You don't find it odd that she makes teas to heal people? Or how she's getting her customers to reveal their secrets?"

"She studied Eastern medicine and she's kind. Something you would know nothing about."

"Kindness will get you nowhere. Remember that. And you would do well to remember what I've told you about the Tellus family. They can use almost anything grown in the earth to heal or to extract the truth. To deceive."

Eric shook his head. This was utter nonsense. Sorrel wasn't like him. But ... she *was* different ... no ... She'd had an unusual upbringing was all. She was an eccentric heiress. It didn't mean she possessed supernatural abilities and ... *the other book.* "She makes wedding cakes and lemonade. She's harmless."

A vicious grin spread across Vincent's face. "Use your power to find out if she has the book. If you don't, the family and I will, as soon as we finish up our business in Paraguay. Your mother," he hissed, "has gotten herself into some legal trouble, and we need to sort it out before we can leave the country."

"You're insane. There is no Tellus family. You've wasted your life on a fool's mission."

"Do it!" his father demanded. "And don't think about lying, because I'll know. I always know. I would hate to hurt your *girlfriend* for no reason, so find out the truth." A shudder went through Eric. "For all you know, she knows who you are and she's trying to find our book. Use whatever means necessary. If she's the one, we need to find her book and destroy it before she figures out how to get ours." He slapped his hand so hard against the table it made Eric jump. "Time is of the essence. Things are changing, I can feel it. And with the book not telling you who to bind yourself to, we need to be more aggressive than ever in our search to end this bloody curse once and for all. Don't disappoint me. Again."

Eric hated himself for feeling as if he had to obey his father, but after years of being subject to his abuse and control, it had exhausted him. So, he gave in to his father's will rather than uselessly fighting back. But he hated himself and the damn book even more for playing its evil games and endangering Sorrel. Once again, he was going to have to protect her, but this time he wasn't sure if he could. Once his father got an idea, he would see it through, even if that meant killing someone. "I'll do it."

"That's a good son. I'll be checking back." He vanished.

Eric woke up, drenched in sweat. "Damn it! Damn it! Damn it!" He pounded his fist against the couch before covering his face with his hands. "What have I done?" he cried out.

He knew in his heart Sorrel had no idea who he was. There was no way she was from the Tellus family. Or . . . no. How could she be? If so, they would be sworn enemies. And Sorrel wasn't his foe. In fact, she'd given him a reason to have hope in this world. Still, what if his father was right? What if she was using her powers to deceive him? He was sounding as insane as his father.

He scrubbed a hand over his face. He'd felt the goodness in Sorrel, and he chose to believe in it—in her. But to protect her, he knew he was going to have to make her tell him all her secrets. He already hated himself for it.

FIFTEEN

LEANN PEEKED HER HEAD INTO the kitchen. "Sorrel," she sang loudly over the music. "There's someone here to see you."

I set down the piping bag bursting with lemon frosting and turned down my phone that was blaring what I'd secretly deemed my breakup playlist. Which was ridiculous, I know, because I'd never broken up with anyone. I'd never even dated. Yet, I imagined this is what it felt like to be tossed to the side by someone you cared about romantically.

"Who is it?"

"It's that reporter, Eric Knight." She wagged her brows.

Before I could react, Mateo looked up to the steel-beamed ceiling. "Thank you, God. If I have to listen to "Endless Love" one more time, I might stick my head in the oven and turn it on high." He grabbed my arms and shook me gently. "Please go out there and do whatever you need to do with him. Just stop it with the sad, cheesy love songs."

I ripped off my latex gloves, my heart about ready to beat out of my chest. "My selection of music has nothing to do with him."

Mateo rolled his gorgeous brown eyes. "Oh, honey, you're such a bad liar. Now go out there and get your man."

"He's not my man." Though that had a nice ring to it.

Mateo gave me a good once-over. "Here's a news flash,

bonita. You could have any man you want. You know, except me, because you're my boss and I would feel like less of a man. However, if you want to fire me and then have your way with me, I wouldn't say no," he teased. At least I thought he was teasing.

"I might fire you anyway." I smirked and threw my gloves at him.

He caught them easily. "Don't excite me like that." He nudged me toward the door.

I let out a heavy breath while forcing my feet to move, more nervous than I had ever been. It had been four weeks and two days since I'd seen Eric. Not like I was counting or anything. I looked down at my pink apron covered in flour and frosting, wishing I looked a little nicer, but there was no time to change. Now that it was June, wedding season was in full swing. Which meant I didn't have time for distractions. Not that Eric would want to distract me. I mean, he'd ignored me for thirty days. He probably just came in to . . . well, I had no idea why he would come here. It's not like he was a huge fan of cake, except he had loved the strawberry cake I'd made him. Or maybe he'd just said that so he didn't hurt my feelings.

Just go out there, find out why he's here, and come right back. That sounded like a good, mature plan.

With a heavy breath in and out, I pushed the swinging doors open. Leann stood near the cash register wearing a big grin and pointing to the corner table where Eric always sat when he came in here. Wow. He looked good. His dark hair had grown out some, and his stubbled cheeks were making me weak in the knees. He caught me staring at him, and we locked eyes. And though he smiled, I could tell something was off. It's not like he was a happy-go-lucky guy by any means, but I'd been around him enough to know that his smile was subdued.

Eric stood, and I walked around the counter toward him, trying my best to refrain from knocking down my customers so I could run and throw my arms around him. What was it about him that made me want to act like a hormone-crazed teen?

"Hello," Eric crooned when I reached him.

His rich voice had me grabbing on to a chair for support. "Can I help you with something?" I said as blandly as I could, trying to pretend he had no effect on me whatsoever.

He stepped closer; his spicy cologne was doing its best to seduce me. "You don't sound happy to see me."

I gripped the chair tighter. "I have no emotions one way or the other about it." Mateo was right, I was a bad liar.

His beautiful eyes sparkled, amused. "Did you not like the article I wrote?"

"You wrote an article?" I feigned any knowledge of the beautiful piece I'd memorized. "Is it about someone I know? Someone, perhaps, who you promised to send it to before you published it?"

The smile vanished from his face. "I'm sorry I didn't get your approval or personally send you a copy after it was published. I've been busy and . . ."

"And what?"

His eyes lowered. "I thought it would be better that way."

I knew it. He was purposely avoiding me. I pushed off the chair, trying to put some distance between us, for the good of my heart. "Why are you here now, then?"

He closed the gap between us, not giving my heart a break. He tucked a tendril of hair behind my ear. "I missed you."

"Oh," I squeaked. "I'm glad we cleared that up."

He chuckled. "You're upset that I didn't contact you."

I shrugged. "Why would I be?"

He leaned in and whispered in my ear, "Because you're just as attracted to me as I am to you."

Shivers went down my spine, making me involuntarily shake. "You told me we couldn't see each other ever again."

He rubbed the back of his neck. "When did I say that?"

Oh. My. Gosh. I. Was. An. Idiot. "Never mind."

He wickedly grinned. "Not never mind. I don't recall ever saying those words to you. Why would you say that?"

My cheeks were on fire. "It's stupid. Don't worry about it."

"But I'm going to, unless you tell me."

I bit my lip. "I had this dream about you . . ."

His brow lifted. "You dream about me?"

"Maybe," I breathed out.

"It's nothing to be ashamed of. I dream about you, too," he admitted.

I rubbed my chest. "You do?"

He nodded.

I pointed to the kitchen and realized everyone was staring at us. It brought me back to my senses. "I should get back to work," I stammered.

Eric took my hand. "Have dinner with me tonight."

I faltered, surprised by this turn of events. "Are you asking me on a date?"

He swallowed hard and steadied me. "Yes."

My heart leapt at the same time my head reminded me I was cursed. Or was I? Maybe the book's silence meant something. Or maybe I was just trying to fool myself because I had never wanted anything more than to go on a date with Eric. But where would it lead? I was opening a door that would eventually have to be slammed shut for his safety. But . . . was it so bad to go on a date?

Eric squeezed my hand. "Sorrel, please have dinner with me."

I closed my eyes. "Um . . . I have to work late. We have two weddings coming up this weekend." I tried my best to resist him.

He pulled my hand up and kissed it like he was Prince Charming or something.

My eyes flew open. My body was tingling in ways I didn't know were possible, but definitely wanted to explore.

"I don't mind eating late." His breath played against my skin.

"Okay," I easily gave in. "Pick me up at eight." *I am an awful, selfish person.*

ERIC

I'm the worst scoundrel imaginable, Eric thought to himself before he knocked on Sorrel's door. He knew he was toying with Sorrel's emotions, though better him than his father, he reasoned to ease his guilt. It's not that he didn't want to take Sorrel out, it was that he knew after he seduced her into telling him all her secrets, he would have to cut all ties with her. This time for good. He would hurt her. He had hurt her. Her eyes had said it all when she'd greeted him this afternoon in the bakery.

Eric knocked with one hand while holding a picnic basket in the other. He was pulling out all the stops. *I'm a pig.*

"The door is open," Sorrel called. "Come in. I'm still getting ready."

Eric groaned. A beautiful woman like her shouldn't be leaving her door unlocked. Although to him it was proof she wasn't from the Tellus family. No way would she be so careless with the book. Eric opened the door to find Sorrel peeking out her bedroom door, her hair half-done.

"I'm sorry I'm running late, we had a cupcake crisis. I'll be ready in ten minutes. Make yourself at home." She popped back into her room before he could respond. *She is absolutely adorable.* He set the picnic basket on her overstuffed chair and looked around. Admittedly, he was looking for a good hiding spot for a book, or any other sign she possessed any supernatural abilities. This way he could tell his father how ludicrous it was to think that Sorrel was a Tellus. And if he was being honest, he could put to rest the shred of doubt that had creeped in about Sorrel. The thought of her being like him didn't sit well with him. Not only did he not want the stories to be true, but if they were, it would mean he was destined to destroy her. The thought made him ill.

Sorrel's cat, Tara, began to brush up against him, begging to be held. He bent down and picked up the white fur ball. "Hello, little one." He snuggled the cat against his chest and scratched Tara's head, while covertly poking around and listening for signs of Sorrel coming out. Currently she was belting out "(You Make Me Feel Like) A Natural Woman." It made Eric smile and wish he could make her feel like a natural woman. That he could peek in her bedroom. At her. And not just to see if she was hiding a book.

But while she was preoccupied, Eric took the opportunity to walk around her place and see if he could feel any "magical" stirrings. Though he didn't think of what his kind did as magical. It was downright frightening. When he felt nothing, he resorted to looking under the couch cushions only to find a tube of pink lipstick. Why didn't that surprise him? He went to the kitchen next and opened every cupboard, only to discover she was a bit of a neat freak in how organized she was. The only thing disorganized in her kitchen were all the notes and cards she had stuck to her refrigerator. Most of them went something like, *Thank you for thinking of me. Your muffins must have magic in them. I felt so good after I ate them, I was able to get out of bed for the first time in a week.*

Magic, there was that word again. It was preposterous. It was a placebo effect. He'd felt wonderful after eating Sorrel's cooking, too, but it was because he was with her. And if she was part of the Tellus family, she wouldn't be so careless as to use her powers out in the open. Wasn't it why this curse had started in the first place, because the Tellus family and his didn't want to share their gifts with mankind? Hadn't his family pounded into him how cunning and wicked the Tellus family was? Words that could never be used to describe Sorrel. She was a gifted herbalist who believed in natural remedies, is all. She told him herself how she felt like preventive care was overlooked in this country and how she'd studied Eastern medicine.

"Eric," Sorrel called, making him flinch. He'd been so absorbed reading the cards on her refrigerator that he'd gotten careless and had forgotten to listen for her.

Eric turned around but stumbled back, feeling as if he'd been hit by a hurricane. Sorrel was dressed in a baby-blue summer dress that fell off her shoulders and showed off her lean legs. Her hair was swept up and was begging to have his fingers run through it.

"What are you doing in the kitchen?" she asked.

He held up Tara, not able to take his eyes off the vision before him. "We needed a drink of water, but the notes on your refrigerator caught my eye." He despised how easily he could lie to her. He felt worse when she smiled at him, believing every word he'd said.

"I'm sorry I kept you waiting."

He set the cat down. "No worries. I enjoyed reading the notes from all your admirers."

She blushed. "People are too sweet."

She really was naive, but he didn't mention it. The world needed more people like her. "Are you ready to go?"

"Where are we going?"

He nodded over to the picnic basket. "I thought we could have a picnic by the river. I found a great spot not too far from here."

Her eyes lit up, which made him feel even worse. He was using her dreams against her. Making her wishes come true. He was a prick, yet he had to be, for her protection. He'd promised himself, though, that he wouldn't live out all her dreams—or his fantasies—by tempting her into the water. Not even in her dreams anymore. He'd realized how real they were to her this afternoon, when she mentioned that he'd told her that he could never see her again. He would only push it as far as he had to, to make her talk.

"I love picnics." She beamed.

"I thought you might."

"Eric." She nibbled on her bottom lip. "I'm really glad you asked me out."

"I am too." He wasn't lying.

119

SIXTEEN

IT WAS LITERALLY LIKE A dream come true sitting by the riverbank off the beaten path with Eric. We were sipping white wine and listening to the cicadas and the babbling river while the sweet, sticky air moistened our skin. The fireflies added to the magic of it by dancing wildly in the hayfield across the river. It was almost perfect, except in my dreams there was a waterfall and Eric would have already been kissing me and coaxing me into the river. Instead, he seemed nervous. No, that wasn't the right word—careful, was more like it. Several times I'd felt like he'd wanted to say something, but he stopped himself. And he kept moving the picnic basket, making sure it kept a barrier between us.

"Thank you for dinner. The berry salad was perfect." I popped a leftover blueberry in my mouth.

"You're welcome." Eric gazed out into the distance.

I followed his line of sight and noticed, under the glow of the moonlight, that the gently rippling river was now rushing. I didn't know a river's current could change so rapidly. But I didn't really care about the water; I ached to be closer to the man who was repeatedly running his hand through his hair. In a bold move, I pushed the basket out of the way and scooted closer to him on the plaid blanket. The warmth of his body added to the heat of the night.

He smiled uneasily at me.

"Have I done something wrong?"

Hesitantly, he reached up and brushed back my hair. "No."

"You seem like you would rather be somewhere else."

"There's nowhere else I'd rather be."

"Then why have you been distant tonight? The last month?"

He peered into my eyes. "I told you not to get comfortable with me."

"Yet, here you are." I inched closer, feeling more than comfortable. More like I belonged.

He rested his hand on my cheek and groaned. "Sorrel, there are so many things I want to say to you, but I need you to tell me something." He paused and closed his eyes. When he opened them back up, consternation was written in them. "You never did tell me if you liked the article."

I leaned into his hand, loving the way he so gently cradled my face. I had never been touched so intimately. "That isn't what you were going to ask, is it?"

"No," he whispered, "but I would still like to know."

"If I tell you, will you promise me you'll say what you were going to say?"

"I have to."

I tilted my head. "Have to?"

His ears pinked. It was kind of cute. "I meant, I will," he stammered.

"In that case. I loved it. Every word. Thank you."

His lips twitched, almost forming a smile.

I had to hold myself back from kissing him. He was so close, and his sweet breath was intoxicating. But I was cursed. Yet, when I was around him, I didn't feel that way. It was as if the power inside of me wanted to bind us together. It was impossible and ridiculous. I barely knew this man. No, I did. That sounded even crazier, but somehow, I knew him. I just didn't know how. I took his hand off my cheek and held it between my own, desperate to connect with him. To figure out why I felt the way I did.

"Sorrel." He gripped my hand like a vise and gazed deeply into my eyes. "Tell me your deepest secrets."

A jolt of electricity shot through me, making me shiver. An unspeakable peace overcame me. I stared at his lips that were pressed tightly together and smiled. I wanted him to know everything about me, even the embarrassing things. "Well . . . from the moment I met you, all I've wanted to do is kiss you," I confessed, before throwing my hand over my mouth. I couldn't believe I'd admitted that.

Eric let out a sigh of relief before he chuckled. His reaction was odd and embarrassing.

I pulled away from him and began to stand. "Maybe we should go."

Eric reached for me and pulled me right back toward him, making me land in his lap. "Sorrel." He gathered me in his arms. There were no words to describe the pleasure coursing through me, despite my embarrassment. It was so overwhelming. I gripped his shirt, not caring about the consequences of my actions.

"Do you want to know my secret?" he whispered in my ear before nuzzling it, driving me wild.

I nodded, unable to speak.

"I want to kiss you too." He kissed my bare shoulder, escalating the sexual tension strung between us so tight, it was like it had a pulse of its own. When he trailed kisses slowly and steadily up my neck, my entire body erupted in goose bumps. His lips eventually found their way to the corner of my mouth. His warm lips excited my own while they lingered and teased. He ran his strong hands up my arms and cupped my face. "I must apologize."

He caught me completely off guard. "For what?"

"For this." His lips came crashing into mine, capturing them as if we were running out of time. His urgency bled into my lips, making them part.

I didn't have time to think about why he'd apologized. I was only sorry he hadn't kissed me sooner. My hands released his shirt and wound their way around his neck, pulling him closer to me. My body applauded my actions and begged that I leave no distance between us. Eric's tongue seemed to be of the same mind as it plunged deeper, tasting every part of me that it could. His hands moved up and through my hair, undoing my updo. He groaned in pleasure as my hair cascaded around us.

This was better than any of my dreams. My imagination had been doing me a great injustice. I savored the way he tasted like strawberries and balsamic vinegar and the way his strong hands ran down my silky legs only to slowly creep back up. When his hand skirted just under my dress, I gasped.

Eric immediately pulled away. "I'm sorry. I got carried away."

"Don't apologize." I had to take a deep breath. "I wanted you to, it's just . . . I don't know how to say this, but I lack experience. I'm saving myself." That's something I'd heard mortals say. Unfortunately, I was saving myself for death, but to say that out loud would have really killed the mood.

Eric smiled before resting his forehead on mine. "I'm not surprised."

"Really? Most people are."

"I love your innocence, Sorrel. The world needs more of it. More of you."

"Thank you." I brushed his lips, hoping to pick up where we left off, but he leaned away. "Are you afraid of me now that you know my secrets?"

"You have no idea." He wrapped me in his arms.

My head landed on his chest. I could hear the beat to my favorite song. This time the rhythm was faster and more jagged.

"Eric, do I really scare you?"

"Yes."

"Why?"

He stroked my hair. "Very rarely in life does one get to hold something as pure as you. It's both an honor and a burden."

"You think I'm a burden?"

"The weight of protecting your innocence is."

My finger drew circles on his chest. "You don't need to protect me. I'm a big girl who is quite capable of keeping herself pure, as you put it." I giggled.

"I'm sure you are." His fingers glided down my arm. "But I'll do my part, as hard as it may be."

"I'll do my best to make it easy on you," I teased.

He remained silent, other than kissing my head.

"Eric, tell me something about you."

"Like what?"

"I don't know. Everything."

"Could you be more specific?" He chuckled.

I thought for a moment. There was so much I wanted to know about him. "Did you always want to be an investigative reporter?"

"No."

"What did you want to be?"

"An artist."

My head popped up. "Really? What kind?"

He tapped my nose. "A painter."

"Can you show me some of your work?"

"I haven't painted anything in years."

"You make yourself sound so old." I rested my head back against his chest.

He went back to stroking my hair. "I feel older than I should."

"Is it because of your family?"

His entire body tensed.

"I'm sorry. I know you don't like to talk about them. But . . . if you need to. I'm here."

The only thing that could be heard were the cicadas that seemed to be getting louder the darker it got and some croaking frogs looking for mates. I felt for the frogs.

After a moment or two Eric pulled me closer. "My parents

are all but dead to me. I have three brothers I do my best to stay away from and a crazy grandmother who should be committed. You're lucky you had such wonderful parents. They obviously shaped you into the person you are now, just like mine made me who I am." Resentment laced his words.

My heart ached for him. "I don't know what your parents did to you, but from where I stand, you grew into a good person despite them."

"Sorrel," he groaned. "You have no idea what you're talking about."

I sat up and looked him squarely in the eyes. "Only a good person with a kind heart could have written the article you did about me. And look what you did to uncover that awful sweatshop ring. You helped save hundreds of women and girls."

Eric looked up to the sky. "It's not that simple."

"Then tell me."

"If only I could."

I rested my hand on his heart. "If you ever want to, I'm here."

He took my face in his hands and drew me to him, only to lightly kiss my lips. "Let's not waste this night on trivial matters."

"You're not trivial," I whispered against his lips.

"Debatable. Besides, you're much more interesting. Tell me more about your travels."

I snuggled back into him. "Where should I begin?"

"I think last time we left off in Iceland."

"Oh yes. The Blue Lagoon is known for its geothermal salt water. Not only is it stunning, they also do massages while you're floating in the water that make you feel like you've died and gone to heaven."

"Holding a beautiful woman by the river will make you feel that way too."

Oh, wow, was he good with the one-liners. They took my breath away. But I knew how he felt. If there was a heaven, I wanted it to be like this—in his arms for eternity.

We talked and talked until the cicadas chirped and the frogs croaked their last good nights. Until my eyes became heavy. Eric didn't seem to mind. It was as if he didn't want the night to end. He gently laid me next to him. His fingers lightly brushed my cheeks. "What I wouldn't give to do this every night."

I gave him a sleepy smile. I think I drank too much wine. I was teetering between awake and dreamland. "Eric," I whispered, "do you want to know another secret?" My eyelids grew heavier and heavier.

His lips skimmed mine. "Tell me."

My muddled brain tried to form what I wanted to convey to him. "If I could, I would . . ."

"You would what?"

"I would . . ." What would I do? Oh yes. "I would bind myself to you forever."

SEVENTEEN

ERIC

ERIC SAT OUTSIDE HIS BEDROOM window on the damp metal fire escape listening to the sirens blare in the background. It was Atlanta's nightly theme music. Most of the time he could drown it out, but not tonight. Even the perpetual smell of curry from the Indian restaurant below, that he normally welcomed, was making his stomach turn. Sorrel's last words on the riverbank haunted him. He repeatedly scrubbed a hand over his face, knowing what he needed to do, yet still trying to convince himself otherwise. Maybe her exhaustion had made her say *bind* instead of *give* herself to him. Or perhaps in all her travels there was some culture she'd come across that used the term he'd only ever heard his people use. *And why would she want to bind herself to him?* he questioned, repeatedly. They hardly knew each other.

Yet he felt the same way.

Had the book manufactured their feelings? The thought made him clench his fists. For once in his life, he wanted something real. Someone to care for him, even if it had to be from a distance. Though it wasn't how he would wish it, he had a sense of peace knowing that Sorrel existed and that she thought so much more of him than he did himself, than anyone ever had. But now that peace had turned to turmoil.

Was she from the Tellus family? Was this just a sick game the book had played with him? Had Sorrel played him for a fool? If so, she was the best damn liar he'd ever come across. He knew she'd felt the effects of his powers. He'd seen it in her eyes, in the way her body had shivered. Her response had seemed true, which had given him more pleasure than he'd ever experienced. Her deepest secret was that she'd wanted to kiss him. Not even he could have made that up on the fly. Perhaps she was more cunning than he was.

No. No. NO! She was innocent and wonderful. She belonged in his arms, contoured against his body as if she were born to be there.

He rested his head against the metal railing and let out a heavy breath into the sultry night. He'd promised himself he would never disturb her dreams again, but he had to know if Sorrel was his sworn enemy. If she had the book that would break this god-awful curse. Flashes of Sorrel's dead body made him squeeze his eyes shut. For him to be set free, she would have to die. But the world needed her. He needed her. Or did he? Was it all make-believe? Maybe his father was right, things were changing. Perhaps the curse had run its course and it was ready for the victor to claim its prize—freedom.

But how would he feel free, knowing Sorrel no longer lived and breathed?

Damn it! He pounded his hand against the metal until it stung.

He crawled back into his bare-bones bedroom, staring at his undisturbed bed, wishing . . . wishing for things he had no right to. Either Sorrel was his sworn enemy, or she was exactly who he hoped she was and the best way to protect her would be for him to stay the hell away from her. Either way, he had to go to her one more time. He had to know the truth.

He lay on his bed, propped against his pillows. He closed his eyes and thought of Sorrel. The way she felt in his arms, her velvet skin. How she tasted like strawberries and hope. The sound of her soft, melodic voice. In no time, he was in front of her pink door. It was left open a crack, as if she were waiting for him to come in. It made him even more confused. Why would she welcome him if she knew he was the enemy? He peeked in and there she was, as always, walking in the vineyard with a man. This time, though, he was able to get a closer look at him.

The man had dark hair, the color of Sorrel's. He was hugging Sorrel and whispering in her ear. Eric had half a mind to march over to him and tell him to shove off; Sorrel was his. But he quickly reminded himself that he knew no matter who she really was, that could never be true. Instead, he waited for her on the edge of the vineyard and watched how lovingly Sorrel embraced the man, how she hesitated to let go. Then the man surprised him and caught Eric's eye. His penetrating gaze seemed to bring Eric closer to the pair. The air around him turned drier, as the sun beat down upon him.

"Don't hurt her," the man mouthed before he vanished. It was enough to startle Eric. He almost turned around to go, but then Sorrel called to him. Her face glowed in the rays of the sun. "Eric." She ran his way, out of the vineyard and into a home he didn't recognize. It was warm and inviting, with large windows and a stunning view of a mountain range with snowcapped peaks. "You're finally here." She wrapped her arms around him. When he hesitated to reciprocate, she leaned away, her eyes doe-like. "What's wrong? Don't you like this place?"

Eric looked more carefully at their surroundings. The neutral-toned furniture, while expensive, looked comfortable and inviting. And the large stone hearth had a mantel filled with pictures. Pictures of Eric and Sorrel, as if they had lived a lifetime together. He longed for them to be real.

Sorrel smiled. "The one in the middle is my favorite. It's the day I became yours."

The picture showed them on a rocky cliff overlooking a

white sand beach. Eric was gazing adoringly at her. Sorrel's hair was done up with pink flowers, and she wore a white, flowy gown. She was perfect. So, this is what she dreamed of? Guilt filled him. Then he remembered she never allowed her picture to be taken, unless you counted her driver's license. Why was that?

"Eric, something's wrong. What is it?" She drew the attention back to her.

"Where are we, Sorrel?"

She took his hand and led him to the plush couch. She practically pushed him down before curling up on his lap and nestling into his chest. Before he could stop himself, he wrapped his arms around her. For a few seconds, all felt right in the world.

"We're home. How could you forget?"

He hated to play along, but he knew he had to, to get to the truth. "Sorry, it's been a long day."

She sat up and gave him a toothy grin. "Well, I have some news that will make you feel better." Before he could respond, she blurted, "I'm pregnant." Tears filled her eyes.

Eric's mouth dropped, at a total loss for words. This was some dream. His dream.

"Are you happy?"

He rested a hand on her wet cheek, so badly wishing this was all true. Still, he couldn't pretend about that. "Sorrel, this isn't real."

"Why would you say that?" her voice cracked.

He took her hands and peered into her eyes. *How could this woman be a liar?* he thought. She was guileless. "Sorrel, you never let anyone take your picture. Why is that?"

She shifted on his lap; her eyes lowered. "There are pictures of us on the mantel."

"Those aren't real."

"Stop saying that."

Eric tilted her chin up with his finger. "You can tell me. I'll keep you safe." He was a lying bastard.

She leaned in and pressed a kiss to his lips. "I believe you," she whispered against them.

"Are you in danger?" The instinct to protect her rose within him first and foremost.

"I don't know." She curled up against him, begging to be held. He easily gave in and held her tight.

"Who would want to hurt you?" Besides his family, potentially.

"I don't know," she cried, frustrated. "I don't know what is real." She clung to his shirt. "Are you real?"

"Yes."

She breathed a sigh of relief. "I only want to be with you. Is that so wrong?"

Her declaration confused him. "Why can't you be with me?"

"Because I don't want to hurt you."

He had a hard time imagining the shaking creature in his lap hurting him. Though what if she was more than who she portrayed? "How could you hurt me?"

"Eric, I don't want to talk about it."

Maybe she was in a relationship with someone else, he hoped against hope. "Is it the man in the vineyard?"

"What man?"

"The man you're always walking with."

She sat up and blinked several times, as if she didn't understand him. "I don't know who you're talking about."

She was confusing the bloody hell out of him. He had to remind himself that this was her dream and she was probably just as confused. Which made him feel all the worse. But he had to extract the truth if he could.

"Sorrel." He stroked her silky hair. "What did you mean when you said you wanted to bind yourself to me forever?"

She stilled in his arms. "When did I say that?" she stammered.

"Tonight, by the river."

"I don't remember."

"How would you bind yourself to me?"

She thought for a moment. "I don't know . . ."

He believed her.

"But . . ."

Eric perked up.

"I wish I did."

Eric's heart raced. He knew he had to carefully construct his next words. "What if I told you I knew how?"

She bit her lip. "You do?"

He nodded. "You just need to tell me where your *book* is."

Fear flooded her eyes. "I can't." She didn't seem confused about the mention of a book, like a *normal* person would be.

Eric clenched his fists, both afraid and heartbroken. This woman was his born enemy. The tales were true. He hated—and longed—to do what he did next. For the last time, he took Sorrel's face in his hands. His fingertips memorized the creamy feel of her skin. He took note of the flecks of violet in her deep-blue eyes that were begging to be loved. Or were they cunningly deceitful? Regardless, he would make her believe his feelings for her.

He leaned in and brushed her lips before resting his forehead against hers. "I love you, Sorrel." The words felt natural on his lips.

"Really?" Tears poured out of her eyes and dripped on his hands.

For a moment he hesitated. Her response seemed heartfelt. She stirred something within his soul, as dark as it was. But there was no retreating now. "Tell me where your book is so we can be together. We can live in this house and make love every day." Eric could feel her cheeks burn. Damn it, he hated himself.

"I want to make love to you. But I don't want to hurt you."

"You won't, if you tell me where the book is. Please, I love you." His heart felt too much truth in those words, and it wanted to break. He reminded himself it was all part of the book's sick game.

"You really love me?"

He swallowed hard. "Yes."

She wrapped her arms around him like a giddy schoolgirl. "There's a hidden drawer in my nightstand," she whispered in his ear. "But there's a plant protecting it that will make you forget why you're there."

"It won't be a problem." He could move within the shadows if he needed to.

"But the book is broken."

Broken? She must be confused. "I can fix it," he lied.

She leaned away from him. Pure contentment radiated from her. "I knew there was something special about you. That you would protect me."

He closed his eyes, wishing this was all a nightmare that he could wake up from. "I told you not to get comfortable with me."

EIGHTEEN

I STEPPED OUTSIDE OF THE kitchen, into the alleyway between my building and the shop next door, debating whether I should call Eric or not. It had been a few days since our date and I hadn't heard a word from him, even though we'd exchanged numbers and he'd said he would call. Though when he'd dropped me off that night, something was off. He hadn't walked me to my door. Which was really a bummer because I'd had this entire kissing montage scene worked out in my head, that included me being picked up and pushed against the door. It was a five-star scene. But he only kissed my cheek and whispered goodbye.

I rubbed my abdomen. There was a knot in my stomach the size of Delaware. Something felt off, but I couldn't put my finger on it.

Maybe Josie was right, I had been ghosted and I needed to leave well enough alone. Except I didn't feel well being left alone. It wasn't like I was a needy person who required a man. I'd lived my entire life without one and had planned to keep it that way. For the curse's sake, I had to. Although, with Eric I felt like there were other possibilities. It didn't help that I was having dreams about him where he promised he could set me free. He told me he loved me. Did dreams ever really come true?

I pulled my phone out of my pocket and ran my thumb across the screen, telling myself not to be one of those women who desperately threw themselves at someone who clearly didn't want them. I thought, on the riverbank, that his kiss had said he wanted all of me. Perhaps I was mistaken, as I had very limited relationship experience. Though I had observed many relationships in the last few years of doing wedding cakes, and even without my special ingredients, I had a knack for knowing who would stay together and who should call it quits.

I pressed my back against the brick wall and sighed. I tapped the first two digits of his number when, from the corner of my eye, I swore I saw someone. I looked down the alley, near the garbage cans. "Hello?" I squinted, trying to get a better look. Great, I was seeing things in the shadows again. I rolled my eyes at myself and did something to make me feel equally as stupid—I called Eric. When his phone started ringing, I swore I heard a phone buzzing. I looked around and still didn't see anyone. To be safe, I moved toward the other end of the alley, near the sidewalk and into the light.

Eric didn't answer, which wasn't surprising. I quickly debated whether to leave a message. Before I knew it, I was speaking. "Hey, it's me. Sorrel. In case you don't recognize my voice. I just wanted to say that I was thinking of you. I feel like we left things on a weird note Tuesday night. Did I snore when I fell asleep on you? I did warn you." I laughed nervously. "Anyway, I'll be doing weddings most of the weekend, but if you're not busy, maybe on Sunday night we could get together. It could just be to talk. I would love to hear more about your days in Prague. Honestly, I would love to hear anything you have to say. Okay, now I'm rambling. I hope you have a good day. Bye."

I hung up and tapped my phone against my forehead. I was such an idiot. He for sure wasn't calling back after that ridiculous message. I didn't have time to dwell on my stupidity.

Mateo popped his head out the side door. "Bonita, come quick. There's someone here to see you."

For half a second my heart fluttered. "Eric?"

Mateo shook his head and gave me a look of pity. At least I wasn't annoying him by playing "Endless Love" on repeat.

"No. It's Rhonda Willis; her baby's sick."

I rushed back in. Rhonda was a single mother who had no health insurance and lived in a glorified shack on the edge of town. I'd been to see her on many occasions to drop off food and "medicine."

When I made it into the bakery, I found Rhonda by the entrance with her three-year-old, Isaiah, clinging to her legs and wearing dirty clothes that were two sizes too big. Her baby girl, just under a year old, was crying against her shoulder. Several customers were staring at her, unkindly, I might add. The poor woman, with frazzled ebony hair and bags under her eyes, felt the stares and cowered in a corner. I ran around the counter and jogged over to her.

I immediately took the baby and bounced her, trying to soothe her. "Why don't we go up to my apartment?" I suggested.

Rhonda nodded gratefully.

I led them outside into the steamy day and around the back of the building to the exterior stairs that would take us straight up to my apartment.

"I'm sorry, Miss Sorrel, for bothering you at work. I didn't know where else to go." Rhonda sniffled. "Jessilee has been crying for two days straight, and her fever is awful high."

I kissed Jessilee's head, and she was warm to the touch. "It's no bother. I'm glad you came."

When we reached my door, I had that feeling again, that I was being watched from the shadows. I knew it would make me sound crazy, but for my own sanity I asked, "Did you see anyone come up here?"

Rhonda looked around the small space. There was nowhere to hide, unless you could fit behind the plant. "No, ma'am," she answered.

I wasn't sure if her answer made me feel better or worse. No matter. I unlocked my door and let us all in.

"Please have a seat."

Rhonda and Isaiah took the couch.

"Kitty." Isaiah lunged for Tara, who hissed and ran off. She was not a people person, unless it was me or Eric. Weird how even my cat was infatuated with him.

"Isaiah," Rhonda scolded, "sit down."

"He's fine. Tara can take care of herself." I sat down with Jessilee on the overstuffed chair to take a look at her. Poor thing was out of sorts, with tears streaming down her cheeks and a snotty nose. I ran my hand over her beautiful black curly hair. "Shhh, sweet one. Tell me what's wrong with you."

As if she could understand me, Jessilee tugged on her ear.

I kissed her warm forehead while placing my hands over her ears. I could feel an unsettled energy emanating from them. "You are so beautiful. Yes, you are." Jessilee quieted and smiled at me. "I think I have just the thing to fix her up." I gave her a good squeeze before standing and handing the sweet baby to her mother.

Rhonda took her baby and cradled her against her chest. "She hasn't been this calm in days. You have a magic touch."

"I just love babies."

"You should have one of your own."

I turned and staved off the tears. I wanted nothing more than to have my own baby, but I couldn't bear to curse her. My only other option was to die childless. "I'll be right back."

"I can't pay you, Miss Sorrel."

"I wouldn't accept it if you could." I smiled at Isaiah, who was now stalking my cat behind one of the large houseplants. "Would you like a cupcake?"

He nodded furiously and ran my way.

"Is that all right?" I asked Rhonda. I probably should have asked before I'd offered.

"Of course." Rhonda seemed grateful.

I took Isaiah's hand, and we headed to the kitchen. I lifted him up and sat him on the counter before giving him a raspberry cupcake. While he devoured it, I got out some fresh gingerroot and garlic to make some ear drops for a now-giggling Jessilee.

I still had this funny feeling I was being watched. I looked around to find Isaiah focused on his cupcake and Rhonda playing patty-cake with Jessilee. I was losing it.

I turned my back to everyone, took the gingerroot in my hand and closed my eyes, feeding my energy into the ginger, allowing it to release the healing powers it held. Making it become what it was meant to be. I probably looked like I was praying over it. When I felt heat emanating from the ginger, and what I could only describe as a pulse, I knew it was ready. I did the same with the garlic. Once the ingredients were ready, I made a paste out of both and mixed it with some of my specially made olive oil. After that, I heated it up until it was perfectly blended. As soon as it was cool enough, I bottled it up. In between steps, Isaiah and I sang the ABC song repeatedly. Isaiah had also managed to eat two cupcakes, a banana, an apple, and some yogurt. I realized they probably didn't have any food at home.

I sneaked into my room and grabbed some of the cash I kept hidden in my sock drawer for emergencies, just like my mother had taught me. But the only emergency I'd ever had was the fashion kind. Which made me feel guilty, knowing I had a starving family in my living room. I grabbed $1000 and, along with the ear drops, put it all in a paper bag and folded the top.

I still couldn't shake the feeling I wasn't alone. Maybe I would make myself an elixir for anxiety after Rhonda and her kids left.

I walked back out and handed the bag to Rhonda, hoping she didn't open it in front of me. "Put one drop in each ear a few times a day. She should be feeling better in no time."

Rhonda looked down at her sleeping baby pressed against her chest and kissed her brow. "Her fever's already down. You're a miracle worker."

Or cursed, but it was kind of the same thing. Though I couldn't explain Jessilee's lower temperature. "I'm glad she's getting some rest. I hope you can too."

Rhonda looked at Isaiah, who was relentlessly chasing Tara to no avail. "I won't rest until that child graduates."

I laughed while saving Tara as she darted toward me. I scooped her up, and she curled against me.

Isaiah was jumping for her, shouting, "Kitty!"

"Let's go," Rhonda said to him. With tears in her eyes, she faced me. "I can't thank you enough. I don't know what I would do without you."

"There's no need to thank me."

"Miss Sorrel, the world needs more good folk like you."

There were better people than me. I'd met many of them during my travels. But it panged my heart that there wouldn't ever be anyone else like me. No one for me to pass my knowledge and know-how down to. The gifts I'd been given that could help the world would be lost forever.

After they left, I had a need to look at the book that silently governed my life. Maybe if I begged it enough, it would tell me what to do. Though I feared that just as much, as it would mean the curse was alive and well. Perhaps, though, it could tell me how to break this curse—without having to kill anyone, that is. Or maybe there were some instructions in it that I had missed. I don't know. All I knew was that I felt out of sorts.

I sat on my bed and looked around to make sure no one was looking, which was ridiculous. When I saw no one, because I was going crazy and imagining things, I twisted the knob to unlock the hidden drawer to my nightstand. It was a clever design. It made it look like there was only one drawer when there were really two. There the green book rested, as always. I picked it up, held it to my chest, and closed my eyes as if I could make a wish on it and have it come true.

"What do you want from me?" I said out loud. I flipped to the back of the book, as if my pleading would make the book finally speak. With one eye open I peeked, hopeful. I was once again disappointed and relieved. "Is the curse dead?" I whispered. Still nothing. "How about, can I have Eric, pretty please?

Maybe you can tell me if he likes me or if I'm just a fool." Silence. Not even a scribble of gold. I shook the book. "Why have you stopped speaking? Is it me? I feel like it is. It seems I'm destined to have everyone in my life go silent. I know it's ridiculous to pine over a man I haven't even known for two months, and talk to a book while I'm at it, but I thought we had a connection. And when I say we, I mean Eric and me. Though I do feel connected to you somehow, even though you've ghosted me too."

I lay back on my bed, holding the stupid book against my chest. "You know, it's funny, I really believed my dad when I was a little girl and he told me I was special and would break this curse. But maybe my mom was right: he was a mortal man caught up in this curse, trying to give me some hope, even if it was false hope."

I sat up, shoved the book back in the hidden drawer, and slammed it shut. "You can sit in there for eternity for all I care. Or at least until we move. Which, thanks to you, will be sooner than I want. I'll be giving you the silent treatment from now on. You can see how you like it."

I couldn't believe I had resorted to talking to a book. It was official, I was crazy.

NINETEEN

ERIC

AS SOON AS ERIC HEARD Sorrel leave, he stepped out of the shadow of her bed that was created by the light filtering in from the large window. Eric always found it ironic that light created the darkness in which he lurked. He shook his body, trying to get feeling back. Anytime he slipped into the shadows it was like his entire body fell asleep. It prickled and stung until the blood properly flowed through him again. The longer he stayed in the shadows, the longer it took for him to feel normal. It would take several minutes after following Sorrel all day. He had jumped from one shadow to the next, even if it was the tiniest sliver, as if he were playing a dark, twisted version of hopscotch.

He sat on her bed, trying to recover and keep himself from imagining how it would feel to share this space—covered in a pink ruffle comforter—with her. For days, he'd been agonizing about what he should do. He'd been trying to reconcile what he knew about the Tellus family with what he'd seen with his own eyes. Especially now that he had proof that the book existed. The book that could end this hellish curse.

He covered his face with his hands. Sorrel vexed him. He'd watched her all day, waiting for her to prove to him that his family was right—that she was a conniving coward who used her powers to deceive. All he saw was a woman who gave her life to helping others, all quietly, never for show. Worse, he saw a woman who he'd obviously hurt. He pulled out the phone that had almost given him away. He should really remember to silence it if he was going to follow people. And though he had heard the message that she'd left in person, he wanted to hear her voice.

Eric played her message, and Tara followed her owner's voice into the bedroom. Eric picked up the cat and snuggled her against him. Tara purred violently. "You wouldn't like me so much if you knew why I was here. What I had done to your owner." What he could do.

Eric stared at his phone. To hear that Sorrel missed him and wanted to get together added to the turmoil he'd been feeling all week. Sorrel was in greater danger than she knew. Not only from him, but from his family. How could she not know? Hadn't she been taught to hunt him and guard her secret as he had been taught to despise her and destroy her at any cost? She lived her life as if she weren't cursed. Was her naivete an act meant to lure him in? Even thinking it almost made him laugh. She was the most generous, genuine person he'd ever met. Or was she?

He groaned so loud it startled Tara. He didn't know what to believe. Maybe because his heart wanted to believe one thing and his head another. He'd never felt for a woman like he had for Sorrel. Yet, destroying her book would give him the freedom he'd longed for his entire life. No longer would he be beholden to the book, or his family. He could live the life he wanted, but did he want a life in which Sorrel didn't exist? Could he live with the guilt? Why had the book led him to her? It had said, *The story to be told has been in the making for many years. But how it ends will be up to you.* He had the power to end it all. Did the book's riddle mean that his family was meant to be the victor? What if he was thinking of the wrong story? The wrong ending? Either way, he knew it wouldn't be a happy one. Regardless of what Eric would do, she was on his family's radar, and they would stop at nothing until she and her book were destroyed.

Eric held Tara up and stared into her blue eyes, reminiscent of her owner's. "You're going to hate me for what I do next." He set the cat down on the hardwood floor and stood, now that his strength was back. Tara wound herself around his legs, making him think that he should get a cat. But he wanted more than just a cat to curl up next to. He wanted the woman who had a dozen plants in her room and a million pillows on her pink bed. He knew it wasn't possible though. Only one of them could live.

He cleared his mind until it was as black as a starless night, then slid into the shadow made by her bedroom door. It was perfectly situated to allow him access to Sorrel's nightstand drawer. Being inside the shadow felt like floating in water. And though it gave him less control over his body, the shadow would protect him from the hallucinogenic plant Sorrel was using to protect her book. Not that it was much of a deterrent in his mind. She really shouldn't have been so careless. The drawer didn't even have a lock. Had her family kept her oblivious to the dangers of the curse? Or was she overly cocky about her abilities? The thought seemed preposterous. He'd watched with his own eyes how she'd taken time out of her busy day to help a young mother. She'd even given her a large wad of cash. He could tell Sorrel fretted about the mother discovering the money before she left, as if she wanted none of the credit. That was not the way of a conceited person.

Eric hesitated to reach for the drawer. He was only going to take the book for research for now, he tried to ease his conscience. He was intrigued as to why Sorrel thought the book no longer spoke to her. Or maybe she had said that out loud to trick him into taking it. On some level she was cognizant that she was being watched, thanks to his phone and this sixth sense she seemed to possess. Or did he want to believe that she was so cunning so that he didn't loathe himself for what he was about to do? He hated himself enough already after hearing her pour her heart out to the book about him. Why the woman cared for him so much he had no idea. Was fate so cruel to bring born enemies together like this? Or was it the damn curse torturing them?

Eric decided to take his chances and steal the book. He reached out, and only his arm was made visible as he turned the knob. The secret drawer popped out, revealing the key to his freedom. He hesitated to reach for the book that shined as vibrant as its owner. And, as if Tara knew what he was going to do, she jumped up, trying to bat his arm away with her paw. He had to know the truth. He swiped the book before what little conscience he had got the better of him.

When he took ahold of the book, it hummed in his hands. He wasn't sure if that was a warning or a congratulations. Regardless, he pulled the book to him and shut the drawer. He took one last look at Sorrel's bright and airy room, smelling the eucalyptus and honey scent in the air. "I'm sorry," he whispered, before jumping to the next shadow. It was trickier to navigate when he was holding an object, and thankfully no one was around, as he could be seen for the split-second he was out of one shadow and into the next. He played this careful game all the way to his car, which he had parked outside of town.

By the time he reached his car, he'd had quite the workout and had broken a sweat. Once he was inside, he took several deep breaths, trying to get the feeling back in his body while staring at the green-leafed book in the passenger seat. Like Sorrel, he didn't know what was real anymore. He hoped to find more clarity as he studied the book, both in his heart and mind.

He raced home and rushed up to his apartment with Sorrel's book. And though he hadn't eaten in hours, he had no desire for food. He hopped onto his bed with her book and retrieved his own from under the bed where it was hidden in the shadows. He settled against his pillows with both, ready to do some serious research. With delicacy, he brushed his fingers over the odd cover of Sorrel's book. For some reason he thought he would feel more connected to her, but all he felt was a tiny vibration, as if the book recognized his energy.

He opened the books and took note of the stark differences between his and Sorrel's, from the pages' textures to the gold ink in hers and silver in his. It made him wonder what the Aelius family's book had looked like long ago. It was sad to think how the families had once coexisted peacefully and now it was down to his murderous family and Sorrel. It made him wonder if Sorrel had been lying about being an orphan. Her mother's death was more than suspicious, and they had never recovered a body. If she was lying about her mother, what else had she lied about?

Eric read the first few of the pages of her book. They contained instructions on how to make elixirs for common ailments—headaches and stomachaches. With each page they got more complex—cures for cancer and heart disease. At the same time, it wasn't all roses and sunshine. There were elixirs for truth serums and even to induce arousal. Had Sorrel used those on him? Her customers? He thought back to their first meeting, and he was naturally aroused by the memory of her. Or was it the damn curse? No. Any man would be attracted to her. Though what if she was taking her own elixirs? He groaned and looked up at his water-stained ceiling, not knowing what the hell to believe.

He flipped to the back of her book, assuming that's where the book spoke to her. He easily found the page, but what he found was unsettling. Sorrel wasn't lying when she said the book didn't speak to her. In fact, it never had. The last line was dated just over five years ago.

The time has come for you and your daughter to go your separate ways. Assume a new identity and leave no trace of your former self behind. A way will be shown to accomplish both. Be ready, the time is nigh. Farewell.

How courteous of the book, though cryptic. Was the book bidding her mother goodbye or signing off forever? Curious.

Still, it was proof the mother more than likely lived. Sorrel was a liar, but he had to lie about his own family, too. Pretend he had brothers instead of a father and grandfathers. A grandmother in place of his insane mother. He rubbed his temples. On one hand, he desperately wanted Sorrel to be an evil liar; on the other, he wanted her to be who he had seen with his own eyes.

So many questions, and her book was giving him more instead of answering any. Why didn't her book work for her? She obviously possessed all the powers of a daughter of the earth. Well . . . that wasn't exactly true. He thought back to today and the child she'd helped—no, healed. Her touch seemed to heal. Even he had felt it, only he hadn't recognized it at the time. How could that be? The gift of healing by touch was an Aelius family trait. What a crazy thought. Or was it? He played in his mind all the times he'd observed her at the bakery and even when they had visited people to drop off tea. Sorrel left each person she touched happier. Was it because she was making them feel better?

How could that even be possible? The Aelius family and their book had been destroyed. His own ancestor had witnessed their queen dying. It was the reason they were in this awful hell.

Eric furiously began to search her book for any instructions on how to heal people by touch. For hours he scanned each page meticulously, making sure not to leave any stone unturned. Page after page, there was nothing but instructions on how to use plants to heal or induce feelings of pleasure, even inflict pain. There was a nasty concoction meant to give the recipient gastrointestinal issues to make them dehydrated enough to die. He couldn't imagine Sorrel being so cruel.

Around midnight he finally returned to the last page, not finding any evidence of how Sorrel was able to heal by touch. Yet, he knew she could. She'd healed that baby's ears today and caused her fever to break. How, damn it?

In his frustration, Eric carefully went through the book's instructions to Sorrel's mother. There didn't seem to be much out of the ordinary, until a particular date and the following message struck him. It was twenty-one years ago on the third of March. *Make haste, cremate your husband's remains, take Sorrel and flee to Tahiti.*

The date and the urgency seemed unusual. He pulled out his own book and flipped to the back page. Twenty-one years ago on the same date, his family was told to *flee* for Prague. If that wasn't odd enough, the date reminded him of something from his investigation of Sorrel. He scrambled off his bed and ran into his living area. On the coffee table he found his notes from the investigation. He frantically searched the papers until he found David Black's coroner's report. His day of death hit him like a freight train—March third. Hadn't his father said there were no coincidences when it came to the book and the curse?

It wasn't lost on Eric how both families had lived in California at the time, only miles from each other. There had to be a correlation between all of it—the dates, locations, and her father's death. But what? The curse seemed more convoluted than ever.

Eric paced the small cluttered room in the semidarkness, the curse's warning running through his head. In the end, there could only be one family. Though, which one? And why hadn't the curse just run its course in California? Why continue the torture and the cat-and-mouse game? And why had Sorrel's book stopped communicating? Most importantly, what about Sorrel? He rubbed his heart.

With each step he took, he envisioned Sorrel. Her smile, the way she felt against his body—like she belonged there. Her soft lips and the way she tasted. The way she made him feel about himself. Why boost him up only to kill him? He thought about the way she used her gifts. He'd only ever witnessed her using them for the good of others. Even when she was "drugging" people to tell the truth, it was for the benefit of their potential spouse. She was beloved by many. On the other hand, he was beloved by none, except perhaps her. Yet that was more than likely the curse's doing.

147

He repeatedly ran his hand through his hair. *Only one could live. How the story ended was up to him.*

What did his family offer the world? Death? Coercion? Spying on people in the shadows and in their dreams?

He threw himself on his couch, mentally and physically exhausted. What did the curse want from him? Because what he truly wanted, he couldn't have—Sorrel. He rested his head on the back of the couch and closed his eyes. A tear or two leaked out. He hadn't cried since he was a child. It was a sign of weakness, his father had taught him . . . more like shamed him, for any emotion. Eric swore he would stop the cycle of abuse.

And that's when it hit him. Here was his chance. It would require the ultimate sacrifice. To destroy either book, blood must be shed. The Aelius queen made sure her revenge was exacted until the very end—life, for the life taken from her. His great-grandfather had been kept around to give his life, if ever they found the Tellus book. The old bastard would probably die soon anyway. But Eric would sacrifice his own life to destroy his book first. It was worth it to protect Sorrel.

He would return her book in the morning, and then he would break the curse. A peace washed over him, knowing that for once in his life he was doing the noble thing. It allowed him to fall asleep, even knowing this was his last night in this life.

His mind rewarded him and allowed him to dream of Sorrel. She was sitting in a hospital bed, more beautiful than ever, holding two babies—a boy and a girl. She smiled up at him. "We did good."

Eric began to approach his little family, until a loud pounding on the hospital room door startled him and the babies. They both began to cry.

"Open up the damn door!" his father shouted.

Eric looked around the room for a safe place to hide Sorrel and the babies, but there was nowhere to be found, not even a closet. He panicked and rushed to Sorrel's side. "Don't say a word," he begged her.

"I'm braver than you think," she replied.

He kissed her forehead and lingered there, trying to soak in her courage.

His father pounded on the door again. "You can't hide from me forever."

"It's going to be okay." Sorrel tried to soothe him. "We'll do this together."

A calm reassurance spread through Eric, making Sorrel and the babies vanish. In their place was the table and chair set he'd previously met his father at, but this time it was in a stark-white room. Eric took a seat and cleared his mind. He knew what he had to do.

"Come in," Eric called.

His father sauntered in, with a sneer so vile Eric had to stop himself from flinching. "What took you so long?"

"You were interrupting an intimate moment."

His father took a seat, chuckling. "Like father, like son."

Never, Eric thought.

"So, what did you find out about Sorrel?" His father got right to business.

Eric shrugged. "It was like I said, she's mortal. But . . ."

Vincent's brows raised and he leaned in.

"I'm in love with her, and I'm willing to do whatever it takes to break the curse so we can be together. I want to help you with your search for the Tellus family book."

Vincent narrowed his eyes and studied his son. After a few moments the corners of his mouth ticked up. "This is excellent news. I must meet this woman."

Eric forced himself not to swallow or clench his fists. He would never allow his father to get near Sorrel. "Of course. Are you planning to return to the States soon?"

"We'll be in Atlanta tomorrow."

Eric's blood ran cold. He didn't have much time.

"You took care of mother, I presume."

"Unfortunately, yes," his father snarled. "She's been more

trouble than she's worth from the day I was forced to bind myself to her. I'd just as soon leave her in the hellhole jail she got herself thrown into, but she has a big mouth. And as you know, she has her uses."

Eric internally shuddered, thinking about the uses his mother had. She was like his father's minion, used for whatever nefarious purposes his father commanded. "Why don't we have dinner tomorrow night? I'll see if Sorrel is available. Just know, she thinks I only have brothers and a grandmother."

"We can work with that."

"Good. There's a great place downtown, the Mandolin. Let's say eight tomorrow night. My treat."

Vincent gave Eric a shrewd look. "This woman must really be something special. I might have to fight you for her."

Eric could only hold his composure for so long. "You'll keep your bloody hands off her."

Vincent shrugged. "See you soon." He vanished without another word.

Eric jerked awake, shaking. It was still dark. His first thought was that he had to get the book back to Sorrel and destroy his. He hurled himself off the couch and ran into his room, not caring that it was the middle of the night. He grabbed both books and barely took the time to slip on a pair of shoes. This was it. The curse would die today. Sorrel would live.

TWENTY

I KEPT TOSSING AND TURNING, debating whether I should get up and make myself an elixir to help me fall asleep. I couldn't remember the last time sleep had eluded me like this. Honestly, I was afraid to leave my bed. I'd even kept the light on. I'd never been afraid of the dark before, but I felt as if something watched me from the shadows. Tara didn't help by walking across my bed for an hour, hissing every now and then, as if she were guarding me. My thoughts of Eric had also contributed to the restlessness. He'd never called. I was an idiot.

With those lovely thoughts, I gave in. I needed to sleep. I had to be up early to finish decorating a wedding cake. I sat up and stretched, trying to talk myself into coming out from under the covers, though I still felt unsettled. Maybe I would ask Josie if I could stay with her the rest of the weekend. We'd had girls' nights before. Hopefully she wouldn't want to hook up with anyone from the wedding we both had to attend much later today. In an act of bravery, I threw off my covers. But as soon as I did, my spidey senses started to tingle. I froze and looked around. I was such a child. Then it dawned on me. Maybe it was the book? Perhaps this was what my mother had been talking about for years when she'd said she would get a tingling feeling. Had it finally decided to speak?

I swung my legs around and planted them firmly on the

floor before reaching for the knob on the nightstand. The hairs on the back of my neck stood up. Maybe this was really going to happen. I wondered what it had to say. It would be a lie if I said I didn't wish it had something to do with Eric. With great anticipation, I twisted the knob and pulled out the hidden drawer. But the excitement quickly turned to panic when I realized I was staring into an empty space. How could that be? I opened and shut the drawer a few times, thinking maybe I'd opened it incorrectly.

I jumped up. Had I looked at the book again after I'd scolded it just hours ago? No. I checked behind the nightstand in hopes it had fallen out somehow. Next, I threw the covers off my bed. Nothing. Then I looked under my bed, only to find a few dust bunnies. The book was nowhere to be found in my room or bathroom. I ran out into my living area and like a madwoman tossed every cushion and pillow I owned. Nothing. Then I tore the kitchen apart searching.

I held my stomach through my pink nightshirt, trying not to toss my cookies. Where had the book gone? How could this be happening? Maybe it just disappeared on its own. That could happen, right? The curse could just be broken. Except I still felt this connection to the book.

I stumbled toward my room, my heart beating erratically enough to make me feel as if I might pass out. I knew who I had to contact. She was going to kill me. The biggest rule of the book was to keep it safe. I'd promised my parents I would, and I had failed. I sat on my bed and tried to calm my mind enough to reach out to my mother.

Mom, I cried.

Sorrel, what's wrong?

I had no idea how to say it.

Sorrel. You're scared. I can feel it. What happened?

I grabbed my stomach. *The book is missing.*

What do you mean it's missing?

It's gone. I can't find it anywhere.

You must be mistaken. Retrace your steps.

I did. It's gone.

That's not possible. Did you leave it out? Did someone take it?

I stared at the empty drawer. *No.*

Sorrel, books don't just disappear.

Are we sure? What if it means the curse is broken?

My mother paused.

What is it?

Sorrel, the only way to destroy the book is to give your life.

What? You lied to me. You said my book might tell me how to break the curse if I ever found the other book. When were you going to tell me the truth? What kind of sick curse was this?

Only if ever we found the Selene's book. I didn't want you to carry the burden. I would give my life so that you could live.

I wouldn't let you.

Which is why I never told you. Sorrel, who took the book? Fear laced her thoughts.

No one.

What about that reporter?

I haven't seen him in days, and I saw the book only hours ago.

Are you sure? Has anyone been to your place?

Yes, I was sure. Eric wouldn't take my book. He had no use for it. Except, I did have that dream about him. But it was just a dream. *Well . . . I helped a young mother with her sick baby, but she couldn't have taken the book.*

I could feel my mother roll her eyes. *Sorrel, you shouldn't be using your gifts to heal mortals. Do you see now the danger you put yourself in?*

It's only dangerous if the Selene family has it. That seems unlikely, right?

I don't know. Have you noticed anything different or unusual?

I was going to say no, but I would be lying. I wrapped my arms around myself. *This sounds crazy, but I keep feeling like someone is watching me from the shadows.* I immediately felt the sense of dread coming from my mother. *What is it? Tell me.*

Sorrel, the Selene family works in the dark.

I thought you told me you didn't know what abilities they possessed.

I don't exactly, but it makes sense, given their powers come from the moon.

My eyes darted around my room. Was I being watched now? *I'm scared. I need you.*

It may be too late.

Don't say that, I pleaded.

Sorrel, you must try to find your book. Or theirs before they destroy yours.

I won't let you die for me.

Sorrel, we will both die if they destroy your book. You must find it.

I don't even know how. Please, just let me come to you. Where are you? I'll get on a plane now. We can die together if it's not too late.

Mom paused and contemplated. *I'm in Saint Augustine,* she breathed out.

Florida? That means I'm only like five hundred miles away from you. I'm packing and leaving now. I couldn't believe all this time we had been so close to each other. My heart leapt.

Find the book first, she begged and cried.

Why? What good will it do?

Sweetheart, if the Selene family took it, it means the curse is alive and well and can be broken. Do you not see that? You could be free.

I don't want to live knowing you died for me. I just want to see you one more time if I can.

It might be too late.

Please, stop saying that. Just give me your address. I jumped off my bed and headed to my closet to change and grab a suitcase.

I'm going to regret this.

I'm sorry, Mom. I failed us.

Never. You lived the life your father wanted you to.

I miss him, and you, so much.

I know, darling. We'll see you soon. She gave me her address, though I could tell she didn't believe I would make it. I memorized it anyway.

I love you.

I love you more than life.

Was this truly the end of our lives? Such sadness filled me. There was so much I had wanted to do. I wanted love and babies. To help more people. And my friends? What would they think when I was gone? What would happen to my employees and Love Bites? Maybe when I got to Florida, I could set up some kind of trust or something. And what about Eric? Why was I even thinking about him? He obviously didn't want me. Unfortunately, that didn't stop my heart from aching for him.

No time to think of him. I haphazardly started ripping clothes off their hangers and throwing them into my large suitcase. When it was mostly full, I headed for my dresser and tossed more clothes in until it was bursting. I grabbed my emergency cash; glad I had listened to my mother about one thing.

"Sorrel."

I grabbed my heart, which felt about ready to beat out of my chest, and turned around to find Eric standing by my bed.

"Eric, how did you get in here?" I stammered.

A sneer filled his hardened face.

Fear coursed through me, and that's when I realized it wasn't Eric. This man's eyes were too cold, and the way he cocked his hip while perusing me like I was his last meal wasn't like Eric at all. Yet, the man dressed in all black could pass for his twin, right down to the way the stubble painted his cheeks.

The man stepped closer, and I backed up against my dresser. He looked around at my stripped bed and pulled-out drawers. "Missing something?" He licked his lips. Then he glanced at my suitcase. "You're not leaving, are you?"

"Who are you?" I was shaking so badly, my voice trembled.

"Not Eric."

"How did you get in here?"

The man inched closer. "I see you don't know the ways of my family."

"Your family?" I backed against the dresser so far, I was practically sitting on it.

"Eric didn't tell you, did he?"

I swallowed hard. "Tell me what?"

He took one giant step toward me.

I held my breath. He smelled like rancid vinegar and hard liquor.

He reached out and ran his scaly finger down my cheek. "You are beautiful."

I turned my head away, yet the rest of my body was paralyzed.

"I see why my son wanted to keep you for himself."

"Your son?" I breathed out, not liking at all where this was going—or what it meant.

"Eric is my son."

"How can that be?"

The foul man leaned in and whispered in my ear. "Don't play stupid. You know exactly how it's possible, daughter of the earth."

"I don't know what you're talking about," my voice cracked.

"Hmm." He breathed me in. "You're an awful liar, like my son."

"Please leave me alone." I tried to push him away, but he grabbed my arms.

"I like feisty women. Too bad I can't have you. Though maybe"—he pulled me against his body—"we can have some fun before I kill you."

A sickening panic overtook me from my head to my toes,

making my knees buckle. The sinister man caught me and delighted in it. Finding some strength, I tried to yank myself out of his arms, but it was in vain. He was too strong. Just when I thought all was lost, from the shadow of my bedroom door, Eric appeared out of thin air. At least I thought it was Eric. It was like a nightmare and a dream. The curse was real, and Eric was part of the Selene family. My born enemy.

"I told you not to touch her." Eric's face burned red with anger.

His father whipped his head toward Eric while keeping a tight grip on me, making me wince. "You told me a lot of things tonight. Most of them lies. To your credit, had I not already known the truth, you may have fooled me. I knew, though, that you would never agree to introduce this lovely creature to me." He yanked me in front of him like I was a rag doll. His arms snaked around me like iron bands. He kissed my cheek, making me want to vomit. "Oh yes, I've been watching her—and you, son. I wanted to give you the chance to do the right thing, but yet again, you have disappointed me. And her. Would you like to tell her what's in your backpack?"

Eric's eyes locked with mine. He shook his head and let out a heavy breath. "Sorrel, it's not what you think."

"Oh, I think it is." His father mocked him.

"Shut the hell up," Eric yelled at his father.

"Eric, what's going on?" I begged to know.

Eric stepped closer, but not too close, as if he himself were afraid of the monster who held me. "Please listen to me. I didn't know who you were when we first met. I only took your book—"

His words stabbed me in the heart. "It was you? I thought you—"

His father tsked, interrupting me. "Did you think he cared for you? Even loved you? Is that what he told you?" He laughed maniacally. "Oh, what a wicked game the curse has played with both of you. Your feelings are all a lie. But don't worry, it will be over soon. The Selene family will rise once again and"—his arm moved up and around my neck, preventing me from breathing—"your traitorous family will die."

I tried to scream, but I couldn't catch my breath. Tears poured down my cheeks.

Eric lunged for me and his father. "Don't hurt her." Eric gripped my arms and tried to extricate me, as two more unworldly beautiful yet vile men appeared out of the shadows and restrained Eric. Tara, out of nowhere, tried to come to the defense of her one true love. Why hadn't she come to mine? Her back arched, and she violently hissed at the men. One of them kicked her away, and she crumpled near me, mewing in pain.

"Nooo!" I screamed.

"Damn you!" Eric fought to get loose from the men who shared a strong family resemblance. Knowing how our family lines worked, I assumed the men were Eric's grandfather and great-grandfather. How could these men treat their own family this way? It explained Eric's rough exterior and the pain he carried around. Or was it all an act, to get my book? Why had he taken it? When had he?

"Should we kill him, Vincent?" the auburn-haired man with Eric's strong jawline asked, while holding Eric's arm back and pulling his head back by his hair.

"No, father. We need all the Selene blood we can get. I will just have to teach him a lesson after we're done killing his girlfriend."

"Maybe he should be the one to die to break the curse," the blond man who was also restraining Eric suggested.

"No, you fool, that's your job. Your life is almost over anyway. Besides, it has to be done willingly, and Eric isn't up for the task. And he is the heir to our book, whether we like it or not." Vincent was obviously disappointed.

"What should we do with him, then?" The grandfather gripped Eric tighter, as Eric continued to fight to no avail. With biceps as big as my head, the men looked like they pumped iron all day.

Vincent roughly spun me around. His calculating aqua eyes bore into mine. "Let's give Eric a taste of what his girlfriend is going to get, then we'll come back for him later. I can't have him trying to get all valiant on us. It's not becoming of him." Vincent gave me a snide grin. "You know he killed a girl once?"

"You bastard!" Eric shouted.

I couldn't believe it. I shook my head, sick to my stomach.

Vincent smiled, victorious. "It's all true. I'm sure Eric would love to tell you all about Karina, but sadly there's no time. Now you are going to feel some of the pain your family has caused mine over the years."

"What have we ever done to you?"

"Again, no time, my pet." He grabbed my forearms and squeezed.

A surge of his energy slammed into me. Suddenly, I was hit with a sharp, stabbing pain in my head, so much so I screamed out. "Stop! Please!" It was pain like I had never experienced. I thought my head might split open.

"Leave her alone!" I barely made out Eric's voice before he was screaming out in pain too.

The pain became so bad I wished for death, but before I blacked out, I called out to my mother. *Mom.*

Sorrel.

The Selene family is here. We're going to die. I love you.

TWENTY-ONE

ERIC

ERIC FELT SOMETHING WET AND rough licking his cheek. He tried opening his eyes, but he was having a hard time. His head pounded, and for some reason he couldn't remember, he didn't want to wake up. The persistent licking kept rousing him. "Stop," he groaned.

He peeked one eye open, and all he could see was white fur. It was then he remembered where he was, and why. Both eyes flew open. He realized half his face was plastered against Sorrel's hardwood floor and his hands were tied behind his back. Even his feet had been restrained.

Tara nudged Eric with her cold nose as if begging him to get up.

"I can't, little one. But I'm glad you're alive." He thought for sure her nine lives had been used up. He felt like at least half of his were gone. His entire body screamed from his sadistic family using their powers against him.

Tara nudged him some more.

"It's no use." Eric noticed the early-morning light filtering in through the window. It must have been hours since they'd taken her and her book. "She's probably dead already." The thought brought tears to his eyes.

160

Tara batted his face, as if slapping him for saying such a thing.

"I'm sorry, I tried to do the right thing. I should have known better. The curse always wins."

Tara continued to assault him. He let her. What else could he do? Besides, he thought he deserved it. But . . . perhaps he could find out if Sorrel still lived. Though if she did, maybe she had woken up already, like him. He debated trying. If she was gone, he didn't want to know, yet he hated to think of the terror she must be in if she still lived. That, more than anything, convinced him to try and break into her dreams.

He closed his eyes and focused in on her. The hurt in her eyes when she found out about his betrayal. Her trembling body in the grasp of his father. Soon Eric saw her door; the pink was paler this time. His heart sank, but at least she was still alive. He slowly opened it, afraid to see what was on the other side. When he got a good look, he was relieved to find her in the vineyard with the same man as always. Though this time she was shuddering against him, sobbing. It broke Eric's heart. Especially since it was all his fault.

The man who held her zeroed in on Eric. "Protect her," he mouthed.

Who was this man? He wondered if Sorrel even knew who he was, or that she was constantly dreaming about him. There was so much about the beautiful woman he wondered about, but there was no time to find out. There never would be.

The man lifted Sorrel's chin, smiled, and spoke to her, too quietly for Eric to hear what was said. As soon as the man vanished, Sorrel faced Eric with her tear-streaked cheeks, wearing the revealing nightshirt his father had abducted her in. The thought gave him chills. His father had better keep his filthy hands off her.

"Sorrel," Eric whispered.

She ran from him into her bakery. A space where Eric was sure she felt safe. How he wished they could stay in her dream and never leave. How he wanted nothing more than to keep her safe.

He followed. "Sorrel, please, stop. I'm so sorry."

She melted onto a white chair and covered her face with her hands. "You stole my book. I'm going to die."

He knelt in front of her and rested a hand on her bare knee. She flinched. "Don't touch me."

Eric dropped his hand. "Listen to me, there may be time. Do you know where you are?"

Her head stayed buried in her hands. "No. I hurt all over."

"I know. You were poisoned with the water in your blood. It will take some time to wear off, but you need to stay strong. Remember, you told me you were brave."

"I don't want to be brave. My mother and I are going to die."

So, her mother *was* alive. It made Eric feel worse.

Eric gently removed Sorrel's delicate hands from her angelic face and kept them in his. She resisted his touch, but this time he didn't let go. "Sorrel, you can do this. You can heal your body. I need you to do that so you can wake up and fight."

"I can't heal myself. I don't have any of my plants."

"You don't need them. All you need is inside of you. Do understand me?" Eric was positive she held some powers not even she knew she had. Some she shouldn't have.

"I don't believe you. You're a murderer and a liar." She ripped her hands out of his.

Eric hung his head. "Sorrel, I have done a lot of things I'm not proud of. But you have to believe me when I say I never meant to hurt you. I was trying to protect you."

"I thought you wanted to be with me." She sobbed and recoiled away from him.

"I did. I do. But we can't. Don't you see that?"

"I don't know what to believe anymore."

"Sorrel, I'm going to find you. You need to wake up and fight. Promise me you will."

Her crying ceased and her eyes narrowed. "Why should I promise you anything?"

He took her face in his hands and pressed a kiss to her lips. "Because it is you who must live."

Eric jerked himself out of her dream and shut her door. She was alive and still had some fight left in her. She was going to need it. So was he. Eric tried to wriggle his hands out of the rope that bound him. His grandfather, Frederick, unfortunately had a knack for bondage. Eric closed his eyes, trying to think of a way out of his predicament. If he could only get to his book and the wolfsbane he'd left in his car. Each member of his family carried around the roots of the plant in case they needed to sacrifice themselves and destroy the Tellus's book. The roots had to be steeped like a tea for hours until they turned as clear as pure water. He hoped his family was still preparing the batch for his murderous great-grandfather, Alexander, to take.

Tara stared at Eric impatiently.

"I'm trying," he said.

Tara's eyes said to try harder.

A thought popped into Eric's head. It was something he'd just told Sorrel. She had what she needed inside of her to heal herself. And he had water inside of him. Water he could control. Maybe. He had never tried. But perhaps, if he could decrease the flow of water in his hands and wrists, he could slip out of the ropes that bound them. He would have to be precise and quick. A loss of circulation could be detrimental to the use of his limbs, which he needed now more than ever.

Eric closed his eyes, breathing deeply in and out, focusing first on the beat of his heart. Once he was tuned into its rhythm, he followed the flow of the blood that ran in his veins. He could feel his energy swell and attach itself to his cells. Carefully, he dammed the current that ran into his hands. Immediately he felt the sting of it. He held strong, though—too much was at stake for pain to stop him. His body shook from holding back the tide, yet slowly his hands began to shrink, and the ropes around them began to loosen. He had barely enough feeling in his hands to wriggle out of their confines. As soon as he was free, he pulled back his energy. A surge of warmth spread through his limbs.

With his hands able to function properly, he was able to right himself and undo the rope around his legs and feet. He stood slowly, still feeling the effects of what his family had done to him. He needed a game plan and to think like his sadistic father. Where had he taken Sorrel?

Tara brushed up against him. He reached down and picked her up. "I told her I would find her. How? I lied to her again."

Tara snuggled against him, purring.

One thing he knew: he needed to take the cat with him. And ... he eyed Sorrel's suitcase overflowing with clothes—many of them pink. She was too innocent for the horror she was facing. The horror he'd subjected her to. "Agh!" he screamed out. "Where is she?"

He sat down on the bed, feeling more defeated than ever. He had no idea where to go. Where to even start. Maybe if he just destroyed his book first, it would kill his dad and grandfathers. It was a long shot, but it was the only one he had.

Just in case by some miracle he found Sorrel, he grabbed the cat and her suitcase. She would want both. He wasn't sure why she had packed a suitcase or where she was planning on going. He'd showed up too late to the party. He should have known his father was deceiving him. Or that he couldn't get away with lying to his father. Regardless, if he could, he would make sure Sorrel got to where she wanted to go safely. Then he would destroy his book, because that was the only way she would ever truly be safe.

There was no way to take the suitcase and the cat with him into the shadows. Small objects were one thing, but an animal and a large suitcase were another story. He was going to have to leave Sorrel's apartment the old-fashioned way.

It was just past seven in the morning. The sleepy town of Riverhaven was, unfortunately, anything but. Eric had hardly made it down Sorrel's apartment stairs before he ran into one of her employees. He thought his name was Mateo.

Mateo was wearing a pink apron covered in flour. If it were any other day, Eric would have smiled at the scene. Mateo waited at the bottom of the stairs, eyeing Eric and his cargo suspiciously.

"Hey, man." Mateo flicked his head. "Have you seen Sorrel? She should have been at the bakery an hour ago, and she's not answering her phone."

Eric hated lying, but he had no choice. He smiled. "Sorry about that. I was keeping her busy, if you know what I mean."

Mateo gave him knowing grin. "It's about time."

Eric held up the suitcase—which was, oddly, gray and not pink—and the cat. "Actually, we were hoping to get away this weekend for some alone time. Sorrel will be down soon to make arrangements with you."

Mateo slapped Eric on the arm, his eyes focused on the rope marks around Eric's wrist.

Damn. I should have covered those up. I don't have time to alter Mateo's thoughts.

Mateo wagged his brows. "Dang! You guys got your freak on last night. It's always the sweet, quiet ones."

Eric had half a mind to punch Mateo for thinking such things about Sorrel, but he was too grateful for his dirty mind.

"You're a lucky man. Bonita is over the moon for you. Now maybe she'll stop playing her sad love songs."

Every word Mateo said was like a stab to his heart. "I hope so too. I wish I could talk longer, but I'm anxious to get going."

"Of course. Of course. Don't let me keep you. But, a word of warning: treat her right or you'll answer to me. If I have to hear "Endless Love" one more time, I may shoot you."

Eric would let him. "Take care, man." Eric sauntered off, trying not to act suspicious. He knew he would be a person of interest once they discovered Sorrel was missing, and if she died, he would be suspect number one. It was true though. He'd inadvertently killed her. *No. She can't be dead.*

He jogged across the bridge to where he had parked his car, hoping his father hadn't seen it or what was in it. He'd obviously been following Eric. For how long, he didn't know. Eric threw Sorrel's suitcase in his trunk before hopping in the driver's side with Tara, who he placed on his passenger seat. With trepidation,

165

he reached into the shadow under his dashboard and breathed a sigh of relief. His blasted book was still there. Eric pulled it out and held it in front of him. "I hate you. She's going to die and it's all my fault." He threw the book in the back seat and started his car. He needed to find a secluded place to destroy his book. His apartment was out of the question now that he'd been spotted leaving Sorrel's place. Would he ever catch a break? He repeatedly slammed his fists against the steering wheel.

With the last slam of his fist, the moonstone book began to glow, and his chest began to burn. It was the sensation he associated with the book speaking to him. He didn't care what it had to say. He was destroying the damn thing. He threw his car in reverse, but the burning and glowing both grew to the point that he couldn't safely see, and he felt as if he were on fire. With a loud groan, he shifted the car into park and retrieved his nemesis.

Tara was curious and crawled into his lap while he opened the book. As soon as Eric flipped it open, it stopped glowing, and the heat in his chest dissipated. Once again, the book was the victor. It always was. But very soon, Eric would be the winner, even though it meant losing everything.

Eric sighed and resigned himself to another godforsaken riddle as he turned to the last page. For once the book showed him some mercy. A single tear escaped Eric's eye and landed on the onyx page.

Sorrel still lives. An abandoned warehouse five miles up the river. Make haste.

TWENTY-TWO

I WASN'T SURE IF I was dreaming, paralyzed, or dead. If I was dead, I must be in hell. Every muscle in my body was seizing. I was having the kind of cramps not even my clary sage elixir could touch. Even though I knew I was in pain, my eyes refused to open. To top it off, I was having weird dreams—or thoughts—about Eric. I couldn't tell. I kept hearing him tell me I could heal myself and wake up. The voice kept getting louder, and I wanted it to go away. He'd lied to me. Used me. He was my enemy. Or was he? My mind was too muddled to think clearly.

One thing I knew—I wanted my mother, and I couldn't reach out to her. Had I already killed her? Us? If I could have sobbed, I would have, but nothing was working right. I was in a deep, dark abyss of pain. It was about to swallow me whole when a thought, like a tiny dot of light at the end of a long, dark tunnel gave me some hope. I could hear my father tell me a story about Princess Sorrel.

Princess Sorrel had a very special light within her heart. That light could vanquish any darkness and heal people who were sick. But she had to be very careful with her light. While light illuminates and helps plants and even ideas grow, if it burns too brightly or for too long, it can destroy anything.

I could see my father using his clippers to cut off a bunch of ripe red grapes from one of the vines in our vineyard. He held it up, and I picked a grape off it, popping it into my mouth. With one bite, sweet juice tickled my taste buds.

These grapes, my love, not only needed the light, but the earth, and even the dark, to grow. Remember that. Promise me.

I promise.

The light at the end of the tunnel was growing brighter. I tried to reach for it but couldn't quite touch it. Eric's voice was also getting louder. *You have all you need inside of you to heal yourself.* Was that true? Even if it was, I didn't know how.

Follow your heart, my father seemed to whisper to me.

I wasn't sure if I could; my heart felt so broken. My mother was going to die because of me. Eric betrayed me. Were my feelings for him even real? His father had said the curse had played a wicked game with us. Those thoughts made the light grow dimmer. I grasped for what light remained, as it was quickly retreating. With it, the pain grew.

Follow your heart, Sorrel.

I was afraid. Afraid to believe in Eric. To face what lay before me if I did wake up. Afraid of death.

You promised me you would be brave.

I know, but I don't know if I can.

You must break this curse.

How? By dying?

What does your heart say?

I tried to quiet my fears and listen. Yet, now that I knew more frightening things existed than I could possibly imagine, it was hard to find any peace.

You must live. Eric's voice broke through the fear and confusion.

I took hold of that thought, and the light began to grow. So much so, I could feel the warmth of it. It started in my chest and trickled slowly outward, like a glaze slowly drizzling down a cake. As the warmth spread, the pain disappeared. My headache was gone, and my body relaxed. That was, until I heard voices and was conscious enough to realize I was lying, bound, on a cold, damp floor. Worse, the stench of dead fish filled not only my nostrils but my mouth and lungs, making me want to vomit. I stopped myself so as not to alert the barbaric men who had taken me.

I dared to peek one eye open to gauge where I was, other than hell on earth. From my limited view, I saw several overturned rotting wood crates, debris from broken bricks, and piles of trash. Based on that, and the fact that I didn't detect any artificial light, just some hazy natural light filtering in, my guess was that I was in an old warehouse. My captors were far enough away that I briefly flashed both eyes open. That gave me a clearer picture of the three men clustered in a circle and ... an old woman with a bent back hovering near them, muttering to herself. I couldn't make out what she was saying, but the way she was rubbing her hands together and the sinister smile on her face didn't fill me with any warm, fuzzy feelings.

I shut my eyes and tried to control my shivering, before they realized I was awake. The warmth I'd felt previously had turned to lingering embers. It didn't help when I realized how much my wrists and ankles ached from being tied up. I had no idea how to free myself or get my book. Where was my book?

As if in response to my question, I heard Vincent say, "Stay away from the book, woman. It's not meant for mortals to touch."

"The bloody curse you thrust on me allows me to, you bastard," the woman raged in a British accent.

Was that woman Eric's mother? How old was she? How old was Eric? He did seem to act older. This was all too much for me to process.

"Focus," one of the other men said. "We don't have time for your marital squabbles."

That answered that question.

"We need to wake up the woman and find out how many of her kind are alive, and where they are so we can make sure the curse is truly broken."

"You really think she's going to tell us? It would be better if we broke into her dreams."

"We can't, you idiots. She has to be willing."

"Maybe you should try. Pretend to be Eric. It's obvious from the way those two looked at each other that they have a connection. No doubt Eric probably visited the little vixen in her dreams. I know I would have."

What? All the seductive dreams I'd had of Eric now took on a different light—a dark one. Had he, little by little, been trying to gain my trust until I told him where my book was? The vomit I had been holding back rose up my throat and into my mouth. I had to swallow it back down. The lingering acrid aftertaste made me cringe.

"Don't remind me of my son's disloyalty," Vincent spat, shaking me out my thoughts. "We don't need the Tellus woman. We'll know the curse is broken when she dies, and the bind that connects me to this ugly wench is broken."

I heard a smack. "You've been no bed of roses, you dirty rotten rakehell."

"Hit me again, woman, and I'll kill you myself as soon as this is all over."

"I would welcome it after the hell you've put me through. But if you even think about touching me, I'll slit your throat." She maniacally cackled, sending a shiver down my spine.

"You two be done. I tire of your endless bickering. Portia, put away your knife. We will keep our end of the bargain; you get your freedom, and we get your silence."

"Fine, you bloody bastards."

"Now shut up. I want my last moments on earth to be spent in peace and quiet."

The mother sounded like someone I should be frightened of, too, but the most pressing matter was that someone was going to be dying soon and destroying my book. I couldn't believe my mother had kept me in the dark about how to destroy the books. Was that all she had kept from me? Did she know I was able to heal myself without the use of any plants or elixirs?

170

"Is the wolfsbane almost ready?" Vincent asked.

Wolfsbane? That was the most poisonous plant on earth and not a pleasant way to go. Not that I was wishing Eric's great-grandfather a cheery death, but why use something that could take hours to kill you? Not only that, but it could cause extreme gastrointestinal issues before lowering your blood pressure enough to stop your heart.

"It needs to steep for another fifteen minutes or so."

They were making it into a tea? I'd never heard of such a thing. If only I could get to it before it was done. What was I even thinking? This wasn't like some movie where I could break free, kick some butt, and save the day. I didn't even know where I was, and I was in a nightshirt of all things. Eric had told me to fight though. But Eric was a liar. Why had he even bothered to break into my dreams one last time? Tears stung my eyes, thinking about his kindness. The way he kissed me. It was all a lie. I squeezed my eyes shut as hard as I could, trying to keep the moisture from leaking out.

I was going to die.

Mom, can you hear me?

Sorrel. You're alive. Such relief flooded her words.

I'm so sorry.

Don't apologize, my love. Where are you?

I don't know. Some old warehouse, I think. I was unconscious. Did you know the Selene family could come into your dreams? I had so many questions.

I did not. So much was lost over time. But it makes sense, given where their gifts are derived. Did they hurt you in your dreams? She hesitated to ask.

If she meant that Eric had given me a taste of everything I'd always wanted, only to use it for his own selfish purposes, then yes. *No, but they poisoned me with the water in my blood and . . . I was able to heal myself by thinking about it. How is that possible?*

Silence.

Mom?

Sorrel, that's not possible.

I didn't think so, either. But Eric, the reporter, he's from the Selene family, and he came to me in my dream and told me I could. I waited for the, 'I told you so,' regarding Eric, but it never came.

You must be confused, love.

Mom, I'm not crazy.

You're scared and not thinking straight. You need to figure out a way to get your book and escape. Then come to me. I have passports and plane tickets for us. We're changing our names and leaving the country.

Maybe she was right. I was going crazy. Maybe the effects of the water poisoning had just worn off, and I'd had a real dream about Eric, not one manufactured by him.

They're going to use wolfsbane to sacrifice the great-grandfather.

They have to.

How do you know that?

Sorrel, there is no time to discuss what I do and don't know right now. The most important thing is you escaping.

I can't. They have me tied up and the wolfsbane is almost ready. Besides, there are four of them and one of me.

You must find a way. Her desperation was loud and clear.

I'm no Houdini.

Is there something sharp nearby you could use?

I peeked my eyes open to see if I could spot something. The only thing I saw was a pair of scuffed-up white nurses' shoes. Portia's soft soles had stealthily hidden her footfalls. I squeezed my eyes shut, but it was too late.

"The pretty little thing is awake." Portia nudged me with her foot. "Don't be shy, love. I want to meet the woman who bewitched my son. Such a naughty girl." She tsked.

Mom, I think it's too late. I'm so sorry.

Sorrel, don't stop fighting. Do you hear me?

I love you. I'll see you and Dad soon.
I love you, she cried.

I could hear the defeat in her voice, which made me feel all the worse. I should have been more careful. I shouldn't have gotten comfortable with Eric. I hated him.

I swallowed what fear I could; it almost strangled me. I opened my eyes and tilted my head back. Up close, the woman was even more frightening. Her long gray hair was greasy and stringy. Her bloodshot, translucent blue eyes were darting all over the place, as if she were paranoid. I couldn't blame her there, living with these men who thrived in darkness and shadows. Men, like her son, who could so easily deceive you. Kill you.

With great effort the woman knelt in front of me. I could hear her bones crack and her joints pop.

I tried to scoot back, to no avail. The restraints were too tight, and I was exhausted.

"Don't fear me, pretty." She reached for a knife in the leather sheath around her thick waist. She held it in front of her and looked at it with a childlike wonder. "So shiny and sharp. Just one wrong move and . . ." She purposely pricked her finger with the tip of the knife. Blood splattered on the filthy floor in front of me, making it look as if tiny crimson flowers littered the dirt.

My body uncontrollably shook.

She rested the knife against my cheek and with a malevolent grin said, "Look at you, so young and eternally beautiful. How old are you?"

My mouth had gone so dry, I couldn't speak.

She applied more pressure, enough to slice my cheek. Blood dripped into my mouth. The saltiness of the blood combined with the stench of dead fish and fear made me vomit and choke.

Portia cackled.

Vincent ran over and hoisted me up with ease while I violently coughed, trying to catch my breath.

One of the other men—the grandpa, I believe—grabbed

Portia. "We can't kill her yet, slag. We should have committed you a long time ago."

"She will die," Portia yelled. "She will die, so I can finally live."

"A lot of good it will do you, old woman." The grandpa dragged her away while she spit at and slapped him.

Vincent shook his head at me. "Ah, what a pity to cut such a beautiful face. Eric's mother was never half as tempting as you. Even when she was younger." With his thumb he roughly wiped some blood off my cheek, making me wince. "You woke up just in time to die."

Honestly, I was okay with that. Better to die by the curse than be tortured.

"Would you like an up-close view?"

I said nothing, but my knees went weak, and with my feet tied I had no balance at all. I crumpled. Vincent caught me and swept me up into his arms. My skin crawled being so close to him, but there was nowhere for me to go. No one to help me. Tears silently poured down my cheeks, making the cut sting. I never pictured my life ending in such a brutal, pathetic manner.

He cradled my body against his and smelled my hair. "I had no idea the Tellus women were so intoxicating. What a waste that we don't have time for me to take a taste of you."

My stomach roiled thinking of him intimately violating me, and I vomited again, this time all down his shirt. I never knew I had such a weak stomach, but how could I know when I had never been so thoroughly afraid? Though I felt no remorse for the mess I'd made on him.

"Ugh." He angrily tossed me onto a large crate. I found my voice and whimpered in pain. I could feel the splinters of the mildewed wood embed in my skin where my nightshirt rode up. If somehow I survived, I was always going to wear pajamas that covered every inch of my body. But I knew I was going to die. From my new viewpoint I could see my book lying on what looked like a makeshift altar made of crates. There was a silver goblet near it, with steam rising out of it. The great-grandfather paced in front of the altar, checking on the contents of the goblet with each pass. The grandfather stood nearby, holding Eric's crazed mother back. She was looking at me as she would a fine meal, ready to be devoured.

Vincent was wiping off his shirt and sneering at me. "Your ancestors were as weak as you."

I tried to sit up to no avail, but I did find the courage to speak. "Better to be weak than a blood-crazed maniac."

He raised a hand to me, and I dared him with my eyes to hit me. I was going to die anyway.

He didn't hit me. He only scoffed and walked off. "Is the elixir ready?"

The great-grandfather checked the goblet that was no longer steaming. "It is," he sighed in resignation.

I guessed he wasn't all that excited about dying today. Neither was I. *Mom, it's time. He's going to drink the wolfsbane elixir.*

Sorrel, I'm here. Her voice shook.

Please stay with me until the end.

Always. She began to sing the lullaby she'd sung to me as a child. It was an old Gaelic song about faeries.

My mother's voice lent me the courage I needed to watch the horror before my eyes. As if in slow motion, Vincent took my book in one hand and held it up as an offering to his grandfather. In the other, he took the goblet. "You know what you must do."

The great-grandfather nodded.

"Goodbye, father," the grandfather, restraining Portia, called.

"There is no time for sentimentality, father," Vincent scolded.

The great-grandfather took the cup from Vincent and, without hesitation, downed its contents. The poison's effect was almost immediate. He doubled over and screamed.

"Put your hand on the book and say the words," Vincent demanded.

The great-grandfather crumpled and lay prostrate on the floor. Vincent placed the book on his chest, and somehow the great-grandfather managed to place his hand on the book. Through labored breathing he began to chant, "I give of my life freely. With this sacrifice of blood—"

My mother ceased singing. *Sorrel, something is happening. I can barely breathe.*

"Nooo!" I cried out.

"—I pay the price. The request written on my heart must be given." My book began to smolder. "I give of my life freely. With this sacrifice of blood, I pay the price. The request written on my heart must be given."

My mother's screams got louder until it was the only thing I could hear. My eyes were glued to my dying book. The smolder turned to flames. Vincent jumped back and watched his grandfather be consumed by the fire. The great-grandfather's chanting stopped, and his cries pierced the air. He was writhing in pain, rolling around on the floor, trying to put the fire out. It was no use, and neither was his family. They each looked on eagerly, as if cheering on the flames.

My mother went silent, and I knew she had died.

I thrashed, trying to get loose. I was going to make them pay for what they had done. Then it dawned on me—I hadn't died. How was that possible? My book was nothing, not even ashes. Vincent barked out a victorious laugh. The great-grandfather stilled and took his last breath. Then all the attention turned toward me.

Vincent's eyes went wide in rage. "You're alive."

I flashed him a defiant smile—it was the only weapon I had available to me, as lame as it was. "I'm sorry to disappoint you."

"How is that possible?" the grandfather roared.

Portia broke free of her captor's grip. With both her hands, she grabbed fistfuls of her hair and started screaming, "I'm still bound. I can feel it."

Vincent and the grandfather scrambled over to the charred body of their father and grandfather to make sure he was truly dead and that my book was gone. While they were distracted, Portia marched my way with a look of unadulterated hatred on her face. "You must die. You must die." She charged.

In my feeble attempt to get away from the deranged woman, I fell backward off the crate and landed in a pile of trash. While spluttering and trying to wriggle free, I heard a door slide open and felt the rays of the sun hit me. For a tiny moment I felt hope, but that died when Portia landed on top of me, gripping her knife, ready to plunge it into me.

"Mother, don't!" A voice that had once given me comfort boomed.

It was too late. It was all too late.

TWENTY-THREE

ERIC

ERIC RUSHED ACROSS THE ROOM and watched in horror as his mother thrust her knife into Sorrel's abdomen. Sorrel's heart-wrenching scream stopped him in his tracks.

Hearing the scream, Vincent jumped up and ran toward the two women. "What have you done, Portia? We need her alive."

Eric would be damned if he let his father get to Sorrel first. He lunged toward her just as Sorrel screamed, "You killed my mother!" Almost out of nowhere, a blinding light tore through the abandoned warehouse, breaking windows and throwing Eric to the ground while glass rained down around him. For a moment he lay stunned, and not because the breath had been knocked out of him. He was in awe of the dazzling bright light that illuminated every inch of the dreary warehouse. How was that possible? There was no time to ponder. He had to get to Sorrel. Bravely, he stood, not knowing where his murderous family was. They were the least of his concerns.

Getting to Sorrel was proving difficult. It was like walking against the wind. As he trudged forward, he caught sight of his father, grandfather, and mother all attempting to flee. Truly, the light emanating from Sorrel was both beautiful and terrifying. It was as if the light she'd created within her called to the sunbeams and combined forces to rain down terror on those who would harm her. Not only that, it was so powerful that there was not one shadow in the building in which they could hide. His family couldn't bear to be in its presence. One by one, they crawled out of the broken windows.

Eric realized there was one family member missing. He squinted, as if looking directly into the sun, trying to see if he could spot his great-grandfather. The last thing he needed was another surprise attack. Toward the center of the warehouse, he spotted a charred body that bore a chain with a crescent moon. It was the same one his great-grandfather had always worn. Eric knew then the sacrifice hadn't worked. Something had gone wrong. But where was Sorrel's book?

He didn't have time to look for it. He needed to save Sorrel, though she was doing a good job of protecting herself. He had no idea how she had the energy to produce the light that seemed to shoot out of every one of her pores. With great effort, he finally made it to her bruised and bloodied body. Fierce anger swelled in him from seeing her so broken.

He knelt near her and took her hand. As soon as they touched, the light instantly retracted and settled back into her. He had never seen anything like it. It was almost as if she were a human floodlight that could be turned on and off with the flip of a switch.

Once the light was out, he could see her injuries more clearly. Blood was spilling out of her abdomen.

He ripped his shirt off and pressed it against her middle. "Sorrel, wake up. You need to heal yourself." She didn't stir.

"Please," he begged. He looked up to the ceiling as if the fungus-covered wood beams would have the solution he needed. When no answer came, he bent down and kissed her brow while continuing to keep pressure on her abdomen. Blood soaked through the shirt and wet his fingers. His fingers began to twitch from the need to control the water within her blood. An idea struck Eric. He tossed the bloodied shirt to the side and carefully placed his hands on her injury. Immediately he felt a powerful connection to her—her pulse became his pulse. It allowed him to become attuned to the rhythm of her heartbeat and the flow of her blood. His energy swelled within him, ready to hold back the life force pouring out of her. Before he could push it into her, her energy captured his and combined forces. The blood flow slowed, and Eric could feel both of their pulses start to tick up. Instead of the normal drain Eric felt when he forced his energy out, this time he felt invigorated.

He kept his hands on her until the blood clotted. The puncture in her skin remained, but there was nothing he could do to heal that. Heal? It hit him that he had used his unholy powers for good. This was no time for reflection. He needed to get Sorrel out of there before his family came back. Carefully, he picked up her limp body. He cradled her against him, grateful to feel her warm breath against his bare skin. When he made it to the door he had come in through, he did his best to make sure the coast was clear. He could never be sure with his family and their ability to hide in the shadows, except for his mother. She had been robbed of her ultimate desire today, and he had no doubt if she saw him with Sorrel, she wouldn't hesitate to try and finish the job she'd started.

Had Sorrel somehow managed to prevent his family from realizing their lifelong quest? Why did Sorrel say they had killed her mother? How did she know that? And if her mother had died, why hadn't Sorrel? These were questions he would have to ask her once he got her to a safe place. If there was such a place anymore. And if she woke up. He pulled her against him tighter, silently begging her to open her eyes.

Eric's heart pounded as he moved as fast as he could across the gravel road, while trying not to make any noise. He entered into the small forest of trees near the warehouse. He had parked his car about a quarter mile away, near an old pavilion that was in serious disrepair. This entire area near the river was like a ghost town. Unfortunately, for him and Sorrel, it wasn't the ghosts they needed to be afraid of. Without seeing any sign of his family, he ducked into the thicket of trees, careful not to scrape Sorrel's bare limbs against the abundant dogwoods and pines that dotted the landscape.

With every snapped limb or scurrying of a squirrel, Eric tensed. He needed to survive, not only to get Sorrel to safety but to destroy his book. Though now he questioned whether his sacrifice would have its intended effect. Sorrel was proof things weren't as they should be, that the curse didn't work how they'd assumed it would. Maybe Sorrel would have the answers—if she woke up. She had to. He had to believe she would. He looked down at her bloodied but beautiful face, more determined than ever to protect her. This time he would make sure he helped her instead of harmed her, even if it meant giving his life.

Eric was relieved when his car came into view. He even smiled when he saw Tara up on his dash playing lookout. Maybe she could get her owner to wake up. With the car in sight, Eric picked up his pace, trying not to jostle Sorrel, who hadn't moved—other than breathing. No doubt her light show and the loss of blood had taken their toll on her.

When he reached the faded and cracked pavement, he heard voices coming from behind him. He wasn't sure if they sounded familiar, but it didn't matter. He couldn't be caught, by friend or foe, while covered in blood and carrying an unconscious woman. In haste he laid Sorrel in his back seat. Tara immediately jumped to her side. He shut the door and rushed around to the driver's side. He had just cranked the ignition when he saw his father coming out of the clearing. They locked eyes before Eric threw his car in reverse. Even from a distance he could see the ire burning like flames in his father's cold eyes. Vincent ran toward him as Eric stepped on the gas. Cranking the steering wheel, he spun the car in a one-eighty and floored the gas pedal.

In his rearview mirror, he could see his father and grandfather running as fast as they could after them on the narrow road leading to the main thoroughfare. There was no way for them to catch him on foot. Unfortunately, he knew how calculating they were and how hell-bent they would be on revenge. It was only a matter of time before they tracked him down.

Once on the main road, Eric looked back at Sorrel and noticed she had fallen to the floor. *Damn.* Tara gave him a disapproving look.

"I'm sorry. Did you want to get caught?"

Tara stuck up her nose, not interested in his apologies.

Eric knew he needed to find a place where he and Sorrel could rest and get cleaned up. And he needed a new mode of transportation. Not only would his family be searching for them, but the authorities would be, too. No doubt Sorrel's friends knew by now that she was missing and that it was under suspicious circumstances. Eric slapped his hands against the steering wheel, trying to come up with a plan. He had contingencies in place in case his secret ever got out; unfortunately, they involved hiding in the shadows and coercing some of his shady informants to help him get the necessary identifications he would need to start over in another country. There was no way he was getting Sorrel anywhere near those people. He'd already put her in enough danger. Plus, a couple of them had enough of a conscience that they would turn him in if he showed up with a bloodied woman.

What they needed was a secluded place off the beaten path. He remembered Raine Peters yammering about her last assignment at some bed-and-breakfast in the Blue Ridge Mountains of Georgia. That was about two hours from where they were. The mountains were probably their best bet until he could figure out a more permanent plan, at least for Sorrel. As it stood, he was still planning on the most permanent of any plan for himself—death.

Once he felt somewhat safe, he pulled over to the side of the road near the river and pulled out his phone to get directions to Blue Ridge. First, though, he jogged down to the river to wash

Sorrel's blood off him. It disturbed him to be covered in it. It was a reminder of his failures and the pain he'd caused Sorrel. The cold, dirty water of the river removed the blood, but not the stains on his heart.

Thankfully, he always kept a gym bag in his car. He only wished he'd thrown his workout clothes in the wash earlier. His black tee was smelling pretty ripe. Still, it was better than no shirt at all. He checked on Sorrel, who soundly slept on the floorboard of his car. She looked so broken and lifeless. More than anything, he wanted to hold her in his arms until she woke up, but time was of the essence. He pulled out his phone and jotted down the directions he needed before turning it off and chucking it into the river. They were going off the grid. He would take the back roads into Georgia and hope he didn't get pulled over. Maybe if Sorrel woke up, she would have a better idea. Though he imagined she probably wasn't going to be happy to see him. The look of betrayal she had given him at her apartment was still fresh in his mind.

Tara hopped onto the passenger seat and looked at him as if to say, *What are you waiting for?* He didn't need the cat to tell him twice. He hit the road and looked back only to check on Sorrel, who still hadn't stirred at all. What had his family done to her? He shuddered to think of all the possibilities.

The back roads were lined by trees and punctuated by towns with populations of less than five hundred people. They all looked the same: a gas station, a small white church, and pickup trucks parked at each. By the looks of it, Eric could have stayed shirtless and not have been out of place at all. Even so, he made sure to draw as little attention to himself as he could, and that included driving the speed limit, though he wanted nothing more than to race to his destination so he could get Sorrel cleaned up and attend to her wounds. He kept reaching behind the front seat just to touch her, to make sure she still existed and breathed. When he wasn't doing that, he was checking the rearview mirror to see if they had been followed.

By early afternoon, they had made it to Blue Ridge. Now

came the tricky part. He needed to find a place for them to stay and regroup. There wasn't any way for him to check into a hotel—using his credit card would be a fatal error, and he only had about a hundred dollars in cash on him. He hated to, but he was going to have to use his "gifts" to secure a place for them. He was doing it for Sorrel, he told himself. Surely that made it okay. There was no other way to protect her. She could never go home until his family was dead.

Eric had seen signs on their drive for cabin rentals near the Toccoa River. He decided those were his best bet. He only hoped they would have one available during the busy summer season. The town was crawling with what looked like tourists. He took the turnoff for the cabin rental office and thought about a good story he could use for his coercion.

When he pulled up to the office, the first thing he noticed was a "Closed for Lunch" sign in the front window. Of course. He was about ready to swear when he noticed an older couple on the front porch, punching in a code on a large lockbox. From it, they pulled out some paperwork and a key. Perhaps a key to a cabin?

Eric took the sunshade for his car and laid it over Sorrel. Tara gave him the evil eye; nonetheless, it was better than someone seeing a half-naked, unconscious woman lying in the back, all covered in blood. "Sorry," Eric whispered, before exiting the vehicle.

The happy couple were dressed to enjoy the outdoors as they stepped off the painted white porch and greeted Eric with friendly hellos.

"You wouldn't know when they'll be back from lunch, would you?" Eric pointed at the office.

"I'm not sure," the gentleman responded. "However, if you're looking to rent a place here, we were told we got the last cabin for the next week."

Eric's jaw clenched, but he kept his cool. He eyed the friendly couple, their Rolex watches, and their luxury SUV. He reasoned they probably had great insurance policies and enough money to recover if, let's say, they happened to have their vehicle confiscated for a noble cause. And they could surely find another place to stay for the weekend. Before anyone could interrupt them, Eric took them both by the hand. The woman giggled and swatted him, but the man tried to pull away, ready to throw a punch. Eric was quick—he connected with them and, using the energy he had built up inside of him, pressed his will upon them. He spun a tale so tall you'd need an extension ladder to make it to the top of it. In the end, though, it worked. The man handed over the keys to his SUV and the cabin, and as an added bonus threw in their cooler full of food. He even helped Eric get Sorrel's luggage in their car. Eric then made them think Sorrel was luggage. Sometimes his powers frightened him.

When it was all said and done, the man and woman drove off in Eric's old sedan with instructions to abandon it at a junkyard after discarding the license plate and to never tell a soul about it. They wouldn't remember Eric or Sorrel, or even that they had planned to spend the next week here. Eric wasn't a total monster: he'd instructed them to book a trip to the Bahamas, which they'd agreed was a splendid idea. While Eric felt awful about it all, he didn't have time to dwell on it.

As luck would have it, the cabin was deep in the woods and far from any other rental. The quaint cabin with a wraparound porch was the kind of place Sorrel deserved. If only the circumstances of their lives were different. What he wouldn't give to be able to not only afford the place, but to take the woman he carried in his arms on vacation here. He could picture them on the porch, sipping wine and watching the fireflies dance among the wildflowers. Instead, he was carrying her limp body up the porch steps while her cat perched on top of her.

Eric took Sorrel straight to the master bedroom and gently laid her on the massive, rustic four-poster log bed that was covered in a dark-green comforter. He ran the back of his hand down her cheek. His eyes welled up with tears. "Please forgive me."

TWENTY-FOUR

ONCE AGAIN, I WASN'T SURE if I was sleeping, paralyzed, or dead. At least this time I was warm and seemed to be on something soft. That led me to believe I was dead, which would explain why my eyes wouldn't open. Or maybe I was paralyzed? But then I wouldn't be able to feel at all? Perhaps I was sleeping, because I kept hearing someone say how sorry they were and begging me to wake up. I thought the voice sounded familiar, even kind, though I couldn't be sure. I wasn't sure of a lot of things lately. The voice asking me to wake up was getting louder and less fuzzy. I didn't want to wake up. I remembered the last time I did, terrible things had happened. Things I didn't want to remember. Regrettably, now they were all coming back.

My eyes flew open.

"Sorrel. Thank God. You've been asleep for hours."

I sat up, scrambled to the other side of the bed and cowered against a log post, pulling a blanket around me as if that would protect me. "Leave me alone. Don't hurt me."

Eric's eyes widened. "Sorrel," he spoke my name softly, "I'm not going to hurt you."

"You did hurt me. You and your family." It was all coming back to me now. "My mother is dead and my book is gone, because of you." Tears streamed down my cheeks, causing a stinging sensation. A reminder of what his crazy mother had

186

done. I grabbed my middle. I had been stabbed, too. Yet I wasn't bleeding and . . . I looked down at my clean pink T-shirt and pajama pants. "How did I get in these clothes?"

Eric swallowed hard. "I put them on you."

"You undressed me? What else did you do?" I pulled the comforter tighter around me.

Eric scooted his chair closer to the bed. "Nothing, I swear—other than clean you up and remove the splinters from your skin."

"Please forgive me if I don't take your word for it," I sneered at him.

"Sorrel, please listen. I couldn't stand to see you covered in blood," his voice cracked. "And I didn't want your cut to get infected. As beautiful as you are, there was no sexual motivation behind me cleaning your wound and changing your clothes."

"How can I believe that?"

"You know the consequences of us having sex. Since we are both still alive, there's your answer."

Perhaps he had a point. Still . . . "You could have done other things to me."

"You're right, but I didn't."

Maybe I shouldn't have believed him. In fact, I knew I shouldn't, but my naïve-yet-broken heart still had feelings for him. At least it thought it did. I tried to tell it that the curse had manufactured my connection to Eric, but it wouldn't hear of it. Instead, it told me to relax and sink against the pillows. I only obeyed because I was exhausted and in pain. It gave me the opportunity to look around at our surroundings. The room was naturally dim, since it was decorated with an abundance of dark-stained wood—wood-paneled walls, a large wooden dresser, and even a large bear made of wood. Thankfully, there was a fair amount of sun filtering in from the large picture window, gently lighting the room. "Where are we?"

"Blue Ridge, Georgia."

"You abducted me too?"

He sighed. "No. I'm trying to save you."

I sat up with the intention of getting out of bed. I stopped when I saw stars and felt a sharp pain in my abdomen. "I don't need you to save me. I need to go home."

"You can't."

I closed my eyes and grabbed my middle. "You can't keep me here."

"Sorrel, if you go home, my family will find you and kill you."

I curled up in a ball and groaned in pain through my sobs. How had this become my life?

Eric rushed to my side. "You're hurt. You need to rest."

I tried to push him away, but it was a feeble attempt. I had zero strength. "Leave me alone."

"Sorry, no can do. Whether you like it or not, we're stuck in this mess together for now. You need to eat and drink. You lost a lot of blood."

I reached under my shirt and felt the tender cut. "How did I survive?" The last thing I remembered was being stabbed. It had felt more like being punched in the gut. Honestly, I'd thought it would hurt more. Regardless, I didn't remember anything after that, except for a bright light.

Eric eased himself onto the bed, and to my surprise Tara jumped up and nudged me with her nose. I cuddled her against me like a security blanket, so happy to see her. "I thought she'd died. How did she get here?"

"She apparently has more than nine lives. I couldn't leave her, and I knew you would want her."

I supposed I should give him props for saving my cat, but I kept quiet. He didn't deserve my thanks after what he'd done.

"Sorrel," Eric whispered. "Where's your book?"

"It was destroyed," I whimpered.

"What do you remember?"

I shuddered while visions of knives, burning flesh, and unwanted touches flashed in my mind. "I don't want to talk about it."

"I understand, but . . . we need to figure out what's going on. And . . . there's something different about you."

With great effort I turned toward him, keeping ahold of Tara like a lifeline. "What do you mean?"

"For starters, you didn't die. And you possess some gifts that haven't been seen in many years. As far as I know, since . . ." He paused and pressed his lips together.

"What gifts?"

He ran a hand over his hair and blew out a heavy breath. "I can't believe I'm saying this, but I think you're a daughter of the sun."

If I could have, I would have spat out a laugh; however, that would have required stomach muscles, and mine were out of order. Eric was out of his mind. "You're as crazy as your family. The Aelius line died a long time ago. If not, we wouldn't be here like this. I would still have my family," I choked out. *We wouldn't be enemies.*

Eric reached out to comfort me, then thought better of it when I scowled at him. Still, part of me longed for him to touch me and make it all better, as if he could. I wanted the feelings I had for him to die, but something inside of me kept fanning the flames of my desire for him as if he were a need. It seemed so sick and wrong.

Eric stared at my cheek. "I can prove it to you."

"How?" I played along.

"Heal your cheek."

"I can't right now. I need some calendula and olive oil."

"You don't need those things."

Suddenly, I remembered the dream I'd had of him while I lay unconscious from being poisoned by my own body's water. He'd told me I could heal myself. The memory also reminded me of another reason to despise him. "Can you enter my dreams?"

His mouth fell open, but not a sound escaped. He rubbed the back of his neck. "I can," he admitted.

"Have you?"

He nodded.

Every embarrassing moment I'd unwittingly shared with him came crashing into my mind. Everything from how I'd dreamed we were married and I was having his baby, to all the steamy kisses we'd shared. Worse, all the lies he had told me— especially how he'd professed to be in love with me.

I recoiled from him and pulled Tara tighter against me. "You used me and lied to me. I thought you . . ." Well, it didn't matter.

He clenched his fists and closed his eyes. "Sorrel, I know you won't believe this, but I had no idea who you were when my book sent me to you."

"Your book speaks to you?"

His eyes fluttered open. "Unfortunately, yes. It told me to take Raine's assignment."

"Why?"

"I don't know. I didn't even suspect who you were until the night on the riverbank when you said you wanted to bind yourself to me."

I narrowed my eyes at him. "I don't remember saying that."

"You were pretty sleepy, and I think a little buzzed from the wine."

I rubbed my temples. My brain hurt. "You tricked me into telling you where my book was."

He stood and began to pace. "I know. I hate myself for it, but I had to know. My father became suspicious of you after reading the article I wrote about you. He demanded that I find out. Then I began to wonder if you knew who I was . . . and if it was you who was playing me."

"Why would you think that? What had I ever done to you to make you think I was capable of being as cruel as your family?"

Eric threw himself onto the fabric-covered chair in the corner of the room and covered his face with his hands. "Sorrel, you have no idea what it was like to grow up in my family. My whole life I've been told stories about the evil, conniving Tellus family. But, I knew it wasn't you. I was going to give your book back and . . ."

"And what?"

"It doesn't matter. Whether you believe it or not, I was trying to protect you. And that's what I'm trying to do now."

"I don't feel protected. How do I know your family isn't hiding in the shadows now? Or that they won't break into my dreams? I trusted you. I thought I was falling in love with you. Now I know it's all been a lie, and everything and everyone I care about is lost to me." I wanted to cry, yet the tears wouldn't come. Maybe I was dehydrated.

Eric padded over to me and knelt by the bed. "Sorrel," he said tenderly, "I can imagine the horrors you witnessed today. I lived them for most of my life. For that I am truly sorry. And I take full responsibility for my part in all of this. But there is something bigger afoot here. I don't know exactly what. But my father is right about one thing—there are no coincidences when it comes to the curse."

Part of me ached for him. I couldn't imagine growing up in his family. Though how could I trust him, or even myself, after everything that had happened? "How do we know that, when the curse doesn't work right? I should be dead."

Eric sank farther to the floor. "I know. Are you sure your book was destroyed?"

I nodded, trying to block the images of it going up in flames along with Eric's great-grandfather. "Except, I still feel connected to it."

Eric pursed his lips together. "Hmm. I hate to ask this, but how do you know your mother is dead?"

I stroked Tara as a tear rolled down my cheek. "I could hear her." Her dying words would forever haunt me.

Eric tilted his head. "How?"

"Can't you speak to your family through your mind?"

"No. That must be a Tellus gift. Or an Aelius gift?"

I shook my head. He needed to quit saying things like that. "No. That's impossible. Besides, my mother would have said something. I think."

"What does that mean?"

"It's just that she didn't know a lot about the other families, and she kept information on how to destroy the books from me. But she would never keep something like that from me. Besides, we both know that family no longer exists."

"We also thought destroying the book would kill you."

"True, but it was broken."

"That's another mystery."

"Well, what about your book? Why haven't you been bound to anyone?"

Eric shrugged. "It's withheld that information from me."

"Why?"

"I don't know."

"How old are you?"

The tiniest of smiles appeared on his face. "Forty-one. How old are you?"

"Thirty."

"Figures, you didn't lie."

"The only thing I ever lied to you about was my mother's death. And now she is dead." Her death was really starting to sink in, and it created within me an incomprehensible void. So much so, it made it hard for me to catch my breath.

Eric took my hand. For a moment I reveled in the comfort I always felt when we touched. I needed it. It filled some of my loss, even though it was all make-believe. I pulled away half-heartedly. "Our connection was never real, was it? You never really wanted me."

"Sorrel." He hesitated.

"Just tell me the truth."

He heaved a heavy sigh. "I don't know."

I snuggled down under the covers with Tara, willing myself not to cry. "I'm tired."

"You should rest. I'll watch over you."

"Why bother?"

He rested his warm hand on my cheek. "Regardless of what the curse has or hasn't made us feel, one thing I know without a doubt is that there is something special about you. Something well worth protecting."

"I don't want your protection," I lied.

His hand dropped. "I understand that. But it's all I have to give to you."

His words pierced my broken heart, and I turned away from him.

"I am sorry, Sorrel."

I was too.

TWENTY-FIVE

ERIC

ERIC COULDN'T HELP BUT SMILE over at Sorrel as she slept against the passenger-side window. Her beautiful tresses cascaded down around her heart-shaped face that still bore the cut from his mother. Sorrel refused to even try to heal it. And she wanted to hear nothing about the light show she had put on. It was almost as if she were afraid to realize the truth about herself. On the other hand, she was tenacious as hell. She'd woken up late last night, intent on going to Saint Augustine to give her mother a proper burial and wouldn't hear a word to the contrary. Eric gave in only when Sorrel informed him her mother had passports and plane tickets for her to use. His plan was to make sure she had safe passage out of the country, and then he was going to destroy his book.

The curse may not have killed Sorrel, but if indeed her mother was dead, it meant that destroying his book should kill his father and grandfather, thereby releasing his mother from the binds that tied her to his father. He hoped that once his mother was free, she would forget about seeking her revenge on Sorrel, though he couldn't count on that. At least she would have no resources and Sorrel would have a new identity. It was the

194

best plan he could think of. Sorrel would have to be on her own to discover the truth about herself.

He ached to reach over, brush her hair back, and tell her that despite the curse he was falling in love with her. How could he not be? But what good would it do? She would never believe it. And after everything he and his family had done to her, it seemed cruel to play with her emotions like that. She clearly had serious misgivings about him, and she was frightened by his family. He noticed the way she purposely avoided shadows and tossed and turned in her sleep, sometimes muttering words like "stop" and "help me." He didn't think she would sleep at all, except her body demanded it after all the blood she'd lost and the energy she had expended. He would do his best to make up for everything. He would prove his love for her by giving his life. Then she would be free to live her life as she pleased. To find love and have those babies both she and he dreamed of having. The world would have more of her in it, and that gave him some comfort.

Eric focused back on driving. The sun was barely creeping over the horizon, and he should have been exhausted, but Sorrel had picked leaves from a plant outside of the cabin and worked her magic on it before telling him to chew it. He teased her that she'd probably poisoned it. She didn't even crack a smile. He ate it anyway. It didn't taste half-bad, and almost immediately he'd felt as if he'd had a full night's rest. He was stumped as to how she could still use her Tellus gifts. He'd thought with the book destroyed she would no longer be able to. Perhaps their abilities weren't tied to their books. There was so much he didn't know. Sorrel's other abilities only deepened the mystery.

They had already been on the road for over four hours, taking all the Georgia back roads they could. They had stopped for gas just outside of Blue Ridge at one of those seedy all-night places—it probably had criminals running it, so they didn't care if their customers were too—and bought an atlas. Thankfully, Sorrel had packed her emergency cash. And no one seemed to recognize them. Without their cell phones they had no idea if they'd made the news yet. Sorrel was so beside herself, thinking about how worried her friends and customers must be, especially Josie and Mateo. She shed several tears thinking about the weddings she'd missed. Eric wanted to tell her that maybe she could go back after it was all said and done, but there would be too many questions surrounding her that would expose her for who she really was. Even with his family gone, that could be dangerous. Honestly, he was surprised no one had caught on before now. Though even he had been fooled. He had known she was hiding something; he'd just never guessed she was a Praeditus like him.

As much as mortals loved to watch movies and read books about supernatural abilities, deep down they didn't want those things to be true. It would throw their world into a panic if they had to believe in things that go bump in the night. Things like his family. No. It was better for the world, and Sorrel, if she kept her gifts hidden. Though Eric knew she wouldn't. She would help people to her own detriment. And that's one of the reasons why he was falling in love with her. He'd never met such a selfless person. He'd had no idea someone like her even existed.

Sorrel stirred and it made his pulse rise. He knew she hated him, but despite that, he wanted to spend every last second with her that he could, even if she only gave him dirty looks. At least if she was looking at him, he could admire her.

She stretched and yawned, giving Eric a nice view of all her lines and curves.

"How are you feeling?" Eric asked.

She settled against the fine leather seat and stroked Tara, who was faithfully curled up on her lap. "Better." She grabbed her water bottle from the console cup holder and took a large drink. She hadn't had much of an appetite, but at least she was drinking.

Eric thought she still looked pale, though he didn't mention it. If only she would believe him and heal the wounds her body bore inside and out.

"How much farther do we have to go?" She stared out at the horizon filled with hayfields and cows.

"Probably another four hours. Are you sure you want to see your mother? What if her body's already been discovered?"

Sorrel's entire frame tensed, and she sniffled. "I doubt anyone knows she's missing. She distrusts mortals and made it a point to never get close to anyone besides my father and me."

Her father? Eric had some questions about him. "How did your father feel about being brought into the curse's power?"

"That's an odd question."

Eric grinned over at her. "I'm just trying to make small talk. It's going to be a long drive."

That approach seemed to make her more willing to speak to him. "He loved my mother. I think he didn't care what he had to do to be with her."

"Your mother was lucky."

"I know. We both were. My father was eternally optimistic and made me believe I would break this curse."

"Maybe you will." Or he would for her.

"I don't see how that's possible now, unless I die."

Eric whipped his head toward her. "Don't say that. You're meant to live."

She seemed taken aback by his abruptness. "That's what you said in my dream. The dream where you told me I could heal myself. Was that a real dream?"

"Yes," he said apologetically. "Sorrel." He paused. "Who is the man in your dreams you're always walking with in the vineyard?"

Her cute button nose scrunched. "What are you talking about? I don't remember walking with any man in my dreams."

Curious. Very Curious. "Are you sure? Every time I visited you," he hesitated to admit, "you were walking with a man with dark hair and penetrating brown eyes. You seemed to have a great deal of affection for him." Eric tried not to sound jealous, although he was envious of the man.

"My dad had dark hair and brown eyes, but I have no idea what you're talking about. While we're on the subject, can you just come into my dreams whenever you want? Because that's an invasion of privacy, and you should take everything I may have said or done in my dreams with a grain of salt. They were dreams, nothing more. People can't control themselves in their dreams."

She was adorable when angry and embarrassed, he thought. "Sorrel, I'm sorry for violating your dreams. It was the safest way to get to know you. I feared if we ever got too close physically, I might make a fatal mistake."

Sorrel gripped the armrest. "Your father said you killed a woman."

Eric's face turned crimson and seemed to pulsate. "I did. Karina," he whispered her name. "I was stupid and careless and didn't put enough stock in the curse. I thought since the book hadn't told me who to bind myself to, it meant the curse was broken. I was wrong."

Sorrel visibly relaxed. "I had some of the same thoughts over the years. Do you think the curse forced us together because it wanted us to, you know, have sex so we would kill each other off?" She blushed uncontrollably.

Eric loved her innocence. "That's an interesting theory, but I don't think so."

"Why?"

He twisted his hands around the steering wheel. "Because my book told me how to save you."

Her mouth fell open. "It did? Why?"

Eric shrugged. "Maybe because I asked it to."

She bit her lip. "Oh. Does your book normally grant requests?"

"Only once."

"Where is your book?" She was eager to change the subject.

He raised his brow.

"I don't want to steal it."

He chuckled. "I keep it hidden in the shadows. I'll show it to you when we get to Saint Augustine. And by the way, I can only enter your dreams if you let me—or want me there."

Her entire body seemed to flush red.

"Don't be embarrassed. I didn't lie when I told you I dreamed about you too."

"Do you like music? I think we should turn on the radio." She flipped on the radio to some pop station before he could respond. Then she leaned her seat back, closed her eyes, and started humming along.

So much for them talking. She hardly said a word to him the rest of the drive, unless it was to tell him she needed to stop to use the restroom. It gave him too much time to think. He wanted to know why she didn't remember the man in her dreams. He wondered if it was her father, or if he was a piece of this bizarre puzzle. When the man in her dreams had spoken to him, it seemed real. Could someone else enter her dreams? Certainly not her father. He'd seen David Black's coroner's report. And most importantly, how did Sorrel possess gifts from both the Tellus and Aelius families? How could she still feel connected to a destroyed book?

If only he could stay alive to see how it all unfolded. But he'd promised Sorrel he would protect her, and he meant it. He had only a precious few hours left, depending on what they found when they reached Saint Augustine. Which was any moment now. Eric wanted to wait until dark to enter the city, but Sorrel wouldn't hear of it. Eric thought she still held out a tiny shred of hope that her mother had survived, just like she had.

Saint Augustine was stunning with its Spanish architecture and ocean views. Sorrel seemed to become more alive the closer they got to the coast. She rolled down her window, breathed in the salt air, and let her hair whip in the wind.

"I hope you're planning on going somewhere warm and near the beach," Eric commented.

Sorrel turned to him with concern in her red, tired eyes. "You're not coming with me?"

Eric thought he detected a hint of disappointment in her tone. Maybe it was wishful thinking. "No. I'll be staying in the States to make sure my family doesn't follow you."

"How will you find them?"

"I have my ways."

"How?" She wasn't going to let it go.

"The less you know, the safer you'll be."

She folded her arms. "I'm tired of people keeping things from me because they think I'm some delicate little creature."

Eric wanted to reach over and caress her cheek, or at the very least hold her hand, but he settled for a quick glance and a smile. "That's not why. You're braver than anyone I know. It's like I told you that night on the riverbank, it's a rare opportunity to be in the presence of someone like you, who reminds us all of what we could be—should be. And I think those of us lucky enough to get to know you all want to preserve your innocence that enchants us all." From the corner of Eric's eye, he could see Sorrel wiping her eyes.

"You know, you really make it hard to hate you." Sorrel's voice was filled with emotion.

"I'm glad." If anything, he didn't want to die knowing Sorrel hated him.

As they wended their way around Saint Augustine, Eric couldn't help but look around and be jealous of all the happy couples and families enjoying the centuries-old architecture and myriad of restaurants. All while he was driving the woman he loved toward what was sure to be a gut-wrenching experience.

Sorrel was also looking out the window as if she, too, wished she could trade places with one of the tourists. "Eric, if you can find your family, can they find us?" Her voice trembled.

"Eventually they will, which is why I'm staying behind. You're sure no one knew your mother's new identity or where she lived?"

"I don't think so—she wouldn't even tell me until I told her the book had been stolen."

"That should buy us some time. Still, you should leave as soon as possible."

"What will happen to you?"

Eric patted her bare knee. "Are you worried about me?"

She took a moment to answer. "Yes, though I don't know if I should be."

"You don't need to worry about me."

She didn't reply, other than to lean her head against the window and hug Tara.

Once they turned onto the road where her mother lived, or used to live, Sorrel sat straight up, on high alert. It was a long stretch of road dotted by coastal homes and palm trees. The back of each house faced the street, and they all looked similar—boxy, with two-car garages in varying shades of tan.

"Her house number is 475," she informed Eric.

Eric crept slowly down the road and, unfortunately, too many people saw them. These damn beach dwellers were too friendly—waving and smiling as if they were in a parade. Eric and Sorrel half-heartedly waved back, trying to act normal. Thankfully her mother lived at the end of the street, and the farthest away from any other neighbor. It made sense to Eric, considering Sorrel had said her mother didn't like mortals.

When they pulled into her driveway, Eric stiffened. The garage door was open, showing off her mother's white Audi. Sorrel faced Eric with her brows raised in suspicion while she tightly gripped her seat.

Eric shifted the SUV into park. "Stay here. I'm going to go check the house."

She grabbed his arm. "You can't leave me alone."

The terror in her eyes killed him. He took her hand, and it wasn't lost on him how well her delicate fingers seemed to intertwine perfectly with his. Their surreal connection was just as strong as it always had been. He didn't care if the damn curse had initially manufactured it, it felt more real now than ever. "Sorrel, it's me who shouldn't want to be without you. You possess a power a hundred times stronger than anything I can do. The light inside of you can overpower my family."

She shook her head. "No. You're mistaken."

He kissed her hand and she didn't flinch, giving him some hope that she didn't hate him. "I saw it with my own eyes. How do you think we escaped the warehouse?"

She nibbled on her pouty lip. "I don't remember."

"You will. Just give it some time."

"My dad told me a story once about Princess Sorrel and the special light she had in her. I could hear his voice reminding me of it when I was trying to heal myself from the water poisoning," she admitted reluctantly.

That piqued Eric's interest. He tilted his head. "Sorrel, are you sure your father was mortal?"

She leaned away from him. "Of course. How could he be anything else?"

"I don't know. But we don't have time right now to discuss him. Please stay here."

"What if something happens to you?"

He placed his hand over her heart. "Then find the light within you and run like hell." He reached under the seat of the car and, like magic, pulled out a book too thick to fit underneath it. The moonstones sparkled in the light of day. "Take my book, and if I don't come out in ten minutes, leave. Use the book for leverage if you have to."

Sorrel hesitated to reach for it.

"I trust you." Eric tried to coax her, while inching the book toward her.

"How can you? We're born enemies."

"Maybe we were born that way, but that's not my choice." He pressed his lips hard against hers without warning. "I choose you."

TWENTY-SIX

I KEPT LOOKING BETWEEN ERIC'S book in my lap and my mother's house, shaking where I sat. It was mostly out of fear of who Eric might find lurking within, and partially because of the feelings I was having for the man I watched disappear into the shadows. I couldn't think about those feelings, no matter how strong they were, when I knew my mother was probably dead inside that house. My only consolation was that she'd spent her last days in this beautiful oasis with an ocean view. She'd loved white sand beaches and the water. And while this place wasn't exotic, it was serene, with sand grass blowing in the breeze and blue, blue skies.

I feared that Eric's family had followed us here or worse, beat us to the punch. I hated to think what they would have done to my mother had they found her alive. What they would do to Eric if he walked in on them. And though Eric promised me I had the power to fight them off, I had no idea how that was possible. Eric had my mind reeling with so many questions. The biggest one being, why did I survive? I had no idea where to get the answers.

The clock on the SUV seemed to be broken. It was the longest ten minutes of my life, waiting for Eric. I clutched Tara, who purred against my chest, like his book seemed to purr on my lap, as if it recognized who I was. So weird. I wanted to peek inside the ethereal-looking book made of what looked like moonstones, but now wasn't the time. And it almost seemed like a violation of Eric's privacy. Though he had apparently searched through mine. But mine was broken. Another question I had no answer to.

With the final minute ticking down, I got ready to go in and find Eric even though he had told me to leave. In good conscience I couldn't do that, despite the fact that if he hadn't come into my life none of this would have happened. I couldn't exactly blame him though. He was bound to obey his book. And he had been nothing but kind and attentive ever since he'd kidnapped me. I glanced at the keys in the ignition and at his book. He was the worst kidnapper ever. Although he was a pretty good knight in shining armor. The thought made me smile. Knight had a double meaning for him. I wondered if he chose that last name or if the book had.

I was about ready to rescue Mr. Knight, or at least pretend to, when he came walking out of the garage door with a regretful look on his face. He came directly to the passenger side and opened my door. The way his head hung, I knew he had found my mother.

Tears trickled down my cheeks. "She's dead."

He only nodded.

"Does she look like she was in a lot of pain?"

"She looks peaceful, as if she had fallen asleep. In fact, she's wearing a designer suit and heels, and her makeup looks flawless."

I laughed through my tears. "That sounds like her. But . . . does she, you know, look dead and discolored? Does she smell?" I wanted to brace myself. The last dead body I had seen was my father's, right after he'd died.

"You don't know a lot about our kind, do you?"

"Not really."

He gave me a small smile. "Since we aren't exactly human, our bodies don't decay like mortals. She looks perfect."

I let out a sigh of relief until I remembered, "Did you see any signs of your family?"

"No. I think we're safe for now, but we should probably pull the car into the garage. The less people see us the better."

That sounded like a good plan. While I wanted to rush in to see my mother, it was also the last thing I wanted to do. She should have lived for another 150 years. I would miss her snarky voice in my head. Even all her warnings that I never listened to. That I should have listened to.

It took no time for us to get the car into the garage. Eric turned to me once we'd pulled in. "Are you sure you want to do this?"

"No, but she would do the same for me. And it's my fault she's dead. I didn't protect the book," my voice cracked.

"I should have never taken it. I'm sorry."

"Why did you try to give it back?"

He tucked some of my hair behind my ear. "Because the world needs your gifts. But mostly because I realized I couldn't imagine the world without you in it."

My traitorous heart skipped a few beats. "You really should stop being so sweet to me. It's confusing."

"I'm sorry to confuse you."

I hated to be so perplexed about him. I took a deep breath. "We should go in."

Eric hopped out. "Let me close the garage first."

I waited until the door was closed before stepping out with Tara into the dimly lit garage filled only with my mother's fancy car. She'd had a penchant for the finer things in life.

Eric met me at the door and reached out a hand to me, and though I hesitated to take it, his hand never wavered. "I'm told everyone needs a hand to hold when someone they love dies."

"Has anyone you love died?" *Like Karina,* I wanted to add.

"My grandmother. She was the only person who ever showed me any kindness when I was growing up. She died when I was ten."

"I'm sorry."

"You don't need to be. She tried to help me believe that I could be different from my father and grandfathers. How she didn't become bitter and hardened like my mother, I don't know."

"You are different from them." I placed my hand in his. I saw that with my own eyes. I wasn't sure I would ever get the visions of his family's evil acts out of my mind.

Eric squeezed my hand and tugged me toward the door that led into the house. "I don't know. I've used my powers in ways I'm not proud of." He flicked his head toward his car. "Just yesterday I confiscated that car from a nice couple."

"What? That isn't your car?" I thought maybe he'd bought a new car, or had two. Never did I think it wasn't his.

"Did I not mention that?" He opened the door to the house. "No, you didn't."

"Don't worry, I'll make sure it gets back to the rightful owners. And to be fair, I gave them my car."

"Maybe the less I know, the better."

"That's probably a good idea."

We walked into my mother's home, right into her mudroom. There were cubbies filled with various flip-flops. Each pair looked like it had been bedazzled. On the hooks hung light jackets and sweaters. The home smelled like her lilac-scented perfume. It made me smile and cry at the same time.

Eric led me to the farmhouse-style kitchen. It was bright and open with white cabinets. There was a teapot on the gas range. Mom drank a cup of her own specially blended tea every morning and night. Her house was also filled with plants of every kind. Through the patio door I noticed some lemon trees.

"She's upstairs in her room," Eric informed me.

I placed Tara on the floor before we went up the wooden steps. She darted off to explore the house.

With each step I gripped Eric's hand tighter, and my breaths became more and more shallow.

"Are you okay?" he asked.

"No," I squeaked. "Though I don't think you're supposed to be in these situations."

"I'm here for whatever you need."

That comforted me probably more than it should have. Our odd connection was maddening, but for now I was grateful for it.

At the first room we came to, Eric paused in front of the whitewashed door. He gave me such a tender look. The kind I had longed for my entire life. Under different circumstances, of course. "She's in here," he whispered.

I swallowed hard and tried to catch my breath.

"You don't have to go in."

"I do."

He opened the door and immediately I saw her lying on the floor in front of her neatly made bed, her luggage surrounding her like a shrine. For a moment I stood motionless, looking at her beautiful body frozen in time. She was just like I remembered her: long golden-brown hair and a petite frame. Oh, how I wished to see her vibrant green eyes that were full of wisdom and sass. I wanted her to get up and yell at me for not listening to her, but she remained still.

After taking a few breaths I tiptoed closer, Eric holding my hand each step of the way, until I was close enough to drop to my knees by her side.

Eric fell right next to me and placed his arm around me. "She's beautiful. You look a lot like her."

I took her cold hand and pressed it against my cheek. It was then I remembered the cut there. A thought struck me. "Do you really think I have some Aelius gifts?"

"Yes . . ."

"Don't they have powers that deal with life and light?"

He squinted. "What are you thinking?"

"What if I could bring her back?"

Eric's countenance dropped. "It's just a theory, and I don't know exactly how that would work, especially since she died by the curse."

"But, what if?" I was desperate to cling to the last shred of hope I had.

"Sorrel, I don't know if it's possible."

"You're the one who told me I could heal myself. What if I can heal my mother?"

He sank to the floor, at a loss for words.

I paid the naysayer no attention and placed my hands under my mother's silk blouse, trying to see if I could feel anything. To see if I could tell where the problem lay, like I had many times with the people I'd made elixirs for. I closed my eyes, focusing, but all I felt was a void. I pressed harder, willing myself to feel something, anything. I thought about my father and the light. I had flashes from when I was unconscious after being poisoned. There was a light. It had come from my heart. I couldn't find it. Tears of frustration poured down my cheeks.

Eric placed his hands on top of mine. "Sorrel."

My name on his lips felt like a key that opened a door to my heart. I could feel the light swell in my chest. The more I focused on Eric's touch, the warmer I felt and the more I felt the light expand. I tried pushing it into my mother; instead I felt my cheek and abdomen tingle. The exhaustion that had plagued me over the last day seemed to disappear.

"Your cheek," Eric whispered, "is healed."

My eyes flew open, and the light dissipated. My focus was solely on my mother, who still lay lifeless. "Why can't I heal her?"

Eric gathered me in his arms, and I sobbed into his chest.

"It's all my fault," I cried.

"Shh. It's not your fault. The curse took her. I think it orchestrated all of this. We're just players in its game now."

"Why? To what end?" What had I done to deserve this? I tried to use my gifts for good. And I loved mortals. It wasn't my fault my ancestors had started some holy war.

He stroked my hair. "I don't know, but no matter what, it's going to be a happy ending for you. I promise."

"You can't promise that." I wasn't sure I would ever feel happy again. The life I loved so much in Riverhaven was over, and the only family I'd had was gone. And soon I would part with Eric, and though it confused me to no end, the thought of leaving him hurt my soul.

"You need to trust me. Can you do that?" he begged to know.

My head said absolutely not, while my heart shouted the opposite. It said some other things, too. I touched my healed cheek, and the voice in my heart beckoned me to remember how Eric's touch had played a part in my healing now, and after I had been stabbed. Vague recollections were flashing in my mind. Mostly I saw Eric in them. "Eric, why didn't I bleed to death?"

His heart pounded double-time against his chest. "I don't know how to explain it. When I was using my energy to stop the flow of blood, your energy grabbed ahold of mine, and the combination of the two healed you."

Words my father had spoken to me slammed into my chest. *Light, earth, and dark all need each other.* I wasn't sure exactly what that meant, but this my heart knew: "I trust you, Eric."

TWENTY-SEVEN

ERIC

TOGETHER THEY DECIDED TO GIVE Elizabeth a water burial. Eric would use his power over the water to make sure she was buried deep in the depths of the ocean. While they waited for dark, they made preparations for Sorrel's departure the next day. She would fly to Lisbon like her mother had intended for her, under a new name—Genoveva Ferreira. Her mother had originally wanted Sorrel's name to be Genoveva, but her father had insisted she be named Sorrel. He'd said it was an old family name. At least it made Sorrel smile that her mother had finally gotten her wish.

To Eric's relief, Elizabeth was well prepared for these situations. Not only did she have the needed passports and visas for Sorrel, she also had several thousand dollars in American and euro bills as well as a credit card in Sorrel's new name. Sorrel would leave bright and early and take her mother's car to the airport. Eric planned to be long gone by then. As soon as they buried Elizabeth's body and Sorrel fell asleep, he would leave and destroy his book.

Knowing he had only hours left with Sorrel, he stayed as close to her as she would allow. She seemed to be more comfortable around him since owning to the fact that there was more to her than she even knew. It wasn't like she was giving him a repeat of their one and only date, but she at least let him hold her hand and didn't shy away from him. He would take what he could get, though he longed to take her in his arms and kiss her until they were both breathless. He wanted to touch her silky skin and, if he was being honest, make love to her. It would be the perfect parting gift. He knew it was out of the question. Not only would it be in poor taste, in light of Sorrel mourning for her mother and everything else she had lost, but it would be deadly. And he refused to let his death be because of a selfish act.

They settled onto her mother's plush navy couch to check the news on Elizabeth's laptop. Eric was anxious to see if there were any reports about them. It didn't take long to discover that there were several local stories about them both in Riverhaven and Atlanta. That story he'd done about Clayton Palmer had once again come back to bite him—his notoriety sensationalized the coverage. Well-known journalist was wanted in connection with the disappearance of Riverhaven's town sweetheart.

Sorrel gripped his hand while they watched Josie and Mateo's interview on a local Tennessee station. Mateo had his arm around Josie while tears streamed down her face.

"I knew Eric Knight was bad news." Josie wiped her eyes. "I mean, why did an investigative journalist want to interview her? It was probably just a ploy," she sniffled, "to lure her into God knows what." She could no longer continue.

Mateo pulled her closer. "She's going to be okay, baby."

Josie turned into him and lost it.

Sorrel's brows raised. "Well, maybe one good thing will come out of this. Those two might finally get together."

"I saw Mateo when I left your apartment carrying Tara and your luggage. I told him we were going away for the weekend. He might have also been led to believe we were intimate," Eric admitted.

"And how did he come to that conclusion?"

Eric held up his bruised and cut wrists from where he'd been tied up. "He noticed these and assumed you were, let's say, adventurous."

Sorrel laughed softly. As subdued as it was, it did Eric's heart good to hear her laugh. Sorrel surprised him further by gently taking his left arm in her hands and tenderly running her fingers across his injuries. "I'm sorry your family treated you so cruelly."

Her touch both soothed and tormented him. How desperately he wished their story could have a different ending. "Not as sorry as I am that they hurt you."

Her entire body shivered. The fear of what she'd been subjected to still lived in her eyes. "Thank you for coming for me. I probably should have said that earlier."

"Shh." He placed a finger on her supple lips. "You don't need to thank me."

She kissed his finger and closed her eyes. Eric immediately felt a surge of warmth down his arm. The cuts and bruises seemed to seep underneath his skin, leaving no trace of them. Eric held out his arm and looked at it in amazement. Sorrel, too, seemed astonished.

"I can't believe I can do that."

"Promise me you'll do what you can to find out who you really are."

"Why can't you come with me? Surely you can use your powers to obtain the necessary documents to travel. I have access to several bank accounts in Europe. We can hide from your family there."

Eric placed his hand on her cheek. "Sorrel, you'll be safer on your own."

She leaned into his hand. "Please. I just lost almost everything and everyone I care about. Why do I have to lose you, too?" Her eyes darted toward the laptop screen that now showed the outside of her bakery. It had become a shrine to her. There were not only hundreds of balloons and flowers but large signs plastered to the windows that said things like, "We Love You,

Sorrel" and "Please Come Home Soon." Her tears dripped onto his hands.

Eric was tempted to give in to her plea, but she didn't deserve a life on the run. Always having to look over her shoulder, avoiding the shadows like he'd watched her do all day. And honestly, what kind of life could they have together when they could never truly be together? It would drive him mad to have to live like friends when he wanted to be her lover and the father of her children. He kissed her forehead and lingered there, deeply breathing her in and memorizing everything he could about her—from the way she smelled like the coconut oil she'd used after showering, to how perfectly smooth her skin was. "Sorrel, the best way for me to protect you from my family is for me to stay."

"But together, we're stronger. You even said yourself that my gifts are better against your family than yours are."

She had him there, though his life was the ultimate weapon. He leaned away from her. "This is the way it has to be."

She narrowed her eyes as if she could tell he was keeping something from her. "I could refuse to leave tomorrow."

His jaw clenched. "But you won't."

She folded her arms. "Watch me."

He was half-exasperated, half-smitten with her tenacity. Still, she would go. He would make sure of it. "There's no room for argument."

"You're right." She turned from him and continued to watch their story unfold on the small screen. Meanwhile, Eric contemplated how he would get the stubborn woman to leave without revealing his plan.

Later that night, while Sorrel said her final goodbyes to her mother, Eric decided to write Sorrel a letter about his plans. He would leave it for her to find after he was gone. After it was too late to stop him. He would convince her that even though she was safe from his father and grandfather, the safest thing would be for her to start a new life away from any speculation—

somewhere away from his mother, who was a loose cannon at best and a murderer at worst.

Well after midnight and following a careful examination of the private beach Sorrel's mother had lived on, they decided that it was safe enough to bury Elizabeth in the water. Under the night sky shrouded in clouds, Eric carried Elizabeth's body wrapped in a sheet. Sorrel silently wept behind him. They trudged through the beach grass and white sand down the coastline several yards away from the house. Once Eric felt comfortable, they neared the water. He placed Elizabeth's body on the beach just beyond the waves' reach.

Sorrel knelt near her mother once more and whispered, "Goodbye. I love you."

Eric rested his hand on Sorrel's shoulder. "I'm sorry, we should hurry. I need you to stand back."

Sorrel obeyed and watched in awe as Eric closed his eyes and directed the water with his hands as if he were conducting an orchestra. A large waved crashed against the shore and swallowed her mother. Sorrel placed her hand over her mouth, stifling her gasp. The ocean almost seemed to roll under itself in a giant rip current. Eric waved his hands about for several minutes while the angry water thrashed and turned like a violent song. Once he was satisfied Elizabeth's body would remain forever hidden, he sank onto the sand to catch his breath.

Sorrel rushed to his side and fell next to him. The now-gentle waves lapped up against them, tickling their feet and bare legs.

Eric gazed at Sorrel, and the half-moon parted the clouds as if Eric had called to the celestial orb from which his powers were derived. Sorrel looked lovelier than ever under the moonbeams, her linen shirt falling off her shoulder. There was so much he wanted to say to her. Instead, he took her face in his hands and pressed the gentlest of kisses upon her lips. His own tears mingled with hers. This was goodbye.

Though Eric hated to, he called the persuasive energy within himself and whispered "Sleep" against her lips, his will bleeding into hers. Before she even knew what hit her, she fell limp into his arms.

He cradled her against his body and stroked her hair. "I love you, Sorrel."

TWENTY-EIGHT

I WOKE UP IN THE dim morning light on my mother's bed, not sure how I got there. I sat up and stretched, running a hand through my hair and feeling completely disoriented. I felt so groggy it was like I had taken an elixir for sleep, though I couldn't remember doing that. The last thing I remembered was watching my mother's body get sucked into the ocean and then . . . I touched my lips. Eric had kissed me. It was the sweetest kiss I had ever had.

Eric? Where was he? My eyes darted around the room, sure he would be watching over me. He'd promised he would protect me.

I tossed the blanket off me. "Eric."

He didn't respond, but Tara gave me a disgruntled look for waking her up.

I jumped off the bed to go search for him when I saw a white envelope with my name written on it in calligraphy leaning against the hurricane lamp on the nightstand. I sat back down on the bed; a feeling of dread washed over me as I picked up the envelope. Carefully, I broke the seal and took out the folded sheet of paper. I unfolded it, and before I even began to read it, a lump had already formed in my throat.

Dear Sorrel,

Where do I begin? Maybe at the beginning. The very first

216

message I received from my book told me that I must prove myself worthy for the destiny meant to be mine. For years I resented the book's cryptic message. Then I met you, and from the first moment I saw you, something deep within me called to me to protect you. I didn't realize it at the time, but it has become apparent what my destiny is—it is to protect you, my love. And yes, I do love you. I know I told you, that because of the curse, we couldn't be sure of our feelings, but I have never been more sure of anything in my life. And that is why I must destroy my book.

"No!" I cried to no one but Tara. My tears splashed against the paper shaking in my hands.

I do not resent sacrificing my life for you—I only regret that we never got the chance to make a life together. Now you are free to live your life as you please. With the curse broken, I hope you find a man worthy of your love and your gifts. I hope you can trust him with your secrets and to be the father of the children you dream of having.

Please forgive me for not protecting you better, sooner. I beg you to get on that plane this morning. It will be safer for you. The less mortals suspect about you, the better, even those closest to you like Josie and Mateo. And though my father and grandfather will be gone, my mother will likely seek her revenge. She can't be trusted to be rational. The curse and my father's cruelty have damaged her beyond reason.

Please, Sorrel, do this last thing for me.

I love you.

Eric

I let the letter drop to the floor and wrapped my arms around myself, sobbing. I couldn't believe he was going to sacrifice himself for me. That he loved me. Flashes of his great-grandfather's burning body made me want to vomit. I couldn't let Eric do that. I had to find him. Or was it too late? I didn't feel any different, so maybe the curse still lived. Perhaps he did, too. *Please let him live.* I didn't know if I would feel a change once the curse was broken, though the fact that I didn't feel different gave me some hope.

I hurried to get dressed, not sure where to search for Eric. I was so angry with him for not giving me a say in the matter, yet I felt overwhelming love for him. What was he thinking?

I rushed downstairs and grabbed the keys to my mother's car off the hooks near the garage. I opened the door, hoping to find him there, but the SUV he had stolen was gone. We would discuss grand theft auto later, if he was still alive.

Driving around the unknown city, I was torn between breaking every speed limit and not drawing attention to myself. The last thing I needed was to get pulled over and have someone recognize me. Even so, I almost risked it to ask for directions to any abandoned warehouses or secluded places. Thankfully my mother's fancy car had a state-of-the-art navigation system. I noticed there was a swamp conservation not too far away. A swamp seemed like a fitting place to drink wolfsbane and destroy a book.

I cried all the way there, while thinking of what I could say to convince him not to go through with this ridiculous plan—that is, if I found him. The odds weren't in my favor. If by some miracle I did find him in time, I would tell him that for the first time since I had left my mother five years ago, I felt truly connected to someone—him. Sure, I loved Josie, Mateo, and basically everyone in Riverhaven, but there was something different with Eric. And I had to believe the curse brought us together for reasons other than him killing himself. After all, he brought out gifts in me I didn't even know I had. Aelius gifts? I was still trying to wrap my mind around that. If that truly was the case, there had to be more to the curse than we knew. I had to believe there was a way to break the curse, other than Eric sacrificing himself. Maybe? The curse stated that only one family could survive. Yet I had survived the curse. The unknowns were all so maddening. Regardless of what we did and didn't know, I would rather live a cursed life with Eric than a free one without him. And I would tell him so. If he still lived.

When I arrived at the swamp conservation, it looked nothing like I thought it would. It was more like a bundle of slash pine trees that looked undernourished. Eric's stolen vehicle was nowhere to be found in the parking area, and I didn't see anywhere he could've taken it off-road. I leaned my head on the steering wheel, crying and thinking of where else I could look. Maybe he went back to Georgia? One of the problems was that I didn't know how long he had been gone. Or when I had fallen asleep. That's when I remembered Eric's last word to me—sleep. Oh, he was so getting a piece of my mind when I found him. He must have used some of his powers on me. I should get a numbered list of his abilities for future reference.

I blew out a deep breath. *Think, Sorrel. Where would he go?* Maybe somewhere dark. The warehouse his family had taken me to had little natural light. This was Florida, the Sunshine State, and today there was hardly a cloud in the sky. So it would have to be somewhere inside. Though did it really matter where the book was destroyed? Maybe my heart could tell me something. That sounded crazy. However, so was the fact that I could heal people by touching them. And apparently shoot light out of me. I was kind of sorry I couldn't remember that, or how to reproduce it.

I closed my eyes and tried to focus on my feelings. All I felt was love—love for the man willing to give his life for me. I knew it was crazy since I hardly knew him, yet when we touched, I knew him in ways I couldn't explain. In a way that told me we were supposed to be together. *Please let me find him.* No direction came, and I found myself aimlessly driving around, looking for his car and trying to will my heart to tell me how to save him. I spent hours doing this.

By the time noon rolled around, I had given up hope. He was probably dead, and once again, it was my fault. And I still felt cursed—cursed to be alone.

Defeated, I used the navigation system to find my way back to my mother's place. I had no choice now but to leave and honor Eric's last request. No matter how much I was ticked off by it, he had forced my hand. After what he had done, how could I choose any other way? It killed me to leave my friends thinking something awful had happened to me, which it had. I'd seen things I would never be able to get out of my mind. I should have died. And what about my bakery? I had employees that depended on me and customers expecting wedding cakes.

Maybe I could go back to Riverhaven. I could tell the police about Eric's mom and get a guard dog. Tara would hate it, but she wasn't going to save me from a knife-wielding lunatic. I would tell the authorities it was Eric's family who had abducted me and their son. That they had killed Eric. That could work. After settling my affairs in Riverhaven, I would say I needed to move on after all the trauma. Then I would go to Europe and assume a new life. Surely Eric would understand me wanting to do right by the people who depended on me. I would give Josie and Mateo the bakery. Mateo had the baking skills, and Josie, well, Josie loved to eat cake. I would stipulate that they hire a business manager.

With puffy eyes and no tears left to cry, I turned down the road leading to my mother's beach house. I couldn't believe Eric was dead. Not only because it seemed surreal but because I still felt connected to him, like the connection I felt with my book that no longer existed. If that didn't say it all. I should just admit I was insane and move on. Yet, there was no moving on from this. I would carry the scars with me for the rest of my life.

I reluctantly pulled into my mother's drive and clicked the garage door opener. I had failed once again. I had caused another person's death. The thought was unbearable to me. And though I no longer had any tears to shed, my body was racked with dry sobs. While my chest heaved, I started to pull into the garage when my brain registered the stolen silver SUV parked there. Eric was here? He wouldn't sacrifice himself here, would he? My mother would kill him if he damaged any of her things—you know, if she were alive. And I would kill him for killing himself.

Then my rational, fearful side kicked in. What if his family had found him and then me? Honestly, I didn't care. Maybe it was time to end this once and for all.

After pulling into the garage, I hurried out of car and into the house, my heart ready to beat out of my chest. I barely made it past the mudroom when I ran into a hard body, a body holding my very content cat.

Without thinking, I slugged Eric in the gut. "Don't you ever do that to me again!"

"Aah," he groaned, while grabbing his middle and setting Tara down. "I would say I was happy to see you, but you should be halfway to Lisbon by now."

I wrapped my arms around him and breathed a hundred sighs of relief.

He pulled me to him as tightly as he could and kissed my head.

"You came back," I choked out.

"You didn't leave." He sounded half-exasperated, half-relieved.

"I tried to find you."

"Of course you did."

"Why did you come back?"

He leaned away and brushed my hair back, looking dazed. "I have something to show you." He took my hand and led me toward the couch in the living room. There on the coffee table sat his book, as whole and as beautiful as ever.

"Did the sacrifice not work?" I shuddered to think of him drinking the poison to which there wasn't a known antidote. Though if he'd survived, that was fantastic news. It meant the curse wasn't all we thought it was.

Eric didn't answer me right away; instead, he took a seat on the couch and pulled me onto his lap. I snuggled into him. As furious as I was with him, I wanted to be near him to reassure myself he was alive. "I thought you were dead."

"I know, and I meant to die, but . . ."

"But what?"

"Sorrel, something happened right as I was going to drink the wolfsbane. My book spoke to me," he whispered.

"What did it say?"

"I think it's best if I show you." He carefully leaned forward, still holding me while he reached for his book. He placed it on my lap. "Turn to the last page."

I bit my lip, unsure. Something told me I might not like what it had to say. Whatever it was, I was grateful it had kept Eric alive.

"Open it," Eric encouraged.

With trembling hands, I opened the cover. The book's pages were made of onyx and contained silver writing. The first set of instructions in his book reminded me of something. "Did you render me unconscious?"

Eric gave me a crooked grin. "You left me no choice."

I narrowed my eyes at him. "You know, I have some neat tricks I can do, too. If you don't want to spend all day in the bathroom or covered in hives, you better keep your gifts to yourself."

"How about this gift?" Eric's lips brushed mine before capturing them.

I forgot about the heavy book in my lap and drank him in deeply. He tasted like cinnamon and felt like home. I ran my hands through his hair, making him moan.

His lips glided off mine and pressed kisses across my jaw and then down my neck, slowly and sensuously. His warm breath against my skin had me tingling and erupting in goose bumps.

"Eric," I stuttered, "do you really love me?"

His lips paused on my collarbone. His hot breath cascaded down my chest. "I shouldn't have told you that."

I leaned away from him, hurt. "You lied."

His head snapped up, and his blazing eyes met mine. "Sorrel, I didn't lie. I do love you, but it was unfair for me to tell you while we both live."

I placed my hands on his stubbled cheeks, happy he loved me, but confused. "I don't understand."

"You will once you read the message." He adjusted me on his lap, indicating it was time.

I would have preferred to keep kissing him, but the book called. Like truly called. It began humming loudly until I flipped to the last page. There, toward the bottom, in beautiful script, the last message was written.

You have proven yourself worthy of your destiny. Now you must help the daughter of the sun find her book. Only then can the curse be broken.

I about fell off his lap. My voice caught in my throat, along with the air that was unable to escape.

Eric steadied me and patted me on the back as if to tell me to breathe.

A huge whoosh of air came out of me. "That's impossible," I stammered. "Maybe it's not talking about me."

Eric tilted my chin toward him. "Sorrel, it can't be anyone *but* you."

"I'm a Tellus."

"Maybe. But why didn't the book speak to you?"

"I have my mother's gifts. And the Aelius book and their line were destroyed. Isn't that why we have the curse?"

Eric leaned back against the couch and took me with him. "I know," he sighed. "But the book never lies. Someone from their line had to have survived."

I bolted up and gripped Eric's arm. "My father once told me that Princess Sorrel was cursed by her mother and she did her part to break the curse, just like I would. What if . . ." My heart thudded so hard it was difficult to say what I needed to. "What if the stories about Princess Sorrel were true, and not just about me like I'd always assumed? What if Princess Sorrel's mother was the Aelius queen?"

Eric's eyes widened. "What do you know about your father's family?"

"Nothing, other than they came from France. I told you my father didn't like to talk about them."

"What if he couldn't?"

"This is insane." I rested my head on Eric's shoulder.

Eric rubbed my arm. "I know it's a lot to take in. Sorrel, you realize what this means?"

"Other than my entire life is not what I thought it was?"

"That. And . . . the Aelius queen meant for her family to be the one that survived. It is you who must live."

My blood ran cold. "No," I cried.

"Only one can survive," he whispered.

I sat up and gazed into his aqua eyes. I saw myself in them. They reflected the love he felt for me. "I won't let another person I love die because of me."

He blinked several times. "You love me?"

I leaned my forehead against his. "I do love you. I think I was meant to love you. And I don't care if we never break the curse. You will not die on my behalf."

TWENTY-NINE

ERIC

THAT NIGHT ERIC WATCHED SORREL restlessly sleep on the couch. He paced back and forth while holding Tara and scratching her head. "Your owner is stubborn," he lamented. If the book had let him go through with his plans earlier that morning, Sorrel would already be free. The thermos containing the wolfsbane elixir had just touched his lips when the book began to glow, brighter than ever. He almost ignored it, but it practically blinded him until he opened it. Now he only had one dose of the wolfsbane left to complete his mission, and an infuriating yet maddeningly wonderful woman on his hands. The woman he loved; and amazingly, she loved him. *Damn the curse.*

Didn't Sorrel know that he wanted nothing more than to live a long life with her? But it was impossible. The curse would have its way, whether Sorrel wanted it to or not. She could protest all she wanted. One thing Eric was sure of was that the Aelius queen would have her revenge. And was she ever vindictive. She obviously wanted to make certain Eric's line paid as heavy a price as possible. She had made sure Eric would die knowing exactly what he would be missing out on. But, Eric would happily die so Sorrel could live. In that way, he felt as if he were defying the curse.

How to get Sorrel to see reason, he had no idea. He also had no idea where to even begin to search for the book of the sun—Sorrel's book. Maybe in France? That was, if her father had told Sorrel the truth about where his family was from. The man was shrouded in mystery. Eric should have investigated him further; then maybe he would know where they should go. He should do some investigative research now. Selfishly, though, he wanted every minute he had left with Sorrel. He wanted to go to her now. Her thin, supple body covered in satin pajamas called to him.

He gave Tara one last good scratch before setting her down. She looked up at him, miffed. "Sorry, your owner is more my kind of girl." Eric strutted over to Sorrel. Although he hated to wake her, he picked her up.

She immediately opened her soulful eyes. "I was having strange dreams."

Eric sat on the couch with her and maneuvered them until they were both lying down. He pulled her body as close to his as he could and relished in the contours of her shape and curves. It was cruel torture, as well as ecstasy.

She naturally snuggled into him and buried her head in his bare chest.

His hand slid down her back. "Tell me about your dreams."

"I was in our old vineyard, with my father. He wants to meet you. He said it was time."

"Time for what?"

She paused. "Time for me to be brave, like I promised him I always would be," her voice cracked.

"What does that mean?"

"I don't know. He wants to tell us together."

"How is that possible? I think you were just dreaming."

She drew circles with her finger on his chest. It drove Eric mad with desire. He was going to have to be careful with her.

"It felt like when I would dream of you. A real dream. My father said you've met him before and would know where to meet him again."

THE BOOK OF SORREL

Eric thought for a moment, and then a light bulb went on. "Sorrel, I'm going to need to go into your dreams again."

She stiffened against him.

"I know what a violation it is."

"It's not that." Her tears tickled his chest. "I'm afraid I'll make a fool of myself. That I'll dream about being pregnant with your baby again. Honestly, I want that to be true more than anything. I know, though, that it can never happen."

"Shh." He cradled her head. "If I could have a dozen babies with you, I would. When we break the curse, you can have those babies."

"Eric, I can't let you die. I would rather live a celibate life with you than marry a man who will never truly understand who or what I am."

The thought of Sorrel marrying another didn't sit well with him, either, but he couldn't be selfish. His destiny was to die so that she could live. Truly live. He had to believe she would meet someone who could make her happy. Someone who could make love to her and give her babies. He bristled at the idea. "Let me meet your father."

"What if I don't dream about him again?"

"You will. You do every night." Admittedly, he was over-joyed that the man in the vineyard was her father and not some Casanova he'd have to beat the hell out of. Sorrel could move on after he died.

"Why can't I remember that?"

"I don't know. Maybe he'll be able to tell you."

"But he's dead. I watched him die."

That one stumped Eric. He knew the man had spoken to him in Sorrel's dream. He was positive the man held secrets they needed to know. "I think it's important that we talk to him."

"I'm too awake now."

Eric nuzzled Sorrel's ear. "I can help with that."

Sorrel's body shivered in delight against him. "And you accused me of drugging people."

He chuckled. "I wouldn't be drugging you. Only persuading."

"Persuading, huh? What other powers of persuasion do you have?"

His hand ran the length of her body. "If only I could show you. But"—he pressed his fingers into her hip—"I won't endanger you for my own selfish desires."

She wrapped her leg around his. "You're the least selfish person I know."

"Sorrel," he groaned, "you don't know me that well."

"I do know you." She kissed his chest.

Her warm lips against his skin was more than he could handle at the moment. "You need to go to sleep before we do something dangerous."

"In my dreams could we . . . make love?"

He could feel her cheeks burn against his skin before he let out a heavy sigh. "Yes, but we won't."

"Why?"

"Because I love you."

"That makes no sense."

"Sorrel,"—he gazed down into her eyes—"I'll admit, when I first met you, I hoped you would allow me to have you in your dreams. That was before I saw the impact of how my actions, even those in your dreams, affected you. It was before you taught me what it means to truly love someone. I will not let you settle for an imitation of the one thing that should be more real and lasting than anything you experience."

She ran a finger down his cheek. "Thank you, Eric."

"For what?"

"Showing me what love is. Please," she pleaded, "don't make me give you up."

"Sorrel, I don't think we have a choice. Let's see what your father has to say."

"Okay," she squeaked.

Before she could change her mind, Eric called up the energy

inside of him that always hummed low, just waiting. Once he activated it, he filled it with his desire. He lowered his lips onto Sorrel's and took a moment to breathe her in before whispering, "Sleep."

Her head fell against his chest, and her breaths became deep and even. He held her tight, enjoying the feel of her, the way she trusted him. He closed his own eyes and almost instantly saw her open door, as if she eagerly awaited him. Eric anxiously entered, and sure enough, there she was, walking in the vineyard with her father. He let father and daughter have a moment before he walked toward them. Sorrel turned to her father, and while David held her, he caught Eric's eye. David smiled and beckoned him to come closer.

Eric walked toward them in the blistering heat, taking note of the vines bursting with red grapes. When he was within a foot or two, David leaned away from his daughter. "Would you mind introducing us, my sweet girl?"

Sorrel wiped her eyes and looked between the two men. "Dad, this is Eric. Eric, this is my father, David."

Eric longed to reach for Sorrel to comfort her, but her father kept her hand in his. David reached out with his other hand to shake Eric's.

Eric gripped David's hand. "It's a pleasure to meet you."

"The pleasure is all mine. I've been waiting for the day we would meet."

Eric tilted his head. "How do you know about me?"

A Cheshire grin appeared on David's face. "I know a lot about many things. However, that's not important right now."

Eric made to disagree, but Sorrel interrupted him. "Dad, who are you?"

David gently swiped his daughter's brow. "I'm your father." He said it as if he couldn't be prouder to hold the title.

"I know that, but do you . . . I mean, are you mortal?"

He pressed his lips together. "Once you find the book, all your questions will be answered."

"Why can't you just tell me?" Sorrel was as tenacious as ever.

He smiled. "Patience, daughter. It's important you take this journey. For both of your sakes."

"Do you know where the book of the sun is?" Eric cut to the chase.

David nodded.

"Where?" Sorrel asked.

Her father didn't answer her; instead, he led her down a row filled with overgrown vines. Eric followed.

"Sorrel." David pointed at the vines that were in need of a good pruning. "Vines need to be pruned—sometimes painfully—so that they can produce better fruit, the best fruit. Do you understand?"

Sorrel shook her head.

David placed his hand on her cheek. "You will. But first you must find the book and break the curse."

"How?" Sorrel begged to know.

"Follow the vines," he instructed.

Sorrel squinted. "What vines?"

David ignored her question. He placed a firm hand on Eric's arm. "You must fulfill your destiny and protect my daughter."

"No," Sorrel cried. "He will not die for me."

Both men faced her. David squeezed her hand. "You promised me you would be brave."

"You promised me I would have a great love."

He smiled between Sorrel and Eric. "And so you have."

"I won't break the curse." She stood defiant.

David only continued to smile at her. "Be brave, Sorrel."

"This is being brave."

"No, love, the bravest thing you can do right now is to break the curse. The world needs you. Follow the vines. I'm counting on you." Without another word, he disappeared.

Sorrel closed her eyes and hung her head.

Eric took her in his arms, and she clung to him. "Your father is right; the world needs your gifts. Needs you."

"But I need *you*."

"And you will have me." *All of me, if necessary.*

THIRTY

ERIC AND I BOTH DECIDED it was too dangerous to stay in Saint Augustine. And his book adamantly reminded him that he was bound to do what it said. That meant we had to find my book, whether I wanted to or not. I was beginning to detest the Aelius queen. She had thought of everything. But I was determined to outsmart her. I wasn't going to lose Eric. Maybe if I thought that enough, it would come true. Unfortunately, Eric had left the research he'd done on me at his apartment, and he was sure his family would search the place. That research had a lot to do with California. And California was the only place we could think to start looking for the book. We would follow the vines there, whatever that meant. So not only could we find ourselves dealing with my vengeful ancestor but with Eric's insane family as well.

Eric was especially convinced that we needed to go to California because he believed something significant had happened there. He'd noticed when he had stolen my book, or what I thought was my book, that my family was told to leave California on the exact date as his family was told the same thing—right after my father died. Eric was sure that was no coincidence. That even if my book wasn't in California, we would find a clue there.

This meant we were going on the mother of all road trips across the country, since Eric was a wanted man and, unlike me, he hadn't been able to obtain a new identity yet. Eric thought renting a small RV would be the best and safest way to travel—allowing for more privacy. It was funny, I'd always been envious of some of the retired tourists that would come into my bakery who traveled the country in big RVs. I would think that they must really love each other if they were willing to spend so much time together in such a small space, day in and day out. I longed for that kind of a relationship, even though I knew I would never grow old with anyone. I would never grow old at all. And now here I was, given the opportunity to be with someone who would never grow old either. Eric was someone I could travel the world with for decades, changing identities as needed. No one would ever question why we were a couple. Except we couldn't really be a couple. Eric was certain that once we found my book it would make sure only one family remained—mine.

Leaving Saint Augustine meant I had to say goodbye to all my mother's things and the last place she lived and breathed. The only thing I took of hers was the diamond ring my father had given her. Even though binding yourself to someone required no ceremony or fanfare, my father wanted my mother to have a wedding ring. I didn't recognize what a sweet gesture that was until I was older. Many years after my father had passed away, I would catch her taking it out of her jewelry box and putting it on. She would stare at it for several minutes with tears in her eyes, until it seemed she could no longer bear the memories of him. In those moments I knew she loved him. That despite how they were brought together, he was the choice of her heart. Just like Eric was my choice.

It's why I drove as slowly as I could, as we started our journey westward across the panhandle of Florida, skirting the southern border of Alabama and into Mississippi. It's why I tried to convince Eric we should stay near the beach somewhere along the Gulf Coast for a few days. He said the longer we stayed in one place, the more likely it was that we would be recognized. His point was valid; still, the thought of losing him ate at me. So much so, I kept glancing his way while I drove the small RV—which didn't feel small at all, since I'd never driven anything bigger than a sedan—just to make sure he still existed.

Eric swiveled his chair toward me, reached over, and placed his hand on my thigh. "It's going to be all right."

I wasn't sure I believed that. "What can the curse actually do if you don't listen to your book?"

Eric squeezed my leg. "The last time I disobeyed, someone died."

Stab to the heart. "I'm sorry, Eric. That was a callous question."

"Don't be sorry. You're scared. And that's understandable. I'm scared too."

"You are?"

His hand made its way up to my neck, where he massaged my tense muscles. If only I could close my eyes and enjoy his touch. As I was driving, it didn't seem prudent.

"Sorrel, I'm afraid I won't be able to protect you."

"You mean die for me?" I could barely say it. I had seen the thermos he'd taken out of the SUV he'd "borrowed" before we abandoned it in a parking lot with no security cameras. I knew what the thermos was for. It was for the wolfsbane, sealed in a baggie, that he kept in his pocket.

He didn't respond to my question; instead, he changed the subject. "Maybe we should play a game."

I glanced over at him with my brow quirked. "Are you serious?"

He flashed me his devastatingly smoldering smile. "Isn't that what people do on road trips?"

"Yeah, but this isn't a vacation. We're possibly going to—"

He pressed his finger to my lips. "Let's not talk about it. I want to enjoy whatever time we have left. Whether we have three days or three hundred years together, I'm going to treasure each day with you."

I wiped a few tears off my cheek. "You know, you should really be a writer."

He chuckled. "I meant every word. So, what game should we play?"

I thought for a second. "Well, my family and I didn't take a lot of road trips, but when we did, my dad always told me stories about queens throughout history. Like Isabella, queen of Castile and Aragon, and Matilda of Scotland. Hmm."

"What?"

I looked out into the vast landscape filled with long stretches of highway and lots of green vegetation. "I see everything my father ever told me through a different lens now. I thought for sure when he told me, when I was little, that I would be a queen, he meant it metaphorically. That I was the queen of his heart or something. Now that I think about it, when he taught me about queens throughout history, he tried to drive home the good qualities a queen should possess. Like how Matilda was compassionate and known for her charity. Or how Isabella insisted that Native Americans be treated humanely. He said the best rulers always thought of others before themselves. They put people above power. You don't think he meant I would be a queen, do you? I mean, who would I rule over?" What a silly notion. I wasn't remotely interested in being royalty.

Eric pressed his lips together in thought. "Did you know our people, the Praeditus, had ruling royal families?"

I nodded. "But they all died out."

Eric shrugged. "So far as we know, but you're living proof we don't know everything. The Aelius family somehow managed to survive."

"Or maybe my father just found their book and kept it hidden." Even I realized how ridiculous that sounded. I loved my father, but I felt like I had been lied to my entire life about who I was. It made me wonder if my mother knew about the other book, too—apparently my book. If she did, how could she keep that from me? And how did my dad know who Eric was and where the book was hidden? Or was the father in my dreams not my real father? It all made my head and heart hurt.

Eric gave me a look like, *You poor naive thing.* I got that look a lot. "Like I said, let's not worry about it until we have to. What game should we play?"

I thought for a moment. It was hard to think of playing a game when life felt anything but fun. I had lost so much and knew I might lose everything. Eric's smile begged me to enjoy what time we had left together, and I gave in. "How about Never Have I Ever. And to make it more fun, we kiss each other if we've done what the other person says."

"I have no idea what game you're talking about, but if it involves kissing you, I'm in."

I was in, too. In over my head.

ERIC

Eric lay wide awake in the dark, holding a sleeping Sorrel against him. He listened to the hum of the other RV generators around them in the campground outside of Jackson, Mississippi. He'd thought Atlanta was humid, but it had nothing on this place. The air conditioner barely kept it on the low end of cool. Sorrel's warm body only added to the uncomfortable heat, yet he refused to let go of her. Even if her cat was giving him the evil eye from the end of the small RV bed. Apparently, Eric had stolen Tara's spot. It didn't help that he was wearing pajamas. He normally slept in his underwear, but the more clothing between him and Sorrel, the better. The touch of her skin did something to him he'd never experienced with any other woman. It was more than the overwhelming desire he felt for her; it was as if every part of him called to her. Besides, he liked wearing the pajamas she had purchased for him. She'd seemed so proud when she was picking them out while he watched over her from the shadows. He'd loved watching her deliberate between the black and blue ones. She had even talked out loud, asking herself which would bring out his eyes more. She'd done that with each article of clothing she bought, until she came out of the department store with two bursting-to-full bags. All for him.

Eric stroked Sorrel's hair, thinking about who she really was. He was certain her father was no mortal. Yet did that make Sorrel the heir of both the Tellus and Aelius families? As far as he knew, the families had never married outside of their respective families, until the Aelius queen bound herself to a mortal. Regardless of who Sorrel was, Eric agreed with her father—she was a queen among women. He would bow down and worship her for the rest of his life. He feared it would be a very short life. Would his family or the curse get to him first?

It was one of the reasons he couldn't sleep—he didn't want his father attempting to break into his dreams. While Eric had to willingly let him in, his father had his ways of bending Eric's will. And Eric feared giving his family any hint of where they were, or that Sorrel was a daughter of the sun. Though they may already be suspicious after her light show. His family's hate for the Tellus family had nothing on their abhorrence for the Aelius family— the most powerful of the three. It made it even more vital that they find her book before his family found them. Sorrel needed it so she could learn how to use her Aelius gifts, not only to help people but also to protect herself against his family. Light always conquered the dark. Though Eric hoped she would never have to use her gifts in those ways.

He was almost certain that once they found her book, the curse would make sure his entire line died. It was only using him now as a pawn. *Hell hath no fury like a woman scorned* took on new meaning to him. The Aelius queen was one pissed-off lady. The woman obviously didn't care that she would be hurting her future descendant. She was going to get her revenge. It made him wonder why she hadn't killed the other two families off by now. Why the centuries-long game? David's odd comment to Sorrel about vines needing to be pruned, even painfully so, had stuck with him. Is that what this had been? Would Eric and his family be the last shoots on the vine to be cut off before the best fruit could grow back?

Sorrel stirred in his arms. He ran his hand down her satin-covered back, trying to soothe her. She needed to rest. She had driven for hours today, and there were many hours left to go before they reached their destination, though not enough for Eric. He didn't think he could get enough of Sorrel to ever satisfy him. With her he finally had what he had longed for his entire life—a place where he belonged. Although their time together would be brief, he would die in peace knowing what he had experienced with Sorrel was something men only dreamed of.

Eric kissed Sorrel's head. "Thank you, my love," he whispered.

THIRTY-ONE

I STARED AT THE TV above the checkout counter, in the truck stop just outside of Tulare, hoping what was being reported was all just a coincidence. The trip had been so uneventful up to this point; in fact, it had been kind of dreamy. Days on end with only Eric reading aloud from one of his favorite books, *David Copperfield*, that we had picked up in Louisiana. Nights in his arms, talking until I was so tired it was only gibberish. And kisses that set my soul on fire. Our time together had been so all-encompassing that I had been lulled into a false sense of security. Or more like I'd had glimmers of hope that California wouldn't be our final destination. That Eric and I would travel the world searching for my book, that hopefully we would never find. And with any luck, his family would never find us either. But those glimmers were dimmed as I watched them flash pictures on the screen of Dr. Ezra Cohen, the retired coroner from Tulare who was found dead in his home three days ago. Preliminary cause of death was cerebral edema. Water poisoning.

I dropped the bottles of water I was planning on purchasing along with paying for the gas I'd just pumped. I picked them up and stumbled toward the cashier, hardly able to catch my breath or hand the inquisitive-looking man, with a crooked nose and smile to match, the credit card with my new name on it.

The man took my card and looked from it to me several

times. "You know, you remind me of a lady who used to live here a long time ago. Real pretty, just like you."

I swallowed and tugged on the brim of my baseball hat. Obviously, it wasn't a great disguise. "Eu não falo inglês," I stuttered, using my best Portuguese accent. Eric and I had been working on it while we drove. Speaking of Eric, I knew he was probably yelling at me in his head to get the hell out of there. He was watching from the shadows, and I was sure he had seen the news report and now this cashier who was too observant. What were the chances of him remembering my mother?

Thankfully, the man seemed to buy my lie and swiped my card without another word. He handed me my receipt. "Have a good day."

I wasn't sure that was possible now. I jogged back to the RV and threw open the side door. It was easier for Eric to enter undetected that way. When I could feel his presence near me, I closed the door, and Eric came out of the shadows. I still wasn't used to it. While it was fascinating, it creeped me out. It would always remind me of his father and grandfathers appearing out of thin air in my apartment. Now to think that two of those men could be nearby.

Without a word, Eric flipped open one of the kitchen compartments and grabbed his thermos.

"What are you doing with that?"

"Protecting you."

I went to swipe the thermos out of his hands, but Eric was too quick and raised it above his head. "Sorrel, we knew it would probably come down to this—please don't make it any harder than it has to be."

"Is it so easy for you to leave me?" Tears welled in my eyes.

He reached out and ran the back of his hand down my cheek. "It's the hardest thing I'll ever do, but I love you enough to do it."

"No. There has to be another way. I'll figure out how to use the light within me. And we don't even know if your family is still here. The coroner died three days ago. Let's just go. We'll find someone who can get you the IDs you need to travel. I'll pay any price." I sobbed.

Eric took me in his arms, and I soaked his shirt with the flood coming out of my eyes, clinging to him like a child.

"The curse will have its way," he whispered.

As much as I hated that, it reminded me. "Your book said you had to help me find my book. You yourself admitted you are bound to do what it says."

He let out a heavy breath. "I will not let my family hurt you."

"Maybe they moved on. I mean, what could the coroner tell them?"

"Enough that they felt they needed to kill him."

A chilling shiver went through me. "We won't go to the vineyard. Let's head to LA and put some feelers out for passports. Or go back to Atlanta where you had contacts."

"Sorrel." He squeezed me tighter, still holding the thermos. "We have to go to the vineyard. There is a reason your father always came to you there. Something happened there. I know it."

"This can't be the end."

"Maybe it's a new beginning."

"For us, or me?"

He remained silent, giving me my answer.

"Eric, I love you." My voice pleaded with him to understand that. Pleaded for him to change his mind.

"I know, and it's why I'll die happy if it comes to that." He kissed my cheek and let me go.

I watched in horror as Eric tipped the wolfsbane into the thermos and filled it with water. He whispered, "I am ready to pay the price." A plume of steam came up out of the thermos before Eric capped it. Eric's eyes met mine. "This is for just in case."

I had no words. I turned from him to head to the driver's seat, but he grabbed my hand and tugged me toward him, letting the thermos drop by his feet.

He brushed his thumb across my trembling lips. "Please don't be mad at me."

"I'm not mad at you. I'm angry at the situation. And I'm confused. My heart is telling me we are meant to be together, while my head says it's impossible. I want to believe my heart."

Eric placed his hand on my chest, over my heart. "It's a beautiful thought. You're beautiful." He took off my cap. My hair cascaded down and fell onto my shoulders. He ran his fingers through it while pressing kisses against my jaw.

I gripped his shirt and removed any space between us. "Please don't leave me," I whispered.

His lips met mine. His tongue urged my mouth to part. He tasted me deeply, making me gasp and him groan. Minute after minute after minute we drank each other in, yet I still felt thirsty for him. It was a quench that would never be satisfied. I felt the need to run my hands over his face, hair, and chest. My fingers wanted to memorize everything about him, from the way his stubble felt like a fine brush to the firmness of his pectoral muscles and the ripples in his abs. He seemed to feel the same way, as his tongue prodded as far as it would go, while his hands gently and carefully trickled down my body like a waterfall in slow motion.

It was a kiss like no other I had experienced or shared with Eric. It was a goodbye kiss.

I wasn't ready to say goodbye.

"Sorrel," he moaned against my lips. "We need to stop before we do something amazingly wrong."

"Amazingly wrong?"

"I have no doubt making love to you would be amazing, but it would be wrong."

I let out a deep breath of agreement.

He kissed my forehead and lingered. "I love you."

"I love you too." And with that, we parted and took our seats.

I hesitated to start the RV. Eric gave me an encouraging

smile, all while holding his thermos and his book. I hated them both. I swore I would save him if I could. Maybe I had enough inside of me to heal him, to overcome the curse's power. Maybe I wouldn't have to today. Still, today would become someday, and someday the curse would end and my heart would be broken.

While I drove, my body shook and my eyes darted every which way, on the lookout for Eric's family. I was more afraid of them than the curse. Not only because I had seen what they were capable of, but because Eric would die to stop them. I didn't think I could bear it. I kept hearing my father's voice telling me to be brave, and my own five-year-old self reminding me of my promise. I remembered when my father had told me I was cursed. Not for a second did it scare me. There was no question I would break this curse. As I'd aged, that courage waned. Yet, it wasn't until Eric came into my life that I became afraid I would break it and remain alive.

Before we drove to my old home, Eric made us wait for hours at a rest stop while his poison steeped. We did nothing but sit on the couch and hold on to each other in silence. My mind raced with how to save him, and us, but I was at a loss. And I had a feeling I would lose it all today.

When Eric said it was time to go, I drove slowly, ever so slowly, hanging on to every minute we had together. And I was nervous to see my old home. I wasn't sure what we would find. The book had demanded we leave so quickly when I was a child, that my mother had been forced to sell it remotely. Did the new owners care for our vineyard the loving way my father had? It had been twenty-one years since I had been back. The landscape had changed a lot because of new developments and homes in the area. I wouldn't have even been able to find it if it weren't for Eric's investigative skills—he could find almost any record on the internet.

It wasn't a good sign when we turned onto the road that headed toward the vineyard and found that the once pristine and beloved place was now in serious disrepair. The potholes were more like craters, and the lines on the road were so faded it looked more like a one-lane street. When we arrived at the long drive that led to our old property, there was a "No Trespassing" sign on the old rusted gate mostly hidden by weeds.

I stopped the RV in front of the gate and looked at Eric for his take on things. "I'm not sure anyone lives here anymore."

"There's one way to find out." He unbuckled his seat belt.

"Where are you going?"

"Relax. I'm just going to see if I can open the gate."

I wasn't sure I would ever fully relax again. "Are you sure your family isn't here?"

"I think you might be better able to judge that. Do you feel as if you're being watched?"

"Not right now."

Eric opened the door and got out, leaving his book on the seat but taking his thermos. I didn't think he trusted me not to dump it out. That was smart of him. Eric approached the gate. I watched his every move, unclicking my own seatbelt in case I needed to rescue him. Not really sure how I would do that, but I hoped the light in me was based on my fight-or-flight response and would kick in when needed.

Eric had to clear away some of the overgrown weeds before he could get to the latch on the gate. With some effort he was able to push it open enough for me to drive the RV through. Once I was past it, he closed the gate and hopped back in the vehicle.

The once vibrant and beautiful property was giving me the creeps. Half of the trees that lined the gravel road leading to the house and vineyard were dead and rotting. There were weeds as tall as me everywhere and even some old abandoned cars and mounds of junk. I was irritated at whoever had let the place fall into such disarray.

"The place almost looks cursed," I said quietly.

"I'm afraid you're right," Eric agreed with me.

At a snail's pace I drove us down the lane, holding back my tears. Some of my best memories happened here. I saw myself skipping down the road and kicking rocks while holding my father's hand. I remembered chasing our old dog Ginger around the yard and the chickens we raised. I'd loved gathering eggs with my mother.

When I saw our old white home with black shutters, a few tears were finally shed. It was covered in layers of dirt, pieces of the roof were missing, and most of the windows were broken. "How could this happen? It used to be so beautiful."

Eric placed his hand on my leg. "I think the book protected itself."

"You think the book is here?"

Eric looked down at his own book, which was flashing and vibrating. Each moonstone was taking a turn glowing. "I'm almost certain. I've never seen the book do this."

My mouth became so dry, I couldn't utter a word. I managed to park the RV by the old detached garage that was in no better shape than the house.

Tara, as if she knew I was frightened, rubbed up against my legs.

Eric turned toward me and took my hand. "You must promise me that you will let me protect you."

"Only if you promise me the same in return."

"What do you mean?"

I stared at the thermos he gripped with his other hand. "Promise me you won't drink that unless it's absolutely necessary."

He let go of my hand and pinched the bridge of his nose. "If I drink it now, you're safe to find your book."

"No. Your book told you to help me find my book, and we don't know for sure if it's here. And there's no sign of your family."

"Sorrel, look at all the shadows that surround us. They could be here."

"I don't feel them. Please," I begged, "give us every chance."

"You know what the curse says. Only one family survives."

"You are my family."

His eyes widened. "As much as I love to hear you say that, I'm a Selene."

"I don't care what blood runs through you. It's what's in your heart and mine. Please, promise me Eric."

His jaw clenched while his eyes searched my own. "Fine. But I won't hesitate to sacrifice my life to save yours. If there is any hint of my family here, I will end it."

The way he said it with such finality made my stomach roil. I bowed my head in acknowledgment, and to say a silent prayer—to someone, anyone—that Eric and I would both survive the day, the curse. All I heard was my father saying, *Be brave.*

I picked Tara up and gave her a quick squeeze. "Stay out of trouble."

"Are you ready?" Eric asked.

"No."

"We need to move. You can do this."

I wasn't sure I could, but what other choice did I have? I knew the curse would have its way.

Eric ran around the RV and met me at my door, clinging tightly to his book and thermos.

"Where's the vineyard?" he asked.

I pointed toward the trees. "Back behind the orchard." Well, what was left of it. The trees looked diseased and had black fruit growing on them. They were knotted and twisted in unnatural ways. I had goose bumps covering my body, though it was blazing hot in the afternoon sun. Eric was right—this place was cursed. I could feel it.

Eric clutched his book and thermos with one arm while wrapping his other arm around me. "Stay close."

He didn't have to tell me twice. I clung to him like Josie would a hot date.

We both seemed to tiptoe through the trees and jump with the snap of every twig we stepped on. It was like walking through a haunted house, waiting for a zombie to pop out at you. Or in our case, a slasher and her two sadistic sidekicks. It felt abnormally cold under the shade of the trees, which didn't help any. I was so glad to see the clearing before us, so much so I broke free of Eric and ran into the light. Eric followed my lead.

We both breathed a sigh of relief before taking note of the rows and rows of overgrown vines before our eyes. There was no green vegetation or red grapes in sight. There were only rows of twisted wood that looked like something out of a Grimm's fairy tale. It broke my heart. My father had so tenderly cared for this land, and now it was unrecognizable.

"Follow the vines," Eric whispered.

"Where?"

"Downhill."

The grapevines were planted on a hill, but it was hard to tell with all the overgrowth.

"Do you feel anything?" Eric asked.

"I don't feel like we're being watched, but . . . I feel more connected to my book."

"We must be getting close."

"I'm not sure that's good news."

Eric gave me a half-smile.

We stayed on the outskirts and followed the vines down the hill overgrown with grass and weeds. I was sure my legs were being eaten alive by bugs, yet I barely noticed because I was more afraid of what lay in front of us, or in the shadows. Every sound not made by us was suspect. Eric was now keeping his hand on the lid of the thermos.

When we reached the bottom of the hill, there was a giant green patch of weeds that seemed out of place. Almost like the hill was missing a piece and the weeds had filled it in.

Eric put an arm out and held me back. "This doesn't seem right."

I was glad I wasn't the only one who thought so.

Eric looked around and said, "Take my hand."

I gripped his hand tightly while he maneuvered us around the weeds and down to the bottom of the hill. His book lit up, and I felt a strange sensation from the top of my head to the tips of my toes.

"I think we're close," I whispered.

Eric reached into the weeds and parted them. "There's a door."

"A door? Like a hobbit door?"

"Something like that." Eric stepped into the overgrowth, pulling me after him. Sure enough, there was an old, wooden, grayed-by-time door with a sun carved into it.

I stared in amazement, my heart pounding double-time. "I had no idea this was here."

"It's probably a wine cellar, or a good hiding place for a *book*."

"I don't see a door handle," I stuttered.

"Here, let me see if I can open it." Eric handed me his book, but kept his thermos. He ran his hand over the wood several times before saying, "Ah." He pushed the middle of the door, and it parted. What I could see with the limited light was a cave that seemed to be carved out of stone. Something in the cave called to me, yet I was too afraid to go in. I shook where I stood.

Eric put his hand on the small of my back. "It's time, daughter of the sun."

Thirty-Two

TOGETHER WE STEPPED INTO THE dark cave. A chill swept over me, making me wish I had worn warmer clothes instead of a tank top and shorts. I faintly made out a candelabra chandelier above us but couldn't see a light switch. The odds of it working after this long were slim to none anyway. However, we didn't need the light. Eric's book provided it.

Eric stiffened. "I don't like this; my book casts too many shadows."

"I'm happy to leave."

"Nice try. Just stay close."

I grabbed Eric's shirt, clinging to it like a child. "Eric, I want you to know that no matter what happens, I'm glad you walked into my bakery that day."

He brushed my hair back. "I hate that I've put you in danger, but selfishly, I'm glad too."

"You're the love my father said I would have. We belong together."

"The curse says otherwise, my love." He trudged on.

I reluctantly followed as we walked past old barrels of wine. I was surprised how dry it felt and that a fruity aroma lingered in the air. Past the barrels was another room with no door. Inside sat a table, and on that table an old chest.

"It's in there." I pointed at the chest. "I can feel it," I said so breathily it sounded as if I'd just run a marathon. I grabbed Eric's hand for comfort—and so he wouldn't have any stupid ideas, like drinking the poison he held.

He must have known what I was doing. "I'll stand guard."

"No. We're doing this together." Even in the semidarkness I could see how exasperated he was with me.

"My family could be here any minute."

"I want every minute I can have with you." I reached up on my tiptoes and pressed a kiss to his lips. "Please."

"Argh," he groaned. "I can't seem to tell you no."

I led him to the chest made of old driftwood and sealed with a lock that looked like a sundial. I stood in front of it, hesitant to touch it though it beckoned me to. My fingers began to twitch and almost ache. I lightly brushed my hand over the chest, and my fingers calmed. "I'm not sure how to open it."

"Use your gifts," Eric suggested, while his eyes darted between me and the entrance.

I closed my eyes and took deep breaths in and out. I focused on my heart. That led me straight to my feelings for Eric. With those feelings, a warmth spread through me. A light formed, first in my chest, where it traveled up to my shoulder and then down my arm until it burst out of my palm, hitting the sundial and making it turn until we heard a click.

"It worked." I couldn't believe it.

"Open it." Eric was even more eager than I was.

With both hands, I carefully lifted the lid. Inside lay a beautiful white, almost translucent, book that seemed to swirl like a kaleidoscope. Of even more interest to me was a letter with my name on it, in my father's handwriting, next to the book. I plucked up the letter and anxiously opened it. "It's from my dad."

"What does it say?" Eric brought his book closer to give me some more light.

I began to read out loud.

My Dearest Daughter,

Please forgive me for keeping who you are and who I was from you and your mother. I, too, was cursed and had to do my part. My family, your family, the Aelius family was to be kept secret from the world until the time was right. It meant that I needed to give my life in order to save you. Now that you have been reunited with your book, the gifts you've always possessed will begin to emerge brighter and stronger. You, too, will come to realize your prophetic gift.

I paused. "Prophetic gift?"

"That makes sense," Eric responded. "In a way, you were already using it by predicting which couples should break up. And you've mentioned many times how you knew you were 'meant' to do certain things."

Oh. That was interesting. But I didn't have time to ponder. I wanted to keep reading.

This gift is more than following your heart, like I encouraged you to do. You will receive visions at times. Just like I did before I died. Sorrel, I was a very old man, only years from death, when I met your mother. It was well worth the wait. However, I knew my death was near. I was shown in a vision that if you and your mother didn't leave California, the Selene family would find you and destroy the Tellus book before the appointed time, and before it was time to reveal the great secret that the Aelius line still lived. There is no telling what the Selene family would have done to you, had you survived as a child after they destroyed the Tellus book. Knowing I wouldn't live long enough to protect you, I gave my life to change the books, just like Queen Vita did many centuries ago when she cast her curse. I sent each family off in different directions until there would be someone worthy to protect you.

I smiled up at Eric, with tears in my eyes.

His eyes were wide with wonder.

I know your tenacious heart must have many questions. For now, know that your birth—and this day—have been long awaited and were foretold even before the curse was cast. There was a great pruning that needed to occur—a curse that would create a family worthy to carry on our gifts. A family so strong that it would best serve our people, and the world. This family needs—

"Did you hear that?" Eric interrupted me.

I lowered the letter and listened. "I don't hear anything." However, a familiar and unwanted sensation coursed through me. I grabbed Eric's arm. "I think we're being watched."

Eric dropped his book and flipped open his thermos lid. Simultaneously, two men walked out of the shadows near some barrels in the corner.

Vincent walked closer, clapping his hands together, and when the light was right, I caught the absolute hatred he had for me etched on his stone face.

"A daughter of the sun," he drawled. "That we can't have. It is our family who is the strongest and will prevail."

"I don't think so." Eric brought the thermos to his mouth before I could stop him.

"No!" I screamed, and tried to bat it out of his hands. Eric's grandfather shadow-hopped and grabbed me before I could reach him.

Vincent lunged for his son, but was too late to stop Eric from getting enough of the poison down. Eric started to violently shake.

"Damn you," Vincent shouted at Eric. "Father, get her book, it must be destroyed."

Eric desperately reached for his book as his father restrained him.

"You've always been such a disappointment, son." Vincent wrapped his arm around Eric's neck, choking him. "I suppose now you will finally be of some use to us."

Eric's grandfather threw me to the side, as if I was nothing. I hit the stone floor and was momentarily dazed, but I forced myself to roll over, and from my prostrate position watched in terror as the man I loved struggled to breathe and began turning shades of purple. His eyes caught mine, pleading with me to help him. Using all my strength, I got on my hands and knees, willing myself to stand, or crawl, to Eric.

The grandfather held my book, as Vincent worked to force Eric's hand onto it, using his powers of persuasion to try to bend Eric's will to his. It allowed Eric enough air to speak. "Sorrel, find the light within you."

I closed my eyes and tried to concentrate. I was too afraid. Nothing would come. I collapsed on the cold, hard ground.

"Sorrel, I love you."

Those words ignited a flame I could scarcely describe within me. The heat in my chest flooded my body, and an enormous pressure built up in me until it couldn't be contained. A burst of light, like a solar flare, surged out of me.

Vincent and his father cowered from its presence and were forced back against the barrels. Eric fell onto the table, and with all his might reached for his book, not quite able to grasp it.

I managed to stand, while keeping the light burning, buffeting his family. I crept toward Eric. "Please don't do this," I pleaded.

"It's too late, my love," he said, stilted, as if it took all his energy just to speak. "Don't let me die in vain. Your family must live. Please," he begged. "Please let me protect you."

My biggest fear had come to life. Eric was going to die. For me. I promised I would be brave, but I had no idea it would come to this.

"Please," Eric begged again.

With every ounce of courage I had left, I reached for Eric's hand and placed it on the book, tears pouring out of me. "I love you."

"That's enough for me." He closed his eyes. "I give of my life freely. With this sacrifice of blood, I pay the price. The request written on my heart must be given."

The book began to smolder.

"I give of my life freely. With this sacrifice of blood, I pay the price. The request written on my heart must be given."

The smolder turned into a spark and then a flame. I pushed Eric away before the Selene book consumed itself. I would not allow him to burn to death. Vincent and his father shrieked and writhed in pain until there was nothing left of the book, not even ashes, and they lay lifeless. The light within me abruptly extinguished, and I rushed to Eric's side.

He was unconscious, and awful rasps escaped him like he was drowning. It was the death rattle. I'd heard it from my own father years ago. I placed my hands on Eric's chest and called up the energy within me to heal him, but it wouldn't come. "Please," I cried. "Please." I touched his beautiful face. "Eric, please don't leave me." I felt more cursed than ever.

Suddenly a light began to burn, as bright as the one that had come from within me. My book, like a flash of burning magnesium, illuminated my father's letter, not allowing me to ignore it. Hating to, I tore myself away from Eric and scrambled over to pick up the letter. The words I hadn't been able to finish reading jumped off the page.

This family needs the blood of all three lines. You, my love, are the first to carry two Praeditus lines, and together with the last known heir of the Selene line—when he proves himself worthy and gives his life—will break this curse. You must bind yourselves together to restore the Praeditus. Queen Vita foresaw this day and sacrificed herself and cursed her own daughter, Princess Sorrel, so that not only would our people be saved, but all mankind.

Use your gifts well, daughter. Always remember people over power.

Save Eric.

All my love,

Daddy

I needed to bind myself to Eric and save him. But how did I perform the binding ceremony? I frantically thought, and as if to answer my question, my book flipped itself open to the last page. Amid a swirl of every color, the binding ceremony appeared.

While Eric labored to breathe, I took his hand. I felt our powers connect and merge into one, and I began to recite the words. "With these words, I bind two willing hearts and three families: Aelius, Tellus, and Selene. The sun, earth, moon, and mortals will forever be bound. Our love will stand as a testament and witness of their combined strength. With the gifts of each, we restore the Praeditus now and forever."

An indescribable feeling swept through me and filled the room. It was as if I could feel the weight of unseen chains lift off of me, while a beautiful peace knitted my heart to Eric's.

Eric took a deep breath and began to cough and splutter. His normal color began to appear in his face and limbs. I took his hand, kissed it, and placed it against my own cheek. I needed to feel his warmth and strength returning.

He smiled up at me. "I'm alive . . . and free."

I bit my lip. "Well, sort of. We kind of just got hitched for, like, forever."

His beautiful aqua eyes popped. "We're bound to each other."

"Believe it or not, yes. Apparently, all you had to do was try to die and be the last remaining Selene heir."

"Explain."

"We had the curse all wrong. There was only one family meant to survive, but that *one* family would have the blood of all three Praeditus lines, plus mortal blood, combined. And we qualify. The Aelius queen foresaw us. We really are meant to be together."

He yanked on my shirt and pulled me down onto him, our lips crashing together. Eric was just beginning to part mine, when we heard a voice from outside that struck a chord of fear in my heart. We both jumped up.

"I'm bloody free! I'm bloody free!" Portia whooped in her English accent.

Eric pushed me behind him, waiting for his mother to come inside. We waited tensely for several minutes, until we thought we should go out and see where she'd gone. After all, she was a liability, and a knife-wielding psycho. Before we walked out, Eric took one last look at his father and grandfather, who looked as if they were sleeping on each other. "Goodbye, you bastards." Eric took my hand and never looked back.

We walked out the door and into the bright sunlight with *my* book in hand. The grounds didn't look any different, yet it didn't feel as creepy.

"Where do think she went?"

Eric shrugged. "Your guess is as good as mine, but stay alert."

I stuck to Eric like glue as we walked back toward the RV, keeping an eye out for his mother. She couldn't have gotten too far, though she was nowhere to be seen.

When we made it to the RV and didn't see her, I asked, "Should we search for her some more?"

Eric looked around and called out her name, "Portia."

No response.

"Will you think ill of me if I say I don't care if we never find her?"

"Not at all. I'm sorry for all the pain your family caused you."

Eric tugged me to him, the book was the only thing between us. "They're not my family." He kissed my head. "I can't believe this is all over. And we survived."

I breathed the hugest sigh of relief. "It seems surreal. But we're together. We were always meant to be together. I think I knew that from the moment we first met."

"I wish I would have given you a better first impression." He chuckled.

"I can't imagine you were very happy to be reporting about a wedding cake shop."

"Not at all, but that day changed my life." He leaned back and tilted my chin with his finger. "You are the best thing that has ever happened to me, daughter of the earth and sun."

My eyes misted. "I feel the same way about you, son of the moon."

He leaned his forehead against mine. "Well, since we both agree, and we aren't cursed anymore, I think we have some business to take care of."

"And what business would that be?" I played coy.

"I'd like to bind myself to you . . . in every possible way," he groaned.

My cheeks flushed. "We are duty-bound to combine all the bloodlines."

"It's probably best not to delay." He swept me up into his arms.

I brushed his lips with my own. "We have all the time in the world now."

A serene look washed over his face. "Do you mind if I want to spend every second with you?"

"I'm counting on it." A small glimpse of the future filled my mind. The person front and center was Eric. Always Eric.

EPILOGUE

"I CAN'T BELIEVE YOU TALKED me into this," Eric whispered. "Mortals are dangerous and unstable creatures."

I pressed a kiss to his lips. "We can't talk like that. I'm part mortal, you're part mortal, and our babies will be part mortal."

Eric groaned and rubbed my belly that wasn't burgeoning yet, but I knew would be soon. Just like I knew I carried twins. I'd seen them in a vision. A boy and a girl. The girl, olive skinned like her father; the boy, fair skinned like me. Both with dark hair and my blue eyes. They were beautiful, and I couldn't wait to meet them in eight months.

"Okay," he murmured. "But if Josie and Mateo do anything to call attention to us or try to call the authorities, I will use my powers."

"Ooh. Don't get me excited."

He nuzzled my ear. "I'll excite you, all right."

"Later," I said breathily. "I want to say goodbye and make sure the bakery is taken care of before we leave for Lisbon tomorrow." It had already killed me to see Love Bites with an "Out of Business" sign on it. Thankfully—by magic, or something like that—a secret would soon would be found, giving the bakery to Mateo and Josie. Mateo and Josie who were now a couple. At least my supposed death had brought about some good.

"So, are we still good with the plan?" I asked. "I'll knock on the door, tell them not to scream and that I have something to show them. You'll come out of the shadows so they're stunned, and then we'll tell them the truth about us."

Eric's perfectly handsome face scrunched. "I don't like it, but since there's no talking you out of it, sure."

I tapped his nose. "You are such a good husband ... or whatever you are." We were more than married.

"I prefer godlike lover."

"I can live with that." I smiled. "Okay, ready?"

He shrugged, so not on board with this plan. Under the cover of darkness, we came out from behind the bushes at Mateo's townhouse. Well, I came out of the bushes; Eric jumped into the shadow on the porch. I made sure no one else was around and knocked on their door.

"Who's knocking on the door so late?" Josie complained. "Did you order a midnight snack again?"

"Baby, I'm only snacking on you tonight," Mateo replied.

I had to keep from giggling—and gagging.

Thankfully, they both came to the door and opened it together. Their eyes bugged out, and they spluttered until Josie burst into tears. "You're alive." She pulled me to her.

I hugged her fiercely.

"Are you okay?" She patted me down as if to make sure I was really there. "We searched and searched for you. We thought Eric Knight had kidnapped and killed you."

She was half-right.

"I'm fine. In fact, I have something I want to show to you. But you have to promise me you won't freak out and you'll listen to me before you do anything rash."

Josie continued to sob as she squeaked out a yes. I looked at Mateo. "Do you promise, too?"

He was so stunned he only nodded.

"Come out, Eric."

Eric appeared out of nowhere.

"What the hell?" Mateo shouted.

Eric quickly walked in and shut the door behind him.

Mateo held up the cross around his neck, and Josie grabbed the baseball bat near the door.

"Whoa, whoa. You promised me you would listen to what I had to say."

Josie pulled back the bat, ready to take off Eric's head. "You evil, rotten—"

I flashed her my left hand, prominently displaying my mother's ring. "We're married."

Josie lowered the bat while Mateo started reciting Catholic prayers.

"Mateo, we're not evil spirits."

He wasn't so sure, and took Josie's hand.

Eric wrapped his arm around me. "I'd never hurt Sorrel."

"Where have you been for the last two months?" Josie cried.

"It's an interesting story. Do you have some time?"

Josie, though still shaking, waved toward the couch.

Eric and I took a seat and explained to them what we could, and who we were. They thought we were yanking their chains until I healed Josie's leg where she had cut herself shaving earlier that day. Mateo jumped out of his seat ready to call his priest, but Josie convinced him not to. It dawned on her how truly different I was the entire time she'd known me. A peace washed over her. And it wasn't by any magical means.

By the time we parted, they mostly believed us, I thought. I was sure they would be fully convinced when they inherited a lot of money the next day.

Before we left, I hugged Josie. "Thank you for showing me what being a friend is all about. I'll never forget you."

Mateo got in on the action and wrapped his arms around us both. "I love you, bonitas."

I loved them, too, and would miss them terribly. But with Eric by my side, I never felt alone. I wasn't sure what exactly we would do with our lives, but this I knew: we would do it together.

When we got into our car, I turned to Eric. "See, that wasn't so bad."

"You were right. Still, we'd better get out of here before anyone else sees us."

"Good idea."

We were about to back out when I got a tingling sensation from my head to my toes and the car filled with light.

Eric and I both looked at each other, puzzled. We'd thought the book would no longer speak to us since the curse was broken. Eric reached into his seat's shadow and pulled out the beaming book, that now consisted of a piece from each of the three families. In its kaleidoscope swirled shades of green and moonstone. I took the book from Eric and carefully opened its pearl pages to reach the back of the book. The last line made me gasp.

"What does it say, my love?"

"Greetings, Queen Sorrel."

If you enjoyed *The Book of Sorrel,* here are some other books by JJ Makenzie that you may enjoy:

The Queen With No Name
Naming of the Queen (Coming in 2023)

ABOUT THE AUTHOR

JJ Makenzie has always wanted a secret identity, so she finally gave herself one. In real life, JJ is a *USA Today* bestselling author of rom-coms and contemporary romance. She also pretends to be a rock star in her car. She's obsessed with 70s and 80s music, but also has a soft spot for a good country ballad. Her days are spent writing among the beautiful Rocky Mountains. At night she dreams of all the characters she has yet to introduce to the world. She may also be a crime fighter with this new secret identity, but that's another story.

* * *

For updates on new releases and all things book related, follow her on Facebook and Instagram.

If you wish to know her in real life, sign up for her newsletter @ https://www.jenniferpeel.com/.

Made in United States
North Haven, CT
25 July 2025

71018340R00156